For Daniel
and
for Max

Prologue

My father took one hundred and thirty-two minutes to die.

I counted.

It happened on the Jellicoe Road. The prettiest road I'd ever seen, where trees made breezy canopies like a tunnel to Shangri-la. We were going to the ocean, hundreds of miles away, because I wanted to see the ocean and my father said that it was about time the four of us made that journey. I remember asking, "What's the difference between a trip and a journey?" and my father said, "Narnie, my love, when we get there, you'll understand," and that was the last thing he ever said.

We heard her almost straightaway. In the other car, wedged into ours so deep that you couldn't tell where one began and the other ended. She told us her name was Tate and then she squeezed through the glass and the steel and climbed over her own dead—just to be with Webb and me; to give us her hand so we could clutch it with all our might. And then a kid called Fitz came riding by on a stolen bike and saved our lives.

Someone asked us later, "Didn't you wonder why no one came across you sooner?"

Did I wonder?

When you see your parents zipped up in black body bags on the Jellicoe Road like they're some kind of garbage, don't you know?

Wonder dies.

Chapter 1

—— TWENTY-TWO YEARS LATER ——

I'm dreaming of the boy in the tree and at the exact moment I'm about to hear the answer that I've been waiting for, the flashlights yank me out of what could have been one of those perfect moments of clarity people talk about for the rest of their lives. If I was prone to dramatics, I could imagine my sighs would have been heard from the boundaries of the school to the town down below.

The question begs to be asked, "Why the flashlights?" Turning on the light next to my bed would have been much less conspicuous and dramatic. But if there is something I have learned in the past five years, it's that melodrama plays a special part in the lives of those at the Jellicoe School. So while the mouths of the year twelves move and their hands threaten, I think back to my dream of the boy, because in it I find solace. I like that word. I'm going to make it my word of the year. There is just something about that boy that makes me feel like I belong. *Belong. Long to be.* Weird word, but semantics aside, it is up there with *solace.*

Somewhere in that hazy world of neither here nor there, I'll be hanging off that tree, legs hooked over the branch, hands splayed, grabbing at air that is intoxicating and perfumed with the sweet smell of oak. Next to me, always, is that boy. I don't know his name, and I don't know why he comes calling, but he is there every time, playing the same music on one of those Discmans for tapes from the eighties, a song about flame trees and long-time feelings of friends left behind. The boy lets me join in and I sing the same line each time. His eyes are always watery at that point and it stirs a nostalgia in me that I have no reason to own, but it makes me ache all the same. We never quite get to the end of the song and each time I wake, I remind myself to ask him about those last few bars. But somehow I always forget.

I tell him stories. Lots of them. About the Jellicoe School students and the Townies and the Cadets from a school in Sydney. I tell him about the war between all three of us for territory. And I tell him about Hannah, who lives in the unfinished house by the river at the edge of the Jellicoe School, and of the manuscript of hers I've read, with its car wreck. Hannah, who is too young to be hiding away from the world and too smart to be merely organising weekend passes for the kids in my dorm. Hannah, who thinks she has me all worked out. I tell him of the time when I was fourteen, just after the Hermit whispered something in my ear and then shot himself, when I went in search of my mother, but got only halfway there. I tell him that I blame the Cadet for that.

The boy in the tree sobs uncontrollably when I tell him about the Hermit and my mother, yet his eyes light up each time I mention Hannah. And every single time he asks, "Taylor, what about the Brigadier who came searching for you that day? Whatever became of him?" I try to explain that the Brigadier is of no importance to my story, that the Brigadier was just some top brass, high up in the army, who had been invited to train the cadets that year, but the boy always shakes his head as if he knows better.

And there are times, like this time, when he leans

forward to remind me of what the Hermit had whispered. He leans so far forward that I catch his scent of tea-tree and sandalwood and I strain my ears to listen so I will never forget. I strain my ears, needing to remember because somehow, for reasons I don't know, what he says will answer everything. He leans forward, and in my ear he whispers . . .

"It's time!"

I hesitate for a moment or two, just in case the dream is still floating around and I can slip back into it for that crucial moment. But the flashlights hurt my eyes and when I'm able to push them away I can see the ignorant impatience in the faces of the year twelves.

"If you want us to scare you, Taylor Markham, we'll scare you."

I climb out of bed and pull on my jumper and boots and grab my inhaler. "You're wearing flannelette," I remind them flatly. "How scared should I be?"

They walk me down the corridor, past the senior rooms. I see the other year-eleven girls, my classmates, standing at their door, watching me. Some, like Raffaela, try to catch my eye, but I don't allow it to hold. Raffaela makes me feel sentimental and there is no place in my life for sentimentality. But for just one moment I think of those first nights in the dorm five years ago, when Raffaela and I lay side by side and she listened to a tale that I have no memory of today about my life in the city. I'll always remember the look of horror on her face. "Taylor Markham," she had said, "I'm going to say a prayer for you." And although I wanted to mock her and explain I didn't believe in anything or anyone, I realised that no one had ever prayed for me before. So I let her.

I follow the seniors down two flights of stairs to a window that is supposedly the least conspicuous one in the House. I have actually mastered the climb down from my own window but have never dared to tell anyone. It gives me more freedom and means that I don't have to explain my every move to the year-seven spies in the dorm. I started off as one of those. They hand-pick you young out here.

A thorn presses into my foot through the soft fabric of my boot and I let it for a moment, pausing until they push me forward. I walk ahead, allowing them to play out their roles.

The trail that leads to the meeting hut is only

distinguishable in the pitch black by the sensation of soft dirt under my feet. In the darkness, one of the seniors stumbles behind me. But I keep on walking, my eyes closed, my mind focused. Ever since they moved me from the communal dorms to my own room in year seven I have been trained to take over, just like the protégés in the other Houses. Five years is a long time waiting and somehow during that time I got bored. So as we reach the hut and enter and I feel the waves of hostility smack me in the face, I begin to plan my escape from Jellicoe. Except that this time I will not be fourteen and there won't be a Cadet who tags along. There will just be me. According to Dickens, the first rule of human nature is self-preservation and when I forgive him for writing a character as pathetic as Oliver Twist, I'll thank him for the advice.

Candles illuminate the canvas-covered dirt floor where the seniors from all the Houses sit with their successors, waiting for the verdict.

"This is officially the passing-on ceremony," the one-in-charge says. "You keep it simple. It's not a democracy. Whoever's in charge rules. They can only be superseded if five of the six House leaders sign a document deeming him or her incompetent. The one-in-charge has final say in what gets traded with the Cadets and the Townies. He or she, only, has the right to surrender to the enemy."

Richard of Murrumbidgee House makes a sound as if he's holding back a laugh. I don't know whether it's because he's sure the job is his or because he is laughing at the idea that anyone would ever surrender to the enemy, but the sound grates on me.

"The important thing is to never give anything away," the one-in-charge continues, "especially not to teachers or dorm staff. Every time your dorm coordinator calls a meeting, just sit there and look like you're taking in every word but don't let them ever understand what goes on around here after hours."

"Which is?" Ben Cassidy asks politely.

"I beg your pardon?" says one of his seniors.

"Well, what exactly does go on here after hours?"

"What are you getting at?" the senior persists.

Ben shrugs. "Everyone's always going on about what goes on after hours but nothing actually seems to go on at all, except maybe meetings like this."

"Then to begin with," the one-in-charge says,

"don't discuss these meetings."

"Well, it's not as if they don't know what's going on," Ben continues. "This one time I was with Hannah and we were eating her scones and she was asking me one hundred and one questions, as per usual." He looks around at the other protégés as if we're interested. "She makes them herself. Hmm hmm. Beautiful. Well, we got to talking and I said, 'Hannah, you've lived in this house ever since I've been here and it's got the best bird's-eye view of all the Houses, so what do you think goes on here out of school hours?'"

"That's a great question to be asking someone who's constantly speaking to the principal," Richard says. "You're a stupid prick, Cassidy."

"We didn't have much to choose from," the leader of Clarence House says, sending Ben a scathing look and whacking him across the back of the head. Ben looks resigned. In year seven he got bashed up at least once a month, mostly by his seniors. He'd go visit Hannah, which I found irritating because he had his own adult looking after his House and the one thing I hated in year seven, after living with Hannah in her unfinished house for the whole year before, was sharing her with the rest of the school. The revelation that she's a question-asker is even more irritating. Hannah *never* asks me anything.

"What type of scones?" I ask him. He looks up at me, but his senior whacks him again.

"Okay, I'm over this," Richard says impatiently. "Can we just get to the point?"

Those-in-charge look at one another and then back to us. And then at me.

I hear the curses instantly, the anger, the disbelief, the hiss of venom under the breath of almost everyone in the room except the seniors. I know what is about to be said but I don't know how I feel. Just numb like always, I guess.

"You're not a popular choice, Taylor Markham," the one-in-charge says, cutting through the voices. "You're too erratic, have a bad track record, and running off with one of the enemy, no matter how young you were, was bad judgement on your part. But you know this place inside out and you've been here longer than anyone else and that's the greatest asset anyone can have."

One of my seniors nudges me hard in the ribs and I guess I'm supposed to stand up.

"From this point on," the one-in-charge continues, "we answer no questions and offer no advice, so don't come to find us. We don't exist anymore. We go home for study tomorrow and then we'll be gone and our role here is over. So our question is are you in, or do we give this to our next candidate?"

I didn't expect a question or an option. I would have preferred if they just told me to take over. There is nothing about this role that I desperately want. Yet being under the control of any of the protégés in this room for even the slightest moment is a nauseating prospect and I know that if I'm not in charge I'll be spending many a night on surveillance, freezing my bottom off in the middle of the bush.

When I'm ready, I nod, and the one-in-charge hands me a purple notebook and a thick crisply folded piece of paper, which I suspect is the map outlining who owns what in the territory wars. Then the year twelves begin to leave and, like all things insignificant, the moment they're gone it is like they never existed.

I sit back down and prepare myself for what I know is coming. Five House leaders ready for a battle. One common enemy. Me.

"You don't want this. You never have." I think the comment comes from the leader of Murray House, who has never really spoken to me. So the idea that he thinks he knows what I want interests me.

"Step down and the five of us will sign you out," Richard says, looking around at the others. "You'll be put out of your misery and we'll get on with running the underground."

"Richard's got some great ideas," the Hastings House girl explains.

"You don't have the people skills, Taylor."

"And you never turn up to meetings."

"And not once did you gather intelligence against the Cadets last year."

"You spend too much time in trouble with Hannah. If she's on your back, she'll be on ours."

"You just don't give a shit about anyone."

I block them out and try to go back to the boy in the tree. . . .

"Are you even listening to us?"

"Let's just take a vote."

"Five says she's out and she's out."

Back to the tree . . . inhaling the intoxicating perfumed air and listening to a song with no end and to a boy with a story that I need to understand.

"This is the worst decision I've ever known them to make."

"Everyone calm down. We just vote and it'll be over."

"She burnt down the bloody laundry when I was in her House. Who can trust her?"

"They were sultana scones."

The voice slices through the others and I glance up. Ben Cassidy is looking at me. I don't know what I see in his eyes, but it brings me back to reality.

"What are you doing, Ben?" Richard asks quietly, menacingly.

Ben takes his time, then looks at Richard. "The one-in-charge gave it to her, so we should respect that."

"We haven't agreed that she's the leader."

"You need five votes against her," Ben reminds them.

"Murray? Hastings? Darling?" he says to the others in turn. They refuse to look at me and I realise they've rehearsed this. "Clarence . . ."

"Raffaela reckons we need to get the Prayer Tree," Ben cuts in before Richard can drag him into it. I can tell they haven't discussed this with him. He's considered the weakest link. Except when they need his vote. Big mistake.

"That's all we want back from the Townies," Ben mutters, not looking at anyone.

Richard glances at Ben in disgust.

"And of course the Club House is a priority." Ben starts up again, and I can tell he's enjoying himself.

Silence. Tons of it, and I realise that I have my one vote that will keep me in. For the time being, anyway.

"Who's in charge of the Townies this year?" I ask.

I'm staring at Richard. He realises that I'm here to stay and despite the look in his eyes that says betrayal, backstabbing, petulance, hatred, revenge, and anything else he's planning to major in, he lets me have my moment.

"We'll find out sooner or later," he says.

But I like this power. "Ben?" I say, still staring at Richard.

"Yes?"

"Who's in charge of the Townies these days?"

"Chaz Santangelo."

"Moderate or fundamentalist?"

"Temperamental, so we need to get on his good side."

"Townies don't have a good side," Richard says.

I ignore him. "Is he going to be difficult?" I ask Ben.

"Always. But he's not a thug," Ben says, "unlike the leader of the Cadets."

"Who?" Richard barks out.

I see Ben almost duck, as if a hand is going to come out and whack him on the back of his head.

"First thing's first. This year we get the Townies on our side," I say, ignoring everyone in the room but Ben.

The chorus of disapproval is like those formula songs that seem to hit number one all the time. You know the tune in a moment and it begins to bore you in two.

"We've never done that," Richard snaps.

"And look where it's got us. In the last few years, we've lost a substantial amount of territory. It's been split up between the Cadets and Townies. We haven't got much left to lose."

"What about the Prayer Tree?" Ben asks again.

"The Prayer Tree is not a priority," I say, standing up.

"Raffaela reckons the trade made three years ago was immoral," he argues.

I try not to remember that Raffaela, Ben, and I spent most of year seven together hiding out with Hannah. I can't even remember Ben's story. Heaps of foster parents, I think. One who put a violin in his hands and changed his life.

"Do me a favour," I say to him, a tad on the dramatic side. "Don't ever bring morality into what we do here."

Chapter 2

When it is over, when I'm the last person sitting on the canvas-covered dirt floor, when the candles have burnt out and the sun has come up, I make my way towards Hannah's house by the river. Hannah's house has been unfinished ever since I can remember. Deep down I think that's always been a comfort to me, because people don't leave unfinished houses.

Working on her house has been my punishment ever since I got to this place six years ago. It's the punishment for having nowhere else to go in the holidays or breaking curfew or running away with a Cadet in year eight. Sometimes I am so bored that I just go and tell her that I've broken curfew and she'll say, "Well, no Saturday privileges for you, Taylor," and she'll make me work all day on the house with her. Sometimes we don't say a word and other times she talks my ear off about everything and nothing. When that happens, there's a familiarity between us that tells me she's not merely my House caretaker. In that role she works out rosters, notifies us of transfers between Houses or exam schedules or study groups or detentions. Sometimes she sits with the younger kids and helps with homework. Or she invites them to her house and makes them afternoon tea and tells them some bad news, like a grandparent being dead or a parent having cancer, or makes up some fantastic story about why someone's mother or father couldn't come that weekend.

Absent parents aren't a rare thing around here, probably because a tenth of the students are state wards. The Jellicoe School is run by the state. It's not about money or religion but it is selective, so most of us are clever. The rest are a combination of locals or children of alternative environmentalists who believe that educating their children out in the bush is going to instil a love of nature in them. On the contrary, most of the students run off to the city the moment year twelve is over and revel in the rat race, never looking back. Then there are those like Raffaela, who is a Townie and is out here boarding with the rest of us because her parents teach at Jellicoe High School in town and they thought it would be better for her not to have to deal with that. Richard's parents are embassy staff who live overseas most of the time, but his grandparents live in the outer district of the area so it seemed like the best option for him.

I don't know where I fit in. One day when I was eleven, my mother drove me out here and while I was in the toilets at the 7-Eleven on the Jellicoe Road, she drove off and left me there. It becomes one of those defining moments in your life, when your mother does that. It's not as if I don't forgive her, because I do. It's like those horror films where the hero gets attacked by the zombie and he has to convince the heroine to shoot him, because in ten seconds' time he won't be who he was anymore. He'll have the same face but no soul. I don't know who my mother was before the drugs and all the rest, but once in a while during our splintered time together I saw flashes of a passion beyond anything I'll ever experience. Most other times she was a zombie who would look at me and say things like, "I didn't name you. You named yourself." The way I used to see it was that when I was born she didn't take time even to give me an identity. Of course there's a story behind it all and she's not that cut-and-dried evil, but my version keeps me focused. Hannah, of course, knows one of the other versions, but like everything, she keeps it a mystery.

Usually, especially these days, we seem to be angry with each other all the time, and today is no different.

"Transfers," she says, handing me the sheet. I don't bother even looking at it.

"My House is full. No more transfers," I tell her.

"There are some fragile kids on that list."

"Then why transfer them to me?"

"Because you'll be here during the holidays."

"What makes you think I don't have anywhere to go these holidays?"

"I want you to take them under your wing, Taylor."

"I don't have wings, Hannah."

She stares at me. Hannah's stares are always loaded. A combination of disappointment, resignation, and exasperation. She never looks at anyone else like that, just me. Everyone else gets sultana scones and warm smiles and a plethora of questions, and I get a stare full of grief and anger and pain and something else that I can never work out. Over the years I've come to accept that Hannah driving by on the Jellicoe Road five minutes after my mother dumped me was no coincidence. She has never pretended it was, especially during that first year, when I lived with her, before I began high school. In year seven, when I moved into the dorms, I was surprised at how much I missed her. Not living in the unfinished house seemed like a step farther away from understanding anything about my past. Whenever I look for clues, my sleuthing always comes back to one person: Hannah.

I take the list from her, just to get her off my back.

"You're not sleeping." Not a question, just a statement. She reaches over and touches my face and I flinch, moving away.

"Go make yourself something to eat and then get to class. You might be able to make second period."

"I'm thinking of leaving."

"You leave when you finish school," she says bluntly.

"No, I leave when I want to leave and you can't stop me."

"You stay until the end of next year."

"You're not my mother."

I say that to her every time I want to hurt her and every time I expect her to retaliate.

"No, I'm not." She sighs. "But for the time being, Taylor, I'm all you have. So let's just get to the part where I give you something to eat and you go to class."

At times it's like sadness has planted itself on her face, refusing to leave, an overwhelming sadness, and sometimes I see despair there, too. Once or twice I've seen something totally different. Like when the government sent troops overseas to fight, she was inconsolable. Or when she turned thirty-three. "Same age Christ was when he died," I joked. But I remember the look on her face. "I'm the same age my father was when he died," she told me. "I'm older than he will ever be. There's something unnatural about that."

Then there was that time in year eight when the Hermit whispered something in my ear and then shot himself and I ran away with that Cadet and the Brigadier brought us back. I remember the

Brigadier's hard face looked as if he was trying with all his might for it to stay hard. Hannah didn't look at him and I remember it took a great effort for her not to look at him. She just said, "Thanks for bringing her home," and she let me stay at her unfinished house by the river. She held on to me tight all night because somewhere in the town where the Brigadier found us, two kids had gone missing and Hannah said it could have easily been me and the Cadet. They found those two kids weeks later, shot in the back of the head, and Hannah cried every time it came on the news. I remember telling her that I thought the Brigadier was the serial killer and it was the first time I saw her laugh in ages.

Today there is something going on with her and I can't quite figure it out. I glance around the room, noticing how tidy it looks. Even her manuscript seems shuffled neatly in a pile in one corner of the table. She's been writing the same novel ever since I've known her. Usually she keeps it hidden, but I know where to find it, like those teenage boys in films who know where to find their father's porn. I love reading about the kids in the eighties, even though I can't make head or tail of the story. Hannah hasn't structured it properly yet. I've got so used to reading it out of sequence but one day I'd like to put it in order without worrying that she'll turn up and catch me with it.

She sees me looking at the pages. "Do you want to read it?" she asks quietly.

"I don't have time."

"You've wanted to read it for ages, so is it okay to ask why not, now that I'm offering?"

"That's new," I say to her.

"What's new?"

"You asking me a question."

She doesn't respond.

"You never ask me anything," I accuse.

"Well, what would you like me to ask you today, Taylor?"

I stare and as usual I hate her for not working out what I need from her.

"Do you want me to ask where you've been all night? Or do you want me to ask why you always have to be so difficult?"

"I'd prefer that you asked me something more important than that, Hannah!"

Like how am I supposed to lead a community? I

want to say. Or what's going to happen to me this time next year? Am I just going to disappear like our insignificant leaders did last night? And where do I disappear to?

"Ask me what the Hermit whispered in my ear that day."

I can tell that she's stunned, her hazel eyes wide with the impact of my request. She takes a moment or two, like she needs to catch her breath.

"Sit down," she says quietly.

I shake my head and hold up the list she gave me. "Sorry, no time. I've got fragile kids to look after."

When I get back, classes have just finished and everyone's making their way back into their Houses. Jessa McKenzie is sitting on the verandah steps. Despite her being in year seven and in Hastings House, somewhere in my worst nightmare she's become surgically attached to me and *nothing*, not anger, not insults, not the direst cruelty can dislodge her.

"Don't follow me. I'm busy." I keep walking. No eye contact because that will encourage her. That someone can want something out of another person who gives absolutely nothing in return astounds me.

I want to say to this kid, "Get out of my life, you little retard." Come to think of it, I have actually said that and back she comes the next day like some crazed masochistic yo-yo.

"They reckon the Cadets are arriving any minute and that this time they mean business." Jessa McKenzie always speaks in a breathless voice, like she hasn't stopped speaking long enough to take a breath her entire life.

"I think they meant business last year when they threw every bike in the school over the cliff."

"I know you're worried as well. I can tell you are," she says softly.

My teeth are gritted now. I'm trying not to but they grit all the same.

I get to the front door, dying for an opportunity to shut it in her face, but Jessa McKenzie still follows, like those tenacious fox terriers that grab hold of the bottom of your pants and tug.

"The kids in my old dorm are scared, you know," she explains. "The year sevens?" As if I've asked a question. "It's because the older kids are going on about the Cadets coming and how bad it is. I think you should speak to them, Taylor. Now that you're leader"—she leans forward and whispers—"of the Underground Community."

My hand is on the door, almost there, *almost* . . . but then I stop because something lodges itself in my brain like a bullet.

"What do you mean 'in my old dorm'?"

She's beaming. Freckles glowing.

I look at the transfer paper in my hands and then back at her. I open it slowly, knowing exactly whose name I'm about to see there, transferred to Lachlan House. *My* House.

"You have no idea how much I can help," she says. "Raffaela thinks I'll be better off in the senior rooms than the dorms."

"What would Raffaela know?"

"She reckons she can work out where the tunnel is," I hear Raffaela say behind me.

"My father used to say . . ."

But I'm not listening to what Jessa McKenzie's father used to say. I'm sandwiched between my two worst nightmares.

"Congratulations," Raffaela says, "although I think Richard and the others are already organising a coup." Raffaela always has this weight-of-the-world, old-woman thing happening.

"Congratulations from me, too." Jessa McKenzie is still beaming.

"We're going to work out where the tunnel is," Raffaela says, "and get back the Prayer Tree and learn how to . . ."

I want to be sitting in front of my computer, where you can press a button to block out your junk mail. These two are my junk mail.

"But Taylor," Jessa continues in that hushed annoying voice of hers. "You have to get to know the kids in your House because Chloe P. says they hardly know you down in the dorms."

"Incoming!" This comes from one of our guys sitting in the surveillance tree.

Raffaela and I exchange looks before she begins bustling the younger lot into the House.

The Cadets have arrived.

I'm in charge.

The territory wars are about to recommence.

They met Jude Scanlon for the first time exactly one year after the accident. At that time Webb thought nothing would make sense ever again. The pain was worse now because up till then Narnie and Tate and Webb had all just felt numb and if it hadn't been for Fitz's spirit blasting them out of their grief, Webb honestly believed that the three of them would have made some crazy suicide pact. But during that year, when they were fourteen years old, the numbness went away, replaced by memories that made Narnie disappear inside herself and him ache. He saw the same in Tate. Despite her ability to enjoy most of their days, sometimes her despair was so great that, in a melancholy moment when she'd allow herself to think of her family, she'd almost stop breathing and he'd hold her and say, "I'm here, Tate. I'm here, Tate. I'm here." Tate had lost her younger sister as well as her parents in the accident. "We were playing Rock, Paper, Scissors," she told him once. "I was paper and she was rock so I lived and she died."

That year, a boys' school from the city had decided to experiment and send all their students from year eight to eleven on a six-week life-education project as part of the Cadet program. They were to live by the river from mid-September to the week after the October holidays ended.

"We can play skirmish," Fitz said, clutching his

gun, his eyes blazing with the possibilities as the convoy of buses drove into town.

As his Cadet troop jogged along the Jellicoe Road, their boots thumping the ground, eliminating anything in their path, Jude Scanlon noticed the damaged poppies. There seemed to be five, bent out of shape, fragments on the bottom of the boot of the kid in front of him—damaged beyond repair. For reasons he couldn't understand a sadness came over him and it was then he saw the girl standing on the other side of the dirt road, her eyes pools of absolute sorrow, her light brown hair glowing in the splinters of sunlight that forced their way through the trees. It was as if he had seen a ghost, some kind of apparition, which haunted him through that night. The next day he found himself returning to the very same spot, after hours, with five seeds in his pocket. Then, on his knees, he planted something for the first time in his life.

"They have to go deeper," he heard a voice say. "Or else the roots won't take."

There were four of them. Two boys and two girls. He recognised one of the girls from the day before and something inside him stirred. He could tell the speaker was related to her, his hair was the same golden brown, his eyes, though, were full of life. The girl on the other side of the speaker was smiling gently and then there was a boy with a wicked grin and laughing eyes.

"Tate," the smiling girl said, extending her hand. "And this is Webb and Fitzy and you kind of met Narnie yesterday."

Narnie.

"I didn't . . . we didn't mean to . . ."

The boy, Webb, shook his head. "It always happens."

"Maybe you should find another spot to plant your flowers."

"There can be no other spot," Webb said quietly.

Jude pulled the rest of the seeds from his pocket and they all took one each then side-by-side on the Jellicoe Road they planted the poppies.

Each day, at the same time, Jude would return and each day they would be there, led by Webb, whose life could not have been more different to his. Where Webb's memories of childhood were idyllic and

earthy, Jude's reeked of indifference. Webb read
fantasy; Jude read realism. Webb believed a tree
house was the perfect place for gaining a different
perspective on the world; whereas Jude saw it as
perfect for surveillance and working out who or
what was a threat to them. They argued about
sports codes and song lyrics. Jude saw the rain-dirty
valley; Webb saw Brigadoon. Yet despite all this,
they connected, and the nights they spent in the tree
house discussing their brave new worlds and not so
brave emotions made everything else in their lives
insignificant. Somehow the world of Webb and Fitz
and Tate and Narnie became the focus of Jude's life.

The next year, as the Cadet buses drove into Jellicoe,
Jude was desperate for a sign. A sign that would
tell him that things would be the same as the year
before. He'd spent most of the year wondering
about them. Had they fallen out of love with one
another? Did Narnie still have that half-dead look?
Had Fitz got himself into trouble? Had they out-
grown him?

But there they were, on the steps of the Jellicoe
General Store, where the Cadets always stopped to

pick up supplies. Waiting. For him.

"Who are they?" the Cadet sitting next to him asked.

Jude looked at Webb's face, the grin stretching from ear to ear.

"They're my best friends. I'm going to know them until the day I die."

Chapter 3

The territory wars have been part of the Jellicoe School's life ever since I can remember. I don't know who started them. The Townies say it was the Cadets from the city who have been coming out here for the last twenty or so years. They set up camp right alongside the Jellicoe School for six weeks each September as part of their outdoor education program. We say the Townies started the wars because they think Jellicoe belongs to them, and the Cadets blame us because they say we don't know how to share land. All I know is that they began sixteen years ago because that's what the Little Purple Book says. In it the founders wrote down the rules, the maps, the boundaries.

The wars take place only for the six weeks the Cadets are here and mostly they are more of a nuisance than exciting. It takes us double the time to get to town because the Cadets own most of the easy access trails. It's always around that time that we get pep talks from the teachers and the Principal about getting out there in the fresh air and taking bushwalks. What they don't know is that most of the House leaders confine their younger students indoors in case they trespass onto enemy territory. That is one thing you don't want happening. Because after the Cadets are long gone and the Townies are back in their rabbit holes, the real war begins. The Houses are at one another, particularly if one was responsible for losing us territory. When I ran away with the Cadet three years ago, Raffaela and Ben went looking for me and trespassed onto Townie territory. We lost the Prayer Tree because of it. Raffaela and Ben were completely ostracised and when I returned we didn't talk to each other much. Then we stopped talking altogether. And now here we are leading Houses together and about to fight a war.

There are Cadet sightings on the northern border of our boundaries for a whole week. The area is at least a kilometre away from where they are camped so allowing themselves to be sighted is a deliberate attempt at intimidation. Just between you and me, it works every time. The other House leaders want me to begin acting on the intelligence we're receiving, but premature action in the past has been the Jellicoe School's downfall and I'll be damned if I make the same mistakes the leaders have made in the past.

On her weekend visit home, I send word through Raffaela to the leader of the Townies that we'd like to make contact. We receive no answer and the cat-and-mouse games begin. Waiting for war is a killer. Not knowing when the first strike will happen, not knowing what the outcome will be. The build-up makes us tense. Sometimes I want to walk right out there and yell, "Bring it on!" just to get the suspense over.

But it's the home front that's the worst. The school has always had a policy that the House leaders, with the help of the rest of the seniors, take care of their own Houses with the assistance of an adult. Every student knows that the leader has been chosen in year seven and is groomed for the next five years. But every year we have elections and pretend that the House leaders and School leader have been elected by the people for the people. The teachers fall for it. They're pretty young and clueless. Most of them only stay three years maximum to fulfil the Board of Education's employment requirements, so patterns among the students aren't really picked up. They are diligent, though. Each time a Lachlan student forgets to turn up to a sports training session or music recital or debating practice, I get harassed by the teachers. From the junior dorms on the first floor all the way up to the year-elevens rooms on the third, those in my House drive me insane with their expectations. Questions about television privileges, duty rosters, computer access, and laundry. There are tears and fights and tantrums and anxiety. And Hannah is nowhere to be found. I'm furious that she has let me take care of this all by myself—almost like some kind of payback for the last time I saw her. In the past Hannah spent most of her spare time in Lachlan, helping out the House leader, but now that I'm in charge she's gone into hiding.

A year-ten girl knocks on my door. "Evie from year seven just got her period."

"So?"

"You have to speak to her. She's crying."

"Go get Raffaela."

"She's not around. Where's Hannah? How come

Ms. Morris is doing roll call?"

"I have no idea where Hannah is."

I recognise the look on the girl's face. It's a do-you-have-any-idea-about-anything look.

"I'll go get Hannah," I say finally, just wanting to get away. Except when I go down to her office and turn the handle to walk in I find it locked. In my whole time at the Jellicoe School I don't ever remember Hannah's door being locked and I put it down to an extended tantrum, which sits uneasily with me because Hannah never has tantrums. I'm about to head back upstairs but I see Jessa McKenzie coming my way, so I walk out, get on a bike, and ride down to the unfinished house by the river.

At this time of the day our grounds are at their most sinister. I can handle it at night but there's something about this time, when the sun begins to disappear, that makes me think the grounds have so much to hide. There's just endless silence. No birds, no crickets. Nothing.

I dump the bike on the ground beside the house and make my way to the front. "Hannah," I yell out angrily.

But the echo of my voice is the only response.

"Hannah, this isn't funny!"

I stand in the silence, waiting for something. For her head to appear out the window on the first floor, looking exasperated and saying, "Help me with these skirting boards, Taylor."

I look around, sensing something . . . someone. The house has an area around it that Hannah tends and mows. "It'll be my garden," she tells me constantly, where she'll plant lilac and lilies and she'll sit there, on the front verandah, like in that Yeats poem that she sometimes recites to me:

I will arise and go now, and go to Innisfree,
And a small cabin build there, of clay and wattles
*   made:*
Nine bean-rows will I have there, a hive for the
*   honey-bee,*
And live alone in the bee-loud glade.
And I shall have some peace there . . .

But beyond the tamed area there is dense bushland, uncultivated, without even a walking trail. Three kilometres of that is what separates us and the Cadets. Rumour has it they've been creating a secret trail for years, which would make getting to us as easy as. The quickest way for them would be via the river, which flows directly behind Hannah's property. But it belongs to us. Here, near Hannah's house, the river is at its narrowest and there's only about twenty metres between the banks. In the last couple of years, because of the drought, the river has been not much more than a trickle. Once in a while, over time, we've almost lost it through poor leadership but somehow we've always managed to hold on to it and maintain that physical distance between us and them. Today, though, somewhere in that dense uncultivated labyrinth, something or someone is watching. I can feel it with everything I have inside of me that keeps me alert to malevolence.

"Who's there?" I call out.

I think of the cat. Although Hannah has never claimed him as hers, she feeds him every time he comes into the area. I hate the cat and the cat hates me. He's feral, with a tail that always looks like it's been caught in a state of fright, and, like everything to do with Hannah, I fight him for her attention.

"Why does he look like that?" I asked her once.

"Because I think he saw something that scared the hell out of him a very long time ago."

The cat has been dying for years and sometimes Hannah wants to put him out of his misery, but she doesn't have the guts. Sometimes, when I get up close to him, I see the suffering in his eyes, but then he'll scratch me on the face and I am forced to forgo the sympathy.

But whatever is out there now, it's not the cat.

I shiver. Whoever it is has the advantage of being able to see me when I can't see them. I decide to turn around and walk away but just as I do, I hear the crunch of footsteps somewhere behind the bushes, moving towards me, slow and measured.

"Jessa McKenzie, is that you?"

If it was Jessa, she'd answer, and there is no answer, just the sound of a presence that keeps me rooted to the spot. I want to walk towards my bike, but I dare not turn my back and I'm too much of a coward to step forward to investigate. So I stay, for what seems like forever, staring at that one spot, frozen like a soldier who's stepped on a landmine. I don't move. I try to convince myself that it's just my imagination. That there's nothing there but some kind of wildlife with a size-nine foot.

The cold begins to snap at my skin and it's getting darker. Cautiously I take a step back and then another and another. I can make a dash, grab the bike, get on it, and take off before whoever it is can make it out of those trees, but some kind of eerie fear keeps me transfixed. I count to ten but I reach eleven and count to ten again and reach eleven again. Eleven. Eleven. Eleven. Eleven. Eleven.

Ten!

I bolt, turning, racing round the back of the house, straight to the bike. My stomach turns. No bike. Any chance of it all being my overactive imagination is quashed when I see that empty space under the tree. I hit the path with all the speed I can muster, my heart thumping like a rampaging jackhammer. The trail is an obstacle course of tangled twigs and assaulting branches, but I'd know this area with my eyes closed. I can hear only two sounds: the pounding of blood in my brain against my temples and the footsteps behind me. One pair. If there were two or more I think I'd be less afraid. I'd just allow myself to be captured and reinforce the rules of the Jellicoe Convention about diplomatic immunity. But one pair means either a rogue operative . . . or something worse.

When I reach the clearing that leads to the Houses and I see the lit path in front of me, there's no sense of relief. My lungs are bursting and every part of me aches. I just want to reach that door and the closer I get to it the farther away it feels.

Then I'm there, flying through it, slamming the door shut, locking it. Only then do I lean against it, sliding to the floor, taking deep gulps of air, slowing down my heart rate, pushing my perspiration-matted hair off my face, and bending my head between my legs, feeling for the reassuring shape of my inhaler. . . .

Three year-seven girls are standing in front of me, Jessa McKenzie in the middle of them.

"Someone used up all the water," Chloe P. tells me.

"Celia's got matches," the other one, whose name I don't know, says in a hushed voice.

I get up slowly, ignoring them, dragging my body up the stairs, but they are still there beside me.

"Where's Hannah?"

I stop and look into Jessa McKenzie's eyes and suddenly I see someone . . . something that I have seen before. I feel an anxiety I can't explain.

I push past them and escape to my room and when it's securely locked, I walk to the basin and lean over it, nausea rising in me.

I want to see Hannah. I'm not sure why but I find myself repeating the need over and over again. Because it's like a voice whispering in my head telling me that there is something so unnatural about her absence. It's like the last line of Hannah's Yeats poem.

I hear it in the deep heart's core.

At lunch I'm forced to sit with the other House leaders in the food hall as part of our "official" prefect initiation. The Principal makes a speech about unity while Richard whispers to the leader of Hastings. She giggles at something he says and they look at me until she passes it on to the person next to her. Richard has the rest of the House leaders eating out of his hand, except for Ben who is hoeing into his lasagne with a passion. I know that I need to act quickly before there's a coup and as I glance around the table I realise, once again, that my only potential ally is a drop-kick moron with tomato sauce all over his face.

"Ben, make contact with the Cadets. Tell them I'm ready to make a deal."

Ben looks up, in the middle of wiping the plate with his bread, his eyes wide with shock.

"Me?"

"Him?" Richard exchanges glances with the others.

"You," I say.

"What are you doing, Taylor?" Richard asks in that voice of his with the warning in it.

"I'm asking my deputy to do what deputies do. To negotiate," I say politely, standing up.

Ben mouths *deputy* to me like it's a dirty word and then Raffaela walks by and he mouths *deputy* to her as well and even she looks a bit worried.

"And by the way, Murrumbidgee and Hastings House," I say, looking at both the girl and Richard. "I read the Little Purple Book last night. Written in 1986 by the first of the UCs. The leader, I think, referred to himself as Chairman Meow. Pretty bad handwriting, but it's all there, including the fact that no House leaders can fraternise with each other in a romantic sense. Don't know why but probably because it takes away the competitive edge." I look at Ben. "Let's go."

Raffaela follows us as well. I don't say a word until we get outside.

"Where were you last night?" I ask her.

"I got town privileges. My best friend's brother's best friend's teammate—"

"Get to the point."

"—had a message for me. The Townies are ready to meet us. Tonight."

The halfway hut where negotiations take place with the Townies is dark and musty. The flashlights offer little light and no one dares sit down for fear of sitting on the unknown. In front of us there are three Townies. I only recognise Chaz Santangelo, far too handsome for his own good, but at least he doesn't have that mean, hard, feral look that Townie leaders from the past have had. Santangelo's sidekicks are typical hoons. Is there a manual out there that says Townies have to have mullets? Raffaela beside me is fidgety and I figure that they are all waiting for me to begin negotiations.

"So let's make a deal," I say.

"What makes you think we're here to make a deal?" Santangelo asks.

"Because river rats don't usually warn us that they're coming up to see us. They usually cruise around the place and create havoc and then expect us to negotiate just to stop the mayhem."

"I don't operate that way . . . *we* don't operate that way."

Judging by his sidekicks I'm not too sure.

"Well then, Santangelo. Is that what I should call him?" I turn to ask Raffaela. She doesn't answer. She's still fidgeting.

"Chaz," he answers for her.

"Santangelo . . . Chaz, whatever they call you down there, let's make a deal."

"Then you start. Tell us what you want."

First rule of negotiation: never let them think you want something.

"We want access to the Prayer Tree," Raffaela blurts out.

Raffaela failed negotiating class in year eight. The seniors in our House once had her in mind for leadership after I went through my arsonist stage and burnt half of the oval. We have a collection of arsonists at our school. There are at least two in year seven in my House who are going to set fire to us in our beds one day.

"We want access to the Club House," Santangelo states bluntly, looking at me and not her.

"Club House isn't ours. It belongs to the Cadets."

"Yeah, but it's a massive hike for them unless you let them use the river. They want access to the path that leads to it, and you've got that."

"Why the Club House?" Ben asks.

"Limited options. We can't get into any of the pubs, so it's hanging out at the Seven-Eleven at night or the car park at Coles. We're looking for peaceful coexistence, here. One night a week, Saturday night, maybe even two."

"You're talking to the wrong people. The Cadets will never allow you in."

"They might if you give them access to the path."

I shake my head. "The path is too close to the school boundaries."

"And the problem is?" he asks.

"We have junior girls," Raffaela says. "We don't want strangers that close to our boundaries."

"Why? Because last time the Cadets got that close you ran off with one of them?" The three Townies exchange looks and I am suddenly suspicious.

"You don't know who you ran off with, do you?" one of the Mullets says, stepping towards me. "You are one stupid—"

"Is this the best you can do?" Raffaela snaps at Santangelo, pointing to his morons, her finger almost an inch away from the bigger Mullet. He growls and makes a bite for it and Ben drags her back.

Still nothing from Santangelo and then I realise he's deliberately ignoring her and that they have some kind of history.

"You two know each other well, I presume."

Just a sigh and pursed lips from her and a hellish scowl from him.

"This is ridiculous," I say, walking to the door.

"No it's not. It's called coexistence." Santangelo blocks my exit. "Once you and the Cadets get it right, we might even try to sell the idea to the Israelis and Palestinians. What do you reckon?"

"You haven't told us what you have to offer us yet," I say.

"The Prayer Tree," Raffaela says immediately.

"I'm not negotiating with her."

I glare at Raffaela. Personally, I'm not interested in the Prayer Tree. I'm curious about what they're going to use as a bargaining tool.

"I've got information," he says to me, "that you might want."

"About?"

No answer, and for a moment I think we're dealing with an amateur who has come with nothing to offer.

"What?" Ben asks.

I glance at Santangelo and I get a gut feeling that it's not about the territory wars or the Club House.

"We have a map that could possibly be the draft for a tunnel," he says, suddenly focusing on Raffaela and Ben.

A ploy. Doesn't mean the map is non-existent but he's holding back and I want to know why.

"Means absolutely nothing to us because they never finished it beyond your school boundaries," he continues. "But it might be important to you."

"The tunnel's a myth."

"Are you calling him a liar?"

The Mullets are angry. Their teeth are showing

again and they almost back us into the door. Ben tries to stand between us but they shove him out of the way.

"Set up a meeting with the Cadets and maybe we'll talk again," I say.

"That might be hard," Santangelo says.

"Make it easy, then."

"I don't think you understand. My father was the cop who dragged you back when you ran away a couple of years ago."

I chance a glance at him again. He knows something about me; that I can tell. Being the son of the cop in charge would mean he knows a lot about most people around here.

"Well, you just make sure you thank him for me and tell him I said hi," I say with mock sweetness, although I do remember the cop's face, kind in a stressed-worried-angry way. The Brigadier, though, was a different story. Cold and tense.

"I don't think you're getting my drift. The guy my father and that Brigadier dragged back with you? Remember him? Well, he's in charge of the Cadets now and rumour has it that none of us want to be dealing with him."

I can't believe what I'm hearing. The Mullet Brothers are smirking. Raffaela and Ben look confused.

"Griggs?" I ask, feigning indifference.

Chaz Santangelo nods. "Jonah Griggs."

Chapter 4

Jonah Griggs.

Not just a name but a state of mind I never want to revisit, although I do keep him at the back of my mind for those times I get my hopes raised about something. So then I can slap myself into reality and remind myself of what happens when you let someone into your sacred space. Jonah Griggs is my second reminder to never ever trust another human being. My mother was the first and these days I feel like Hannah might have joined that small and intimate group of traitors.

Raffaela and Ben haven't said a word, but I can hear what they're thinking as they follow me out into the clearing. I want to tell their brains to shut the hell up but I know the only way to do that is to speak and I can't.

The lights of the Houses beam through the bush and mark out the path. Finally, after fifteen minutes, silence takes its toll.

"Did you make contact with the Cadets, Ben?" I say finally.

"Me?"

"Me?" is Ben's standard response to everything.

"Ben Cassidy, could you please tell the class why crossing the Rubicon was considered the catalyst for the fall of the Roman Republic?"

"Me?"

"Ben Cassidy, someone's on the phone for you."

"Me?"

"Ben Cassidy, I think one of the Darling girls has a crush on you."

"Me?"

"Ben Cassidy, who's the biggest loser in the Western World?"

He'd have that "is this a trick question?" look on his face.

"Me?"

"Seeing as Raffaela made contact with the Townies, you can make contact with the Cadets," I tell him now.

"I think that Cadet might want to talk to you, Taylor."

I stop and he walks into me. "What's that supposed to mean?"

Ben shuffles for a moment, looking at his feet, before he dares look at me. "Well, rumour has it he's not the easiest person to speak to and seeing you guys have a history it might make some sense. . . ."

"Do you know what a history is? It's what Raffaela and Chaz Santangelo have. Lots of stories to tell, lots of anger to vent, lots of baggage to check into I-Don't-Give-a-Shit Airline. The Cadet and me? Nothing to tell. I ran away one day. He was running in the same direction. We ended up on the same train in the same carriage. The train derailed, we walked the same road and hitched a ride with the same postman in Yass. We got caught because the Cadet got scared and rang the powers that be. We came home in Santangelo's father's paddy wagon. End of story. No history. No sequel. Nothing."

I can't see their faces because it's too dark but they know I'm lying. I lie all the time about those three days. Probably because I can't explain it. It reeks of supernatural bullshit and hunches. It stars the boy in the tree in my dreams who took me by the hand and made me stand on a branch and asked, "What can you see?"

"Nothing," I had said.

"Know what I can see? From this distance, everything is so bloody perfect."

And I looked harder into the distance and what I saw was my mother. There was a radiance about her that I had never seen before. So I went looking for her and in that dream I found her soul, but when I woke up in the morning, I knew that I had to go looking for the rest of her.

That's when I first saw the Cadet, on the platform of the Jellicoe Station. I knew who he was in an instant. It's not every day that you hear a story about a boy who killed his father. That was the rumour, anyway. Standing on the platform alongside him, I believed every word of it. There was a caged fury to him. A feralness that seeped out of every pore.

"Do you know when the next train to Yass is coming?" I had asked.

"Go to hell," he said, but there was a desolate fear in his eyes and I couldn't look away.

"Been there. Trust me. It's so overrated."

And for reasons I will never understand, I received a smile from Jonah Griggs, and there was a yearning in it, touching a nerve inside me that still freaks me out to this day. On that train something was unleashed in both of us. He didn't say much about himself except that it was his first time away from his mother and brother and he had a desperate need to know that they were all right without him. And I told him everything. About my first memory, sitting on the shoulders of a giant who I know can only be my father. Of touching the sky. Of lying between two people who read me stories of wild things and journeys with dragons, the soft hum of their voices speaking of love and serenity. See, I remember love. That's what people don't understand. And what I also remember is that in telling that tale to the Cadet on the train I got a glimpse of peace.

When the train derailed and we decided to hike, there was never a question that we wouldn't stick together and find my mother. Except on the third night he had a dream and betrayed us.

"What do I say to him?" Ben asks, bringing me back to the real world.

What should he say to the Cadet? Ask him why

he called his school to come and get us when we were so close to wherever both of us wanted to be. Ask him why he had made that call when he knew I was two hours away from my mother.

"Tell him we want to make a deal."

I walk past the year-seven and -eight dorms, where Jessa McKenzie has already taken over. The others hang off her every word and I haven't seen them this animated . . . actually ever. The Lachlan House leaders were always strict. Commandments number one to ten ranged from No Fun to No Fun. But down here, Jessa McKenzie and her posse are either giggling hysterically or spooking one another out. The rest of the girls are engrossed in her tale and I even notice Raffaela amongst them, sitting on one of the beds, intrigued.

"He's killed ten people in twenty years," I hear Jessa say.

"But nowhere near here?" That comes from Chloe P. who, in all probability, will now be paralysed with fear all night.

"Those kids who went missing a couple of years ago were from Truscott, which is halfway between here and the city," one of the year eights says. "That's close enough."

"Lights off," I say.

They look my way. Scrubbed little faces of kids who don't really know who I am. Just that I'm in charge.

"I'm telling them about the serial killer, Taylor, and how he—"

"Is nowhere near us," I interrupt.

I walk over to her as they begin to disperse. I catch a glimpse of the newspaper clippings spread out all over her bed. The faces of the dead or missing, so young and happy that all I can think of is, how can they be dead? Toothy grins, mostly those school photos that you keep hidden.

But the worst photos are those of the parents. Their faces are so drawn and grief-stricken. They want their children back. I look at the faces of the girls around me and wonder who would look that grief-stricken for half of them. If something happens to me, whose face will be on the front page of the paper begging for me? Is a person worth more because they have someone to grieve for them?

I look at Jessa McKenzie and I wonder what type

of warped person carries around newspaper clippings of dead kids and despairing parents. What kind of a freak is this kid who's giggling hysterically with the girls in the neighbouring beds, each with a crush on the other for being the same age when the rest of the world seems so old?

The three of them are snuggled up together, talking like they haven't seen one another in years. Sometimes I look at the girls in my form, in my very own house, most of them now on the third floor with me, and I realise that I hardly know them.

For the first time since they made me leader of the community, I realise why I told Hannah I was thinking of leaving. It's fear. Not of having to negotiate territory, fight a war, and make sure we come out of it with more land than when we started. I can do that blindfolded.

It's this that scares me.

My seniors have left the House.

I'm in charge of fifty kids who don't give a shit about the territory wars. They just want to be looked after.

And I have no idea how.

Chapter 5

He went missing on one of the prettiest days Narnie could remember in her whole sixteen years. One of those days when she woke up and actually wanted to be alive.

Over the next twenty-four hours the four of them called his name, first with annoyance, then urgency, hysteria, rage, grief.

And then with despair.

By the third day everyone else at the school joined in, as well as the Townies and the Cadets.

But the birds still sang and the river still flowed and the flowers were in full bloom.

And then their voices stopped and their souls stood still and they ceased being who they had been.

Because who they were had always been determined by him.

—

Five days after his disappearance she scraped the words and numbers on the trunk of the Prayer Tree.
 MATTHEW 10.26
 And she vowed that she would never leave this place until he returned.

Chapter 6

The boy in the tree in my dreams comes calling again. His visits are more frequent these days. I ask him why and he tells me it's because he's waiting for someone. For the first time ever I feel a chill slice through me. I ask him who it is he is waiting for but he doesn't answer. For some freaky reason, Hannah comes to mind and just when I'm about to ask him another question, I sense that there is someone else in the tree with us. Someone at the edge of the branch, like a shadow, but I can't quite see their face. The boy stands up tall on the branch and dives into the water below and I hear a whimper from the shadow at the end of the branch. It frightens me so much that, with shaking legs, I stand as well. Ready to jump. Just about to.

"Taylor?"

I look at my clock. Six A.M.

Raffaela is standing by my bed. "It's Ben. You should see what the Cadets have done to him."

They went for his fingers like they knew how much he needed them. His House leaders would always do that to him, too. Ben's a muso. Loves anything that produces a tune, so naturally it's always his fingers that get smashed when someone is pissed off with him, and Ben has one of those personalities that invites pissed-offness. Raffaela has his fingers taped and it's a while before he looks up at me. I flinch at what I see.

I'm presuming the eye will go a purply colour and that it will be difficult for him to eat for a day or two, judging by the amount of blood around his mouth. Raffaela cleans him up with the practicality of someone who has spent a lifetime doing it and I try to keep my mind on the semi-carnage in front of me but I just can't help thinking back to my dream.

"So you made the offer," I say.

He nods but even that seems painful.

"And they didn't like it?"

"He wanted the negotiations to take place

between him and *the girl*. 'Isn't she in charge over there?' That's what he said. Like I thought he would. Remember that part where I said he'll want to speak to you?"

"And he's a coward who gets his thugs to do the dirty work for him."

"Oh no," Ben says, trying to shake his head and pushing Raffaela's hand away. "He did all this himself. You've got to hand it to him. He does his own dirty work."

I can tell Ben's angry.

"I am allowed to delegate," I say to him, speaking more sharply than I should.

"Yeah, I know. But you weren't delegating. You were avoiding someone and I got caught in the middle. Look at me. I'm five foot four. I'm a weakling. My specialty is medieval jousting and violin. I'm not built for pain. He, on the other hand, is a ten-feet-fricken-tall unit."

"Then we try again and give him want he wants for the time being," Raffaela says.

"We have no idea what he wants."

"Did this happen on our territory or theirs?"

"Does it matter? It hurts the same. They have

booby traps everywhere. It's like one of those bad Chuck Norris–Vietnam War movies from the eighties."

"So they're bored?" I ask.

"Out of their tiny brains. They just worked out that you can't get mobile coverage out here. So no text-messaging means more terrorising. You can't walk a metre without a trip-wire getting you. You need to call a meeting with Richard and the other leaders. Remind them of exactly where the boundaries are because if one of the younger kids gets caught in the wrong area, there'll be casualties and the teachers will start asking questions and the other Houses are going to go apeshit."

"Then we'll go check the boundaries later today."

"I'm not going!"

"Yes you are, Ben. You're my second-in-charge."

"Only chosen because you didn't want Richard. Don't think for one moment that I thought you picked me for any other reason. I don't get chosen for things unless there's a motive. You know why I'm head of my House? Because Number One Son found Jesus Christ and is now a happy clapper with those Hillsong People in Sydney, and I'm about this close to joining him."

"I'll get Richard, then. He'll be the best of a bad bunch of backstabbers. Is that okay with you?" I snap. I walk out and slam the door, thumping furiously down the stairs.

The teacher who has replaced Hannah is calling the roll in our dining room and everyone acts as if it's the most natural thing in the world. Everyone except for me and Jessa McKenzie. She sits at the bottom of the stairs wrapped in her nightgown, with that perfect yearning concern on her face.

"Go get some breakfast," I say firmly.

"Are you going to Hannah's?"

"It's none of your business where I'm going," I mutter, slamming out the front door.

Hannah's house has begun to lose her scent. These days it smells musty and still. I walk to her room in the attic and lie on her bed. It's been a week since I've seen her and I know that it's time to go and speak to one of the teachers. To ask casually where she is. I bury my face in her pillow. I can't remember one day in the last five years that Hannah hasn't been around and for a moment I want to cry. I'm angry that I want to cry because I feel like I've been manipulated by the soundtrack in my head—the same one that made me cry in some shit sentimental movie with Julia Roberts where the mum is dying of cancer. I get off the bed and walk down to the kitchen. Hannah's manuscript is there on the table, but it seems thinner and the pages are spread out like someone's just read them, like someone's just been here, which makes me feel uneasy. The pages aren't numbered, so I don't know whether I have the beginning or end or whether it's in sequence but these days I'm not really looking for continuity.

All I'm after is something that makes sense to me.

In between setting up a bilateral agreement with the enemy, banning rumours about serial killers, and fobbing off an attempted coup d'état by Richard and the other House leaders, I go to see our Principal about Hannah and realise that in the whole time I have been at the school, I've been in this office only once. John Palmer moves from behind his desk and sits me down in one of his "guest" seats like he's promoting the notion of some kind of warmth and familiarity. It's not that I don't like the adults around here; it's just that they don't stick around long enough. The Jellicoe School is their stepping stone to some other place and there have been three Principals since I've arrived. That's what makes Hannah different. Rumour has it that Hannah went to school here and just never left. That's another of what I call the Hannah mysteries. Why would a woman who's not even in her mid-thirties hide herself away from the world out here? Worse still, why would she choose to leave out of the blue and not tell me?

"You're not privy to that type of information, Taylor," Mr. Palmer says gently but firmly.

"She's been my House co-ordinator for five years, sir. She brought me to this school. I think that entitles me to be privy to something. Added to that, I have a House of kids who need her."

He's nodding, like it's all occurred to him already. "Ms. Morris will be staying at the cottage just outside Lachlan House, so anything you need, you just call her."

"Do you know whether Hannah's coming back? Did she put in notice or warn you? Anything?" I am desperate for something.

"Let's just say that she was in a rush. She left a letter saying that she had something to attend to in Sydney and that she'd contact us when she knew her plans. She apologised for any inconvenience and signed it."

"Can she just do that? Walk out on her job without an explanation? Has she been picking up her salary?"

"Taylor," he says, a perplexed look on his face. "Hannah's not an employee. She doesn't work for the school. She owns the property by the river and has helped out around here for as long as anyone can remember. She can come and go as she pleases, something she hasn't elected to do in the past, so I'm certainly not going to turn around and demand that she return here, even if I did have her number. You know Hannah better than I do; it would have had to be something important for her to have left. She'll ring you at your House any day now. You're panicking for nothing."

"Did she mail the letter?"

"It was hand-delivered by a friend of hers."

"Who? Who's her friend? I know all her friends.

I promise. Ask me any question about her and I'll be able to answer. Just let me speak to this friend of hers."

He leans forward in his seat. I am humiliated by the pity in his eyes. "I promise you that if she contacts me I will tell her that you want to speak to her."

I nod again, swallowing. "Can I just see the letter?" There's a pleading tone in my voice and suddenly I am every pathetic kid who has ever been dumped in this place. I'm the pining in Jessa McKenzie's face and the desperation in those poor kids who would hang off every one of Hannah's words just because she took notice of them. I always felt that I was above that. I'm not sure why until this moment. From the day Hannah picked me up from that 7-Eleven I knew I meant more to her. That we were somehow connected.

Mr. Palmer walks away for a moment and retrieves something from a filing cabinet. He returns with an envelope in his hands, which he shows me and I take in every detail. On the envelope, in writing not belonging to Hannah, are the words To be given to John Palmer. The writing is amazingly neat and precise. Mr. Palmer sees the look of doubt on my face and takes the letter out of the envelope and I recognise the handwriting instantly. Hannah's.

I stand up, nodding again. "I'm sorry."

"What's there to be sorry about Taylor? That you miss a friend?"

There's been too much sentimentality for me already, so I walk to the door. "If you hear from her . . ."

"You have my promise."

When I get back to the House the juniors are doing their homework.

"If Hannah rings," I say from the door, "you make sure you call me."

Jessa McKenzie looks up and, like every single time she looks at me, I get a sense of familiarity. She holds up her hand and gives a small wave. Unexpectedly, a fierce sense of protectiveness comes over me. Except I fight it back because I can hardly look after myself these days.

I lie in bed and words silently tumble out of my mouth. Some people say their prayers at night. I don't. What I say is always the same. *My name is Taylor Markham. I live on the Jellicoe Road.*

In the tree hanging over the ridge, Webb made his plans to build a house. He'd make it out of gopherwood, like Noah's ark, two storeys high, with a view he could look out on every day with wonder. His father had built their home on the farm. It was one of the things Webb had loved about him and the times he missed him most were when he remembered the sounds of hammering and the humming of a saw and his father's voice joining in the harmony of some song that seemed to play in all their minds. Webb remembered how he and Narnie would hold nails between their teeth just to be like him, tapping away with their hammers, knowing they were part of something big.

He told Narnie and Tate his plan. Sitting in that tree, he told them he was going to build a house and that he needed their help. For a long time Narnie didn't say anything. She just curled up around the branch, staring into the valley below. She told him that from this angle the treetops looked like cauliflower and she had once heard them beckon her to jump, promising her that if she did, they'd bounce her back in the air again. Some days, like today, he was petrified she'd listen to them.

So he made them both stand on the branch, tightly holding their hands.

"Don't worry. I'll never let go."

"What can you see?" Narnie asked.

"Nothing."

"Know what I can see?" Tate said. "From this distance everything is so bloody perfect."

Chapter 7

The next afternoon I walk to Clarence House to find Ben. With hands shaking, I knock on the door and wait. The kid who answers looks at me nervously and I wonder why, until I remember how often I'd come across the UC leader in the past. Rarely. They didn't do house calls. Even within their own Houses they became deified. The kid doesn't move, still staring at me, and thankfully Ben appears and puts his hand on the kid's shoulder.

"Go back to study," he tells him. "I'll be in soon."

Ben doesn't say anything to me, but his look says, *And?*

"So what did you tell your House co-ordinator," I ask, pointing to his face, "about that."

"That I've taken up football."

I nod. "Naturally. You look like a footballer."

"He was very grateful for the lie. Means he doesn't have to investigate."

We look at each other for a moment and for once I feel awkward. It's not that I'm not into humility; I've just never had to practise it.

"You want me to come out there with you?"

"Yes I do," I say honestly, realising there is no point beating around the bush.

"Year eight have assignments due tomorrow," he says, pointing behind him. "It's not really a good time."

"You do homework with them?"

"I'm their House leader."

"My House leaders never did homework with us. Hannah did."

"And my House leaders used to flush our heads down the toilet. Consequently I'm going for a more pastoral approach."

"Consequently? I would have used 'naturally.'"

"You've already used it. Anyway, as a consequence of how I was treated I have chosen to act in the exact opposite way, so I'm sticking by 'consequently.'"

"If I send Raffaela over to help these kids, then will you come?"

"Raffaela's probably sitting there helping your year eights."

"Naturally."

More silence. Humility now has to give way to begging.

"Ben, my first seven days on this job are over and I have nothing to show for it. In the past, our leaders have always made contact with the Cadets and succeeded in at least re-establishing boundaries. I don't even know what to say to these guys. I'm admitting that to you, and I don't know why I'm admitting it to you."

"Because you have no respect for me and you don't care whether I think you're weak or not."

I resign myself to the fact that I'm down to one ally: Raffaela. But Raffaela isn't a House leader, she's my second-in-charge, and there's no way she can save me from defeat at the hands of Richard and his five signatures.

"Fine," I say, turning away. I make it to the bottom stair and turn to find him still there at the door. "And for your own information, I don't know whether I have respect for you. But I chose you over Richard and the others because I trust you. That's my motive and at this moment, trust is beating anything else in my life and if it's not good enough for you then I don't know what to say." I begin walking.

"What's in it for me?" he calls out.

"Nothing," I call back to him. "I'm not even going to pretend there is."

He catches up with me. "No. That's what you have to say to them when you negotiate. I always used to hear the leader say it. 'What's in it for me?'"

He keeps on walking farther away from his House and I experience a sense of relief when we reach the clearing and he's still with me. My stomach begins to twitch and I realise I'm nervous about the prospect of the Cadets.

"We could be lucky," Ben says, sensing my nervousness. "They might be carving up a pig they've just slaughtered for dinner and ripping the flesh off the bones with their teeth as we speak and—"

"—as a consequence?"

"—Won't be interested in us lurking around."

I'm unconvinced.

We're out there for quite a while, marking the map with all the important checkpoints. For most of the year we don't have to worry about boundaries, but come September the map is our bible. I follow its instructions and I don't realise how close I am to the edge of the ridge until Ben grabs my shirt and pulls me back. But I like being this close. Just one step and those cauliflower trees below could bounce me right back up again.

Ben is staring at me. "Are you blind? You almost went over."

I'm about to tell him not to be ridiculous when he holds up a hand.

"Did you hear that?" he whispers.

"What?"

"That?"

He looks at me and I open my mouth to say something but he puts two taped fingers to his lips. "I think we've crossed the boundary without realising," he continues, whispering.

"According to the map, this eucalyptus tree is the boundary."

"According to the map there are two trees this size and we passed the other one about ten minutes ago."

I stand still for a moment. Birds sing, trees rustle

in the wind, but there's something else. The feeling of being crowded in, despite one hundred acres of bush around us, stretching as far as the eye can see.

I hold up one finger, then two, then three, and we bolt. But not even one step later I'm flying through the air. I make contact with the ground in no time, face first in an exfoliation of dirt, leaving my face feeling scratched and bruised.

I try to kneel but I realise that some kind of trap has grabbed hold of my foot and then I see the boot in front of me. Big, black, laced-up, army regular, polished clean, with the ability to wipe out a whole universe of ants in one step. I look a tiny bit farther up and I see the khaki pants tucked in but I stop there. This is not the position I want to be in for this meeting. So I keep my eyes forward as I slowly raise myself, and then we're eye to eye, give or take the ten centimetres he has on me.

Jonah Griggs is a tank. His face is blunter, meaner than I remember. Hair cropped. Eyes cold. Arms folded. He has perfected the art of looking straight at someone while avoiding eye contact.

Two of his Cadets have Ben by the arm and I can tell by the look on Ben's face and the angle of their strongholds that he's in pain.

"Let him go," I say.

Jonah Griggs looks over my head, as though he's contemplating my request. As if. He ponders for a moment, placing his thumb and finger on his chin, and then shakes his head.

"Maybe another time," he says, his voice so unlike the one about to break three years ago.

"We might just take him around for a tour of the boundaries and when he comes back, he can pass them on to you," his second-in-command says.

"I'd prefer you took me for that tour."

Jonah Griggs feigns contemplation again and leans forward as if he didn't hear but still there's no eye contact.

So I grab his face and look straight in his eyes and it's like a punch in the gut holding that stare. "You want to make this personal, Jonah? Then let him go."

I don't know what possesses me to say his name but it slips off my tongue easily and I watch him flinch.

"No deal," Ben calls out. "I don't go without you."

"That is very touching," Jonah Griggs says, shaking free of my hand. "There is so much love in this space."

Ben blows him a kiss and all hell breaks loose. The impact of boots on fingers makes it clear what happened the night before. I jump on Jonah Griggs's back but I can't even pull his hair because Cadet regulation haircut doesn't allow for it. He shrugs me off easily and I land on the ground for the second time in less than five minutes.

"What happened to the scary folk that we were warned about?" he mocks, looking down at me. "You and the Townies are making this too easy for us."

"You want scary? We can do scary." I pick myself up. "Let's go," I say to Ben, who is almost speechless from the pain.

"Scare me, then," I hear Jonah Griggs say.

I turn around to face him. "The treaty? The one that says we control any access with water? The one that you guys have been able to violate for the last four years because there has been no water? Well, while you were away it rained. That means there's a river. That means you have no access unless we give it to you. That means you are restricted to a tenth of the land you've been used to using in the past."

"So what are you saying?"

"This is war."

Griggs shrugs arrogantly. "Well, I guess we're better dressed for it."

Chapter 8

She stood at Webb's door: Tate, with the wild hair and the grin that went on forever. Sometimes Webb believed that he would never experience a better feeling than when he was looking at her, would never see anything or anybody bursting with more life and spirit. Sometimes he felt he needed to inhale it and place it in a storage area in his soul. Just in case.

When he said that to Tate she'd be perplexed. "But Webb, I'm like this because of you. You're everything to me."

On Narnie's sad days, he wished he could be all that to her, too.

"Is that what you want?" his sister had asked once while they sat dangling their feet in the river.

"In a different way because you're my sister but

yeah. If it keeps you happy . . . or wanting to live, yeah, I'd want to be everything to you."

"You do all the work, Webb," she said tiredly. "Don't you get sick of that?"

He shook his head. "Not if you and Tate are okay."

"But what happens to all of us when you're not okay? What then? We'll become pathetic. Even more than I am now. So why would I want someone to be my everything when one day they might not be around? What will be left of me then?"

"I'll never ever leave you, Narnie. You're my sister. You're all I've got."

And Tate, standing at his door now, smiling her hypnotic smile. "The Cadets are here," she said. "This is going to be our last year doing this. Let's go get Narnie and make some trouble."

The three of them stood their ground on the Jellicoe Road, directly in front of a bus-load of Cadets. In the distance the sound of a shotgun rang out and a cloud of dust hovered just above the trees in front of them.

"Townies," Tate said. "At full throttle, by the looks of things."

The bus driver kept his hand on the horn, lazily.

"Surrender," Webb yelled. "Send out your leader!"

"You get off this road or you'll be the ones surrendering your little arses," the driver yelled back.

The doors opened and after a moment a boot appeared on the road and then another.

Tate and Webb exchanged looks. Narnie felt her heart knock against her chest.

A Cadet stepped out from behind the bus door, dressed in full military school uniform. He strode towards them, only looking back once when he realised that the car that had been making the ruckus up the dirt road was almost upon them. He reached the trio and searched their faces.

"I've never understood the strap across the chin," Webb said. "It has to be the most moronic thing I've ever seen."

"How can we take you seriously?" Tate said.

"Bloody uncomfortable, too," Jude agreed, taking it off.

When the shooting got louder they all turned in the direction of the on-coming car.

"Fitz?"

"Psychotic as ever. He got expelled from his school about three times this year."

"And you know how excited he gets when you come a-calling." Tate grinned.

Jude grinned back. He punched Webb in the shoulder and Webb punched him back.

"Where are the others?" one of the Cadets called from the bus window.

"Parent weekend," Webb called back. "We're the only ones around."

As the bus drove off, a car swerved around it, twisting to a halt. Then Fitz was out of the car, jumping on Jude's back with the feverish madness they were all used to.

"Why haven't they arrested you yet?" Jude said, throwing him off and diving on top of him. They wrestled until Fitz victoriously had Jude straddled.

"Loving that position, are we?" Tate laughed.

Webb helped them both up and the five of them made their way down the Jellicoe Road towards the school.

"Guess what?" Fitz said.

"I don't know," Jude said. "What? Narnie smiled?"

He glanced at her for the first time.

"When you guys see a Narnie smile, it's like a revelation," Webb said, gathering her towards him.

Jude stopped in front of her and, with both hands cupping her face, tried to make a smile. Narnie flinched.

"Leave her alone," Tate said.

"I need a revelation," Jude said. "And you're the only one that can give me one, Narns."

"Let's get back to 'Guess what?'" Fitz said, hyped beyond control.

"What?"

"Phase one of the tunnel," Webb said in a low voice. "It's finished."

Every year the town puts on a welcome for the Cadets and invites us along for the gala event, if one can give a sausage sizzle and rugby league game such a title. I get word halfway through the day that a meeting is to take place between the three factions after the official part of the ceremony. I send Ben around to gather the other House leaders and we work out our strategy, which none of us can agree on. In the end we decide that a rental of the river may be allowed;

however, the numbers of Cadets using it at any one time is to be no more than twelve.

As usual, the Cadets are in their fatigues and the bulky frame of Jonah Griggs stands out among them. He surveys the field and beyond, handling his team as he would his troops. I can tell that his team is first-class. Santangelo is tenacious and what his team lacks in skill, they make up for in endurance and speed. Our league team is abysmal and, halfway through the round robin, I realise that we are not even players in this whole territory war.

When the games are over, the official part of the ceremony begins. Behind the microphones, a band sets up and I see the Mullet Brothers tuning their guitars alongside a girl with dreadlocks and heaps of piercings.

Santangelo's mother is the mayor and I hear her whisper, "Behave," to her son as she lines us up for a school captain photo. She's indigenous, which makes sense when I think of his colouring. Even for an Italian, his skin seemed dark. We have photos taken with her and then they place the three of us in front of the stage and take more photos.

"Chaz!" Santangelo's mum is trying to get his

attention from where she's standing with some of the school officials. She mouths *smile*, waving her fingers under her mouth.

"Chaz," Jonah Griggs says snidely. "Your mum wants you to smile."

"And yours wants you to eat shit and die."

I'm standing between these two intellectuals while the local photographer snaps away, asking us to say words like *holidays* and *pornography*.

"Yours thinks you should loosen up," Griggs continues to bait.

"Really?"

"Yeah. She told me last night."

The first strains of the national anthem screech across the stage, causing everyone to wince.

"What did you say?" Santangelo asks quietly.

"Your mum. Nice lady. *Really nice.*"

Santangelo flies into it first. Fist straight into Jonah Griggs's stomach and next minute they're both rolling on the ground pounding each other. Then there's a war cry and it's a free for all, present company excluded, of course, and believe me, I do feel excluded but there is no way I'm joining in. The leader of Murray House goes flying through the air and lands at my feet, groaning. I try to help him up but then I realise he's getting off on this. They all are. It's like some Neanderthal skirmish for the pathetic. Some of the Townie teachers try to stop it. Big mistake. It gets boring for at least four more minutes and even the girls from Jellicoe High acknowledge me with a roll of the eyes. Judging by Santangelo's mum's expression, I wouldn't want to be at her dinner table tonight.

Then the police arrive. I recognise Santangelo's dad, who saves police brutality for when he gets to his son. Then I see Ben disappear under a heap of bodies and I go in to assist because the Mullet Brothers have fallen into the body jam with their guitars still attached to them, causing more pain than is necessary. Except just as I'm about to pull Ben's head out of the scrum, a whistle shrills in my ear and this cop is grabbing me by the arm. And then it's over.

They separate us into groups. The Ringleaders and the Others. I belong to the Ringleaders because my weak, pathetic, traitorous, fundamentally base peers point to me when someone asks them who is in charge. The only positive thing in this whole situation is that because this stupid town is so small, you don't have to actually get into the paddy wagon to be taken to gaol. They march you there. The worst thing is I'm placed in the same cell as Jonah Griggs and Chaz Santangelo and they are still so filthy with each other that I know it's not over and somehow I'm going to be caught up in it. In the cell next to ours there are about thirty other kids, combinations of all three factions. I look for Ben but can see only some of the other House leaders, who are proudly comparing scars.

In my cell I don't even seem to exist. The dust and grime begin to get to me and I feel a shortness of breath that I know spells trouble. On the other side of the cell Jonah Griggs and Santangelo are too busy sizing each other up like two demented pit bulls who have to prove who's got the biggest . . . attitude.

I lean against the bars that separate us from the others. "So let me get this right," I say to one of the Townie girls. "All it takes is to insult someone's mother?"

"No," she explains. "That's the beauty of it. They don't actually have to insult. The words *Your mother* are enough."

"So if I said to you, 'Your mother is a . . . ?'" I shrug.

"Just 'Your mother.'" But it doesn't work if girls say it to each other," she continues. "You have to have a penis for it to affect you in such a way."

"Oh funny, funny," Santangelo says.

The bonding with the Townie girls is a highlight. I spend my first hour of incarceration in conversation with one of them—who happens to be the girlfriend of one of the Mullet Brothers—about the myths around eyebrow piercing. When I have the courage, I ask her the burning question about why the Mullets but I'm short of breath and I can recognise the tell-tale signs of an asthma attack coming on, so I have to go and sit down and don't get to hear the answer.

The first lot of parents come in at around five P.M., including the House master of Murray House, so within half an hour the cell next door is empty and it's just Griggs, Santangelo, and me. They put me in the cell next door on my own and we get to order takeaway for dinner.

"You promised us a negotiation about the Club House," Santangelo says, still eyeing Jonah Griggs, but speaking to me.

"Negotiations are over," I say flatly.

"You can't do that."

"Any which way, we've got the Club House and you can't stop us from getting there," Jonah Griggs says arrogantly.

"Watch me."

"If we make a deal over the Club House, it will be profitable for all of us," Santangelo says.

"Come within an inch of our property . . ."

"And what?" Jonah Griggs calls over to me.

"Unfortunately the state persists in using our school as a juvie centre when it suits them. We have arsonists."

"So you'll burn us down?" he says, feigning fear.

"No, but we will burn down every single building you own on our property. Beginning with the Club House."

Now I have their attention.

Raffaela is allowed to see me based on the fact that she knows how to sweet-talk Santangelo's father, who I find out is her godfather.

"We've called Mr. Palmer but he's at some Rotary Club do and Mr. Grace from Murray House says he's not authorised to bail you out so we have to wait until Sal— sorry, Constable Santangelo," she says, looking up at him and smiling, "speaks to Mr. Palmer . . . which could be after midnight."

"Where's Ben?" I ask.

"I think I saw him go after the Mullet Brothers."

"As if he can take on the Mullet Brothers. Is he insane? Find him, Raffaela. He could be hurt."

"I'm staying with my parents tonight so he can bunk at my place."

I hear the sound of heavy boots enter the station and the next minute Jonah Griggs jumps to his feet saluting, a shocked look on his face. Santangelo mocks the salute behind his back.

"Hey!" his father bellows, and Santangelo sits back down, sulking.

I strain my neck to see what has surprised Jonah Griggs so much and my heart begins racing wildly.

It's the first time I've seen the Brigadier this close since he delivered me back to Hannah's place three years ago. In my memory he has always been a giant but today I notice that Griggs towers over him. I slouch against the gates, watching the interaction between him and Griggs.

"I don't think it will kill you if you stay the

night," he says to Griggs in a tone that isn't open for negotiation.

I don't know how it is that a voice I've only heard once can stay in my mind, but it's as recognisable to me as Hannah's.

I see a flicker of shittiness on Jonah Griggs's face but he holds the salute. "Yes, sir."

"You, too," Santangelo's dad says, pointing at his son. Santangelo swears under his breath.

"Sorry, what was that?" his father asks loudly.

"Nothing," Santangelo mutters.

And then the Brigadier is looking at me and I hold his stare, despite the fact that a part of me feels sick. He looks younger than I've remembered him to be all this time. Younger than Santangelo's dad, anyway.

"Do you want me to take her back to the school?" he asks Santangelo's dad.

"No!" I almost yell.

Santangelo's dad shakes his head. "John Palmer's coming down soon. She'll be fine."

The Brigadier continues to hold my stare, like he's taking in every detail of me and it seems like a million years later that he turns to go.

"I hear you're going to be sticking around for a couple of weeks," Santangelo's dad says to him as they both leave. Only then does Jonah Griggs relax.

"Since when do real army brigadiers run the Cadets?" Santangelo asks.

"They don't."

I can tell that Griggs is confused about the Brigadier's presence. He looks at me and I walk over to the other side of my cell, settling myself as far away as possible from both of them.

Gaol's not that bad, especially when you're used to crap food at school and you get Thai takeaway.

"How's Hannah these days?" Santangelo's dad asks me as he hands it over.

"You know Hannah?"

"Since she was your age."

I shrug. "She's away."

The phone rings and the other police officer comes in holding it.

"It's Clara," he tells Santangelo's dad. "She wants to talk to Chaz." Santangelo takes the phone through the bars and Jonah Griggs snickers and makes himself comfortable on the bunk while Santangelo tries to speak as quietly as possible.

"Hi . . . look . . . I know . . . Yeah, like I did it on purpose, Mum. . . . Okay . . . *you're what?* Don't go to their place. . . . She's a liar. . . . She only pretends to be that sweet in front of . . . Oh, good, believe her over your son. . . . No. He's being an a-hole. . . . I didn't say "arse," you did. . . . Fine, take his side. . . ."

He hands the phone to his father. "She said not to forget to pick up the bread." He sulks.

By ten o'clock I make a pact with myself that I will never commit a crime because gaol is the most boring place on earth. Even more boring than the Jellicoe School on a Sunday afternoon. It's so boring that when Santangelo comes over to my side of the cell, I welcome the conversation.

"Chewy?"

I reach over and take a stick. Up close he is truly a good-looking guy and I'm curious about the Raffaela connection but don't dare ask him about it. Santangelo has this way of looking at me, not in a pervy way or like someone who's interested. He's staring at me like he did in the negotiating hut. Like he has a question to ask or something to say, but doesn't quite know how to say it.

"Spit it out," I say.

"Spit what out?"

"Whatever you want to say."

He's about to deny it, but then he seems to change his mind. "The guy . . . the Hermit? My dad used to take me out there sometimes, to see how he was going."

I move closer. No one at the Jellicoe School has ever mentioned the Hermit. Their way of dealing with it has always been to pretend it never happened.

"You knew him?"

He nods. "He was a bit mad. Like obsessive compulsive, you know. He'd stand on a tree branch and dive into the river in the same spot all the time and just let the current take him away. I thought he'd die doing that, not . . ."

We don't say anything for a while.

"Do you remember much about that day?" he asks.

Only that when I woke up I was in Hannah's bed and I heard someone crying like an animal. I remember opening my eyes and seeing the blur of her body holding on to another—a man. He was clutching onto her with grief and they were both so distraught. I wondered if he was a friend of the Hermit. I remember that I never saw the clothes I was wearing that day ever again, which was a pity because I so liked my Felix the Cat T-shirt and grey cord jeans and whenever I asked Hannah for them, she'd just shake her head.

I don't answer. "What did your dad say?" I ask instead.

He doesn't look at me. "I don't know. Just that it was messy," he mumbles.

"How messy? What do you mean 'messy'?"

He looks up at me. "You know . . . messy."

I see Jonah Griggs get up from his bunk and walk towards us. "Why are you telling her this?" he snaps at Santangelo.

He ignores Griggs. "My father cried. . . . I'd never seen him cry. . . . He told me that the Hermit had a kid. . . ."

I feel sick. Up till now the Hermit had never possessed a life. He was just this madman who lived in the bush. But to know that he left someone behind . . . And then a horrific thought enters my head.

"Was he my father?" I whisper. "Is that what your dad said?"

"Why would you think that?" he asks, surprised.

Griggs grabs Santangelo by the arm. "You're stressing her out."

"Why is this your business? You don't even know her."

I feel my windpipe constricting and I know what's about to happen. I'm trying to work out where my backpack is so I can get my inhaler but I realise that it's out there with the cops.

Jonah Griggs looks at me for a moment and I see a frown appear on his face. "Sit down. You're going to faint."

The chewing gum makes my mouth feel sweet and next minute I'm throwing up mucus that is making me gag.

"Look what you've done, you arsehole!"

I can see them both glued to the bars that separate us. The retching never seems to end, like it's carving out my insides and I can't breathe. My windpipe feels like it's choking me and I can smell the Hermit's blood, the sickly sweet smell of it, and suddenly I see it, plastered all over my clothes, and I see the Hermit out there on that day when the sun was so hot and I hear his whispers and I try to keep my eyes closed, but I can't and there are parts of him around me and the blood smacking at my face and I can't breathe and I can hear Jonah Griggs shouting and Santangelo calling out, *"Dad, Dad, get in here."* I'm making this gurgling sound because I just can't breathe and although I'm bent over away from the bars I feel hands grab hold of me, pulling me towards them. I feel arms around my chest, a mouth against my ear whispering . . . whispering . . . Jonah Griggs whispering, "Just breathe, just breathe, come on, Taylor, just breathe . . . just breathe."

Mr. Palmer is wiping my face. Santangelo's dad is there as well, placing a glass of water in my hands and helping me drink. I'm gulping it down, feeling weak and pathetically teary.

"We're going home," John Palmer says quietly. "Can you stand?"

I nod. "I'm sorry about the mess," I tell Santangelo's dad.

He smiles. "We'll live."

As I walk past the other cell I see Santangelo sitting on the floor with his back against the bars, his head in his hands, and Jonah Griggs standing, watching me. Like he did on that station platform. Like he did those times we lay side by side on our way to Yass. Staring like he's never stopped. For a moment the mask slips from his face, but by that time I'm almost out the door.

It's not until we reach the Jellicoe Road that Mr. Palmer speaks.

"Hannah's fine."

"How do you know?" I ask, raising my head from where it's been leaning against the door.

"I spoke to someone who knows her. She's in Sydney looking after a friend . . . who's sick."

All of a sudden Hannah has all these "friends." Friends who have known her since she was seventeen. Friends who hand over letters. Friends who are sick.

"Who? You don't understand. I know everyone she knows."

He is keeping something from me. I can tell by the way he can't look me in the face and that scares me. He seems to sense this and once again I'm surprised by his kindness.

"She calls her friend, 'Mrs. Dubose.' That's all I know."

Mrs. Dubose.

"Have you heard of her?" he asks.

"Yes," I say sleepily. "She lived in the same street as Jem and Scout Finch."

Chapter 9

I'm riding as fast as I can. The faster the pace, the less thought-process, and being thoughtless suits me fine. I pedal hard, my face sweating, my hands clenched on the handlebars until I feel the blood stop in my fingers. I pedal on with eyes closed and we travel, the bike and I, as if it has a mind of its own and I have no control. I skid suddenly to the side and realise that I've reached the ridge, an inch away from going over the edge. My face is drenched with perspiration and I look at the space below. The world sways and I sway with it until it's like being in a hypnotic dance, almost enticing me to step over.

But my attention is drawn away by the rustling above me. In the tree. There's something watching. I throw the bike to the side and crane my neck, my heart pounding hard. For a moment I think I see the boy, his limbs nimble and quick, his eyes piercing into me, and then he's gone. The knocking at my ribs in no way subsides and for a moment I don't move because I'm petrified. Until there, in the corner of a branch, I see something else. The cat. Without thinking I start climbing. I don't know why but somewhere at the back of my mind is the thought that the cat was the last to see Hannah. When I reach his eye level, I straddle the branch and get as close to him as possible, my arm stretched out as far as it can go. I find myself having to lean my torso onto the branch to balance and for a moment I get close, but he hisses and swipes at me and goes flying through the air, while I half fall off the branch, hanging on with both hands.

I see his shadow first, and the shock of what I see makes me gasp.

Standing under the tree, holding the cat, is the Brigadier. With the cat so compliant in his arms, he resembles some kind of Mephistopheles. As I cling on for dear life, I try to control the breathlessness within me that spells trouble.

"It's an easy drop," he tells me. "You'll be cush-ioned by the leaves."

I'd be happy to stay hanging off the tree for the rest of my life just so I don't have to deal with him. But my hands begin to hurt and I know I have to let go.

There is nothing easy about the drop. It hurts when I land and when he holds out a hand, I ignore it.

He's looking at my face closely and like every other time this man is around there is havoc in my stomach. Like a warning against malevolence. I could easily put it down to the fact that I'm still angry at him for being the one who stopped me and Jonah Griggs that time. But it's more than that.

"Give me the cat," I say when I get to my feet.

"Mightn't be a good idea. He doesn't seem to like you."

I grab the cat from him and he goes back to his feral self, scratching and writhing in my hands, but I'm not letting go.

"Hannah—who lives here—she wouldn't want you hanging around her place or stealing her cat," I say.

He's still looking at me. It's unnerving and although I don't want to have my back to him, I turn and walk away, clutching the cat.

The strange thing is this. In crazy dreams when I relive that moment when Jonah Griggs and I were sitting in the postman's van in that township two hours away from Sydney, ready to set off on the final leg of our journey, I remember the Brigadier. I remember the look on his face when he pulled up in front of the postman's van and got out of his car and walked towards us in that measured way he has. That look was directed at me and a thought has stuck in my head for all these years: that maybe the Brigadier did not come looking for a Cadet that day.

That maybe, in some way, it was me he was hunting down.

The next day, Raffaela, Ben, and I decide to do an inventory of every piece of property the Townies and Cadets own on our land. We split the page in three and list them, beginning with the most valuable: the Club House. There are bike trails, walking trails, bridges, and sheds. Finally there is the Prayer Tree, which Raffaela believes should be on the top of the list. We discuss and argue about the importance of each item. The access path for trail bikes owned by the Cadets. The falling-down shed owned by the

Townies. The more we discuss, the more I am convinced of the stupidity of my past leaders. The access for trail bikes, for example, would be our quickest way to town. During the Cadet season our means of transport is limited and our journey to town is twice as long. The shed once housed a car for us, which the leaders would sneak out in during the night, especially if a band was playing in one of the larger towns. But Raffaela always comes back to the Prayer Tree.

"What's so important about it?" I ask Raffaela on one of our morning checks around the river. Apart from the fact that all three of us feel somewhat guilty that it was handed over because of us.

"Spiritually or pragmatically?" she asks.

"What do you think?"

"I swear to God, if you go out there it will change your perspective on the world."

"Don't believe in God. Love the world just the way it is."

"Okay, then come and look at it from a pragmatic point of view."

"Townie territory," Ben says. "If it's booby trapped . . ."

"It's seven o'clock in the morning," she reassures

us. "They'll never be up this early."

The Prayer Tree is located smack in the middle of the property within easy distance of the Jellicoe Road. It's the area I am the least familiar with because it's closer to the township and there are no proper tracks to reach it from where we are. In actual fact it is a chore getting to it and in the future Ben advises that we should hit the Jellicoe Road and access it from there.

By the time we reach the clearing we have grazes from flying branches and our bodies itch from insect bites. The clearing is small and the tree takes up most of it. I look up and am shocked at just how massive it is. It's almost like Jack's beanstalk and probably one of the highest trees I've ever seen on this property. Right at the very top, lodged amongst the branches, is a small house, cleverly camouflaged by a creative paint job. But it's the trunk that fascinates me the most. There are carvings and symbols and messages and history.

So much romance and so much ugliness. A girl named Bronnie, her name in love hearts with almost every boy around; a boy named Jason who hates wogs, Asians, coons, and towel heads. And poofters, too. The patience it would have taken him to carve out so much hate.

The messages are everything rolled into one. Wise and uncool. Profound and repugnant.

We circle the tree over and over again, trying to decipher all the messages.

Do you remember nothing stopped us on the field in our day?

I stare at the words, tracing my fingers in the grooves created by the carving.

"Your hands are shaking," Ben says.

Because I've heard these words so many times before.

"Check this one out," Ben says to me.

Kenny Rogers Rules.

"Who?" I ask, still wanting to return to my dream lyrics.

"You don't know who Kenny Rogers is?" Ben asks like he can't believe it. "'Coward of the County'? 'Don't Fall in Love with a Dreamer'? 'Islands in the Stream'? 'The Gambler'?"

It's like he's speaking another language and he shakes his head with great disappointment.

"You need to get in touch with the seventies and

eighties, my friend."

I find myself reaching up and touching words engraved right in the middle of the tree. It's bigger writing than the rest. *MATTHEW 10:26.*

"Maybe it's one of those 'God is Love' quotes," Raffaela says, coming up behind me. I think of Hannah's manuscript until I realise that Ben and Raffaela are staring.

"So where's the pragmatism you promised me?" I ask.

She points up. "We have to go up for me to show you that."

Hanging off the tree is one of those floppy rope ladders like in a trapeze act, except that here there is no net. Raffaela grabs hold of it.

"How do you know it's secure?" I ask.

She tugs at it and shrugs. "I just do. Santangelo's anal about things like this."

She begins climbing and the ladder swings around. "One at a time, though," she yells down.

I look at Ben. "You're next."

It's not like I'm scared of heights. There's been many a night that I've climbed out of my window and swung off the tree just outside it. But this thing is massive and I think I'd rather be climbing branches than a flimsy ladder that's attached to nothing I can see.

By the time it's my turn, Ben has already freaked me out with his dramatics. I begin the ascent, concentrating hard on each step, making sure that my foot is on the next rung before I step off the previous one.

When I reach the top, Raffaela and Ben help me up.

"Close your eyes," Raffaela instructs.

"Are you insane?"

"You're on solid timber," she reassures me. "It's very sound and we're holding on to you, anyway. You've got to close your eyes."

I'm convinced that if I hear something about being able to see tomorrow and it's bloody beautiful I'll throw myself off. I stand up straight, however, and close my eyes.

"Open."

I'm standing on a landing, the wall of the tree house behind me. Directly across my torso is a piece of wood, preventing me from falling over the side.

Raffaela points in front of me. "The town." She

turns me to the left. "Cadets." Then she turns me to the right. "Us."

The tree house has the most amazing and comprehensive view I have ever seen. Hills and valleys and houses and steeples, symmetrically cut farm blocks and vineyards. It is lush and hazy in the morning glow and I feel a rush of something inside me. I turn to the right and look in the direction of our Houses. I can see the six of them, looking closer than they actually are to each other. I see the little cottages in between that belong to the House co-ordinators and beyond that I see Hannah's unfinished house by the river.

"They can see everything," I say.

"With a good pair of binoculars they'd be able to see inside our rooms," Raffaela says.

I turn to look at the Cadets, already out of their tents and preparing for the day.

"Who needs satellites?" Ben says.

"That's what interests them the most," Raffaela says pointing. The Jellicoe Road.

"They have a bird's-eye view of every single part of this area. If they are up to no good, they know exactly when someone's coming up or coming closer."

"So they're spying on us."

"I actually don't think so. I think they love the view and it's a pretty good space for just hanging out," she says, walking inside the tree house. Surprisingly it is solidly built and we follow her in, sitting on the floor, taking in the space and possibilities. "I think the eighties mob named it and built a makeshift something up here. I don't think it's ever been as solid as it is now, but that's a Santangelo thing. I think he even wants to tile it. That's the wog in him."

"So you used to come up here when we owned it?"

She nods and smiles. "Anyone who was at the school and came from the town did. Come on. Look at the view. It's awesome. God's country."

"You can take the girl out of the town but you can't take the clichéd Townie out of the girl," Ben says.

"Well, it is!"

"Bet you've been up here with Santangelo," Ben says.

She goes red and walks out onto the landing. We follow her and breathe in the freshness.

"They want to meet again. Tomorrow night. This

time in the Club House," she says.

"Have the Cadets agreed?"

"They think so. They reckon you're never too sure with Jonah Griggs."

On the Jellicoe Road a car appears in the distance.

"Townies," Raffaela says. "We've got about ten minutes to get out of here."

I go down last, taking a closer look at Hannah's unfinished house by the river. Except I realise that it's almost finished. It's only the stuff inside that needs to be done, and the idea of its near-completion frightens me beyond comprehension.

Later on that night, I'm awakened by a sound. I stay still for a moment, my ears alert, heart racing, wondering if it was just one of those loud bumps in dreams that don't actually exist. When I can't get back to sleep, I get out of bed and quietly make my way down the stairs. I hear the breathing of those in the dorms and stand at their door for a while, watching them. I notice Chloe P. in someone else's bed, clutching onto her for dear life, and there's Jessa in the corner, snoring quietly and contently. The music of it all brings a smile to my face. A candle burns in the corner and I go over and blow it out.

I open the front door and step outside and the cool wind brushes my face, almost caressingly. As I stand looking out into the darkness, it's like I can hear the pulse of everything out there. I remember the Prayer Tree and all those names and scratchings, every one of them with their own story, and I wonder where they all are now. Is Bronnie still in love with any of those boys? Does Jason still have so much hate? Do any of them still think of their time on the Jellicoe Road?

I'm about to go inside when I notice that at the bottom of the steps of the House is my bike, which had disappeared from behind Hannah's house. I look out again, wondering if whoever has returned it is out there watching.

When I walk back inside, I pass the common-room and I find myself looking for a bible. Matthew, chapter ten, verse twenty-six. *Whatever is now covered up will be uncovered and every secret will be made known.* I wonder where such a message belongs amongst the Bronnies and Jasons of the world.

I go to sleep thinking of Hannah's character, Webb, who speaks of things I sometimes dream, and suddenly I'm sitting in the tree with the boy. He leans towards me and speaks but no sound comes out of his mouth and I ask him over and over again to say it louder, until I exhaust myself. So I read his lips, my eyes straining, every part of my senses aching, until I'm miming his words, and when I wake, Jessa and Raffaela are standing at the end of my bed, staring.

"Was I shouting?" I ask, my voice croaky.

"You were crying."

"The whole time?"

Jessa shakes her head. "Your mouth was moving but nothing was coming out," she says.

"What was I saying?"

Raffaela shrugs. "I'll get you some water."

She leaves the room and Jessa sits on my bed. After a moment or two I know that she's worked out what I was mouthing.

"Taylor," she says quietly, confused. "You said that your mother wants to come home."

Chapter 10

I'm dreaming. I know I'm dreaming because I'm in a tunnel and in reality I don't do tunnels. And down in the tunnel I smell something vile. I can't identify it, but it consumes my whole being and I start to choke, unable to breathe. But then a hand grabs me and pulls me out and I know it's the boy in the tree in my dreams and he tries to resuscitate me, but his mouth is rotting and his breath is foul. And I scream and I scream, but nothing comes out.

Thoughts of my mother begin to consume my every moment and they sweep me into an overwhelming feeling of bleakness and a desperate need for Hannah. Sometimes in the middle of the night, Raffaela knocks on my door when she sees the light coming from my room but I ignore her. I just sit up and try hard to stay awake because sleeping isn't safe anymore. I find myself Googling any name I remember my mother using. It was never the same name for long and that probably had to do with the profession she was in. She tried to change my name once or twice, convinced that someone was after us.

"They'll take you away from me," she'd say. "They've done it before."

But I didn't want my name changed. It was all I had.

The cat is no more settled than when I brought him home but I refuse to let him go. Sometimes I head to Hannah's place straight after school and try to get some rest there or I sit up in the attic and read. In this room I feel comforted. I like the box-like quality of it, the way the roof slopes, the perfectly cut square in the floor, the trapdoor that blocks out the world below, the skylight that on a clear night allows you to see every star you would want to see in the galaxy. Sometimes after we had been working all day on the house, Hannah and I would sit up here and just talk. She never spoke much about her family except a few times in this room. If I asked her anything about them she'd just say they were all gone and that if she allowed herself to give in to the whole sadness of it, she'd never ever be able to operate like a normal person again.

"I've been in that void," she told me once. "Don't you ever give in to it."

But I want to give in to it sometimes, only because I'm tired and the feeling that I've had for a while—that something is hunting me down—becomes all-consuming and I'm frightened that one morning there will not be enough to keep me going. Except maybe the pages I'm holding in my hands. They comfort me, these characters, like they're my best friends, too. Like Jude felt when he returned that second year and they were waiting for him. Give me a sign, I keep on saying to whoever can hear me in my head. Give me a sign.

But most of the time I wonder how much Hannah is a part of this story and this school. Was she the leader of a community who thought she was weak and usurped her first opportunity they got? Did she experience a coup at the hands of a Richard-like, fascist-loving, backstabbing creep? And where did she get this idea that there was peace between the Townies and Cadets and us?

I find some chapters to read that seem intact.

I'm running out of them because so many are half-finished or written in a scrawl that I can't quite understand. There's this part of me that doesn't want to deal with the fact that one of these characters is lost to them and I'm frightened that I will come across the chapter where they find him, because I know, deep down, that it's not going to turn out the way I want. That someone in this story is not going to get out of it alive. It's how I feel when I think of the boy in the tree in my dreams. Is he there to prepare me for something so devastating that it will lodge me in that void that Hannah spoke about?

Just when I'm about to work out a sequence of pages, I hear a window smash and I jump. I had locked the front door on purpose. Because Hannah's house without her didn't seem so safe anymore.

Quietly I crawl to the hole in the floor and peer all the way to the bottom. I see nothing but shadows and hear nothing but the sounds of breathing. I want to call out but something frightens me into silence and I sit and wait. Listening. I hear the heavy sound of footsteps on the wooden stairs as they make their way to the second floor. My heart is rattling uncontrollably. I reassure myself that nothing out here can be too frightening but I'm anxious all the same.

There seems to be nowhere to hide except under the stretcher bed in the middle of the room. The space beneath it is tiny, but I squeeze myself under and take a deep breath and then there's total silence. From where I'm lying, I can see half the manuscript sitting on the floor. The other half's with me. I reach out my hand until it aches, trying to touch it to drag it over, but as I do, my shoulder lifts the stretcher bed above me. I drop my arm and the stretcher bed hits the floorboards. Suddenly the footsteps begin again, slowly ascending.

Whoever it is has reached the second landing. I can imagine them standing there, looking up at the hole in the ceiling, taking hold of the ladder—one step, two steps, three steps, four. And there it is. The back of a head appears through the trapdoor but I can't quite make out who it is. He lifts himself up and then crouches to pick up the pages on the floor and I know what his next step will be. To turn around and look in the only place there is in the room to hide.

I know it's the Brigadier. I know because of that thumping sound inside of me and the only option I have, apart from being caught, is to lift the stretcher bed across my head and just throw it. Quietly I roll up the papers in my hand and stick them down my jeans and I get ready. The footsteps come closer and the boot stops right in front of my nose. I can hardly breathe but I need to move. *Just do it*, I tell myself. *Just do it and bolt!*

"Are you okay under there?" I hear him ask. He uses a soft tone, like he's trying to entice me out with the good-guy approach. But good guys don't smash windows to get into someone's house and good guys don't freak me out as much as this man does.

"It's okay. You can trust me."

Just do it, I tell myself again.

"I don't want to scare you but I'm coming down," he says, and I block out his voice because it is so familiar and the familiarity makes my heart beat fast and I know I have to get out. *Just do it*, I tell myself. Slowly I watch him crouch and then there is his hand on the sheet ready to pull it up, ready to grab me out of that space and do whatever he wants to do, whatever he may have done to Hannah. The rage inside of me at the idea of it makes me scream and I shove the legs of the stretcher to the side. I hear the impact of steel on his head and a grunt of surprise and next minute I bolt, crawling to the trapdoor, down the ladder, down the stairs, out the front door, and racing for my life, my hands flailing as if I am trying to grab as much air as possible to pull me forward, like freestyle swimming on land. When I feel as if I've run as much as I can without being winded, I take a detour off the track and huddle under one of the oaks and I stay there. Just breathing. Softly.

I realise, after a moment or two, that I am not alone. Slowly I look up, beyond the tree trunk, higher than the branches, to the very top. There, in broad daylight, is the boy in my dream staring down at me. It's like he has climbed out of that nocturnal world that I refuse to visit anymore and has decided to track me down. The sun blinds me as I look up, trying to cover my eyes, but then I hear a sound and I realise that he has brought the sobbing creature from the tree.

I feel hunted, with no place to hide. No solace, no belonging. Just an empty need to keep moving away from whatever or whoever it is that's after me.

As usual, what awaits me when I get home is dependency. Ten questions before I can even get to the bottom of the stairs. About maths equations and parent pick-ups and permission to go to town and laundry crap. Then there is the nightly job of looking through every item of clothing and through the cupboard of our latest resident arsonist, checking to see if she has attended her weekly counselling session and having her sign a contract stating that she won't burn us in our beds that night.

Once I've been assured of that I go to the kitchen to see if those on duty have prepared dinner. There are about sixty kids in the House usually, but with the year twelves gone we're down to fifty until next year's year sevens arrive. For dinner, mostly, we have spaghetti bolognese or risotto, and jelly for dessert, so hampers sent by parents are quite popular, as are the recipients.

On most days the roster works perfectly and on other days it is a total disaster. By six that night I haven't even reached the stairs to my room and when word comes that our House co-ordinator is coming around to check our rooms, the juniors especially are in a frenzy.

Later, I pass the phone stand and give it a glance before I begin walking up the stairs and I see two words on the notepad that stop me dead in my tracks.

"Who wrote this?" I manage to say, breathlessly.

No answer because I don't think they've heard me.

"Who wrote this?" Still nothing. "*Who fucking wrote this note?*"

Silence. But a different kind. The year nines, tens, and elevens appear on the second and third landings, their faces shocked. The juniors come out of study, standing in the corridor watching me.

"I . . . I did." Chloe P. stands there, Jessa next to her, an arm on her shoulder like some kind of angel of mercy.

"When did she ring?"

"I don't . . . I could hardly hear . . ."

I walk over and grab her by the arm. "What did she say?" I'm shaking her. "I told you to call me if she rang. Doesn't anyone listen to me around here?"

I don't realise until she's crying that my fingernails are pinching into her and Jessa is gently trying to dislodge me. She's crying as well, as are half the year sevens. The rest of my House are looking at me like I'm some kind of demented monster. I leave them standing there and start to walk upstairs, my hands shaking, clutching the note, wanting it to have more than the words HANNAH CALLED on it. I want a number or a message. I want *anything*.

Raffaela comes down the stairs towards me. "You look terrible. What's happening?"

I want to slow down the pace of my heart but I can't. The more I hear her speak, the harder it beats.

"Everyone's . . ." she begins.

"*What*? Everyone's what? Disappointed? Thinks I've lost it? Thinks someone else should be doing this?"

She stares at me for a moment, a cold angry look on her face. A look I've never seen before. "You know your problem?" she asks quietly. "It's that you're never interested in what anyone else is feeling. What I was trying to say before you rudely, *as usual*, interrupted me, is that all of us are worried about *you, not* about this situation, and we think you should just try to get some sleep and let us take over but you don't care because the difference between you and us is that you fly with . . . with . . . I-Don't-Give-a-Shit Airline and we fly with a friendlier one."

It draws a crowd. I think Raffaela raising her

voice tends to do that. It's mostly seniors and year tens, but I know that the juniors are listening from downstairs. The past leaders of my House would be rolling in their graves if they knew about the shouting and mayhem that has taken place in this House since they left.

"You're right," I say, walking up the rest of the stairs. "I don't give a shit."

In my room I lie on my bed, sick to the stomach, and I want to cry because my mind is working too much. All I know is that there is something not right. It's in my dreams, it's inside my heart, and without Hannah here, it's an all-consuming feeling of doom. Like something's coming and it's something bad. I try to feed the cat but he scratches me until my arms are red raw, and I let him because I want to feel something other than this emotional crap. Sometimes we sit, the dying cat and I, staring at each other like in a Mexican stand-off and more than anything I want to ask him what he has seen. What was the last thing Hannah said to him? But he stares at me; even in his sickly old age he is feral with fury, his hair matted beyond the point of no return. I try again and even though he seems as if he's going to drop dead at any moment, he scratches until I feel tears in my eyes, my bloody hands trembling with despair.

Chapter 11

It is dark, surreally dark, and I'm hanging upside down from the tree. My legs are hooked over a branch and my arms stretched as far as they can go. From upside-down I see the silhouette of the boy, but this time he is on the ground.

"If I fall, will you catch me?" I call out to him.

He doesn't answer and begins to walk away. I feel myself slip. One leg first, the position so painful that I am perspiring like hell.

"Hey!" I call out again. "Will you catch me?"

He turns around. "Catch yourself, Taylor."

I can no longer hold on. My scream hurts my own ears. The ground comes quickly and I hit it with a sickening thud.

I avoid the House front. I notice that most of the students have started eating dinner in their rooms.

Probably to avoid me. The common area is empty and silent. News has already hit the streets that I'm losing control of my House and Richard is all ready to take the reins.

I begin to develop a pattern. During the day I hide outside Hannah's house. The peace I feel here is overwhelming. Monkey Puzzle trees and rose bushes are scattered all around and the result is a mix of scents and colour and sounds of birds flying low and nature in such perfect harmony that it seems wrong that the very person who created it is nowhere to be found.

There's a point just outside Hannah's house where the river makes a sand bar. I sit there often and one day I see Jonah Griggs standing on the bank on the other side, against a gum tree. I don't know what to feel. For a moment it seems like the most natural thing in the world for him to be there, for one of us to call out a hey rather than ignore or accuse each other. The distance between us is no more than twenty metres and neither of us move for what seems like hours. There is a question in his eyes; I can see. That and something more. I can hear the ducks in the distance but no one stirs, except for the finches, which have no idea about the territory wars and boundaries. They leave my side and make their way over to his, as if to say, "Don't involve us in this; we're just enjoying the view."

At night the Prayer Tree becomes my shrine. I spend most of my time searching the carvings on the trunk while the rest of the world is dead silent, sinister phantoms seemingly absent from their sleeping dreams. Unlike mine. I look for anything. Links, I'd call them. There are phrases that sound like song lyrics and the biblical references are there and as I shine my torch on every single carving, I come across another piece of the puzzle. I find the names. Narnie. Jude. Fitz. Webb. Tate.

All scattered but there. Like they exist, not just in Hannah's imagination but in real life. A little voice tells me that the Prayer Tree could easily be the inspiration for her story but I know deep down it's more than that. Worse still, one of them is dead. I know that from the story. And I grieve like I've known them all my life. I copy down the song lyrics and back in my room I enter the words in a search engine. I find the bands and the songs and in one there's a line about Brigadoon and a rain-dirty valley that reminds me of something in Hannah's manu-script. I download them all, creating a soundtrack of the past. When I finally hear the song that the boy in the tree in my dreams plays to me, I cry for the first time since being on the train with Jonah Griggs. I wrap myself in the music, curled up in my bed, thinking of Hannah, eyes wide open, forcing myself to keep awake. Unlike Macbeth, who has sleep taken away from him, I take sleep away from myself. And Hannah's sick pathetic cat sits in the corner, still huddled in its state of fear.

Chapter 12

Over the weekend Ben gets word through Raffaela that the Townies and Cadets want to meet at the scout hall in town. It's about the last thing I want to do but these days I can't give Richard any more of an excuse to take over and I certainly don't want to be at home.

I don't talk much on the walk there. Ben keeps on stealing glances at me, about to say something a few times and then changing his mind before finally giving in.

"Rough week?"

I shrug.

"Raffy's worried that the Townies and Cadets will have more to bargain with," he says.

"I don't think Raffaela has much faith in me."

"Well, you're wrong," he says, serious for a change.

"I don't think anyone in my House does."

He grabs my arm gently and stops me from walking any farther. "Don't say that. Because I know it's not true."

"You weren't there this week, Ben," I say quietly.

"No, but they told me stuff and all I remember hearing was concern in their voices. And I remember something else. Hanging out with you and Raffy in year seven, skating around that Evangelical church car park. All those Christians were praising the Lord at the top of their voices and you stopped for a moment and asked us, 'Who do you believe in?' I wanted to be all mystical and Mr. Miyagi-like from *The Karate Kid*. Do you remember what Raffy said?"

But we reach the scout hall and I see Raffaela waiting there for us.

"People like Raffy don't lose faith," he says quietly as we walk in.

Santangelo and the Mullet Brothers, who are clutching guitars, are sitting on the stage and then Jonah Griggs enters with his second-in-command, Anson Choi, and we all sit down at a trestle table.

"You guys don't seem happy," Santangelo says.

"It was a long walk. We need some of those trails," I say.

"I've got a proposition, so can we begin?" Santangelo asks.

"It would be smart of you," Griggs tells him. "Because out of everyone here you've got the least to offer."

There's a silence between them and I know that at any minute there will be a full-on brawl.

"Wouldn't you say that letting *any of you* walk down our streets on weekends is a great deal to offer?" Santangelo threatens icily.

"You can't control that. Too many of us belong here," Raffaela says.

"You haven't belonged here for years." He sneers.

"What are you implying?" Raffaela asks, and I see hurt there as well as anger.

"Accusing, not implying. Would you like me to point out the difference?" he asks.

"He beats me in one spelling bee and now he's Mr. Intellectual," she says, looking at me as if I'm really going to get involved in this ridiculous exchange. "In second grade," she continues. "Get over it, Chaz!"

"Are we finished?" Griggs asks politely. "Because

we'd like to get into a discussion about having access to at least one of the water ways."

I look at him, shaking my head. "No chance. It'd be like cutting off our hands."

"Then learn to live without your hands."

"No, because then we won't be able to do this," Ben says, giving him the finger. Jonah Griggs calls him a little bastard and almost leaps across the table and everyone's either pulling both of them back or swearing or threatening.

"Let's talk about the Club House!" Santangelo says forcefully.

"Then talk!"

"I don't want to talk about the Club House," Griggs says. "We want water access. That's what we're here for."

Santangelo is shaking his head. "You know what you are? You are a—"

"What? Say it!"

They are both on their feet now, fists clenched and it's on for young and old. Yet again.

"Santangelo!" I yell above it all. "The proposition. Now. Or we walk and we are not coming back. *Ever.*"

It takes him a moment to calm down and I point to the chair.

"No interruptions," he says, sitting down. He stares at Raffaela and I turn to her and put my finger to my lips. She takes a deep breath and nods, as if it's the most difficult thing she'll ever have to do. Anson Choi gets Jonah Griggs back into his chair and it's semi-calm again.

"Okay. Seniors only and that means year eleven. We open three nights a week, hours eleven thirty to two A.M. Cover charge five dollars. No more than a hundred people per night. For each of those nights, one of us is in charge so that means organising entertainment, food, alcohol, et cetera."

"Alcohol is an issue," I say. "First, how do we get hold of it, and second, what happens when some moron gets plastered, breaks his neck trying to get back into dorms and Houses or . . . tents, or drives back to town under the influence? The teachers will be on us like flies and we'll get stuck inside forever."

"She's got a point." This from Jonah Griggs. "Anyway, Cadets signed a contract saying no drugs or alcohol while we're out here. If we get caught, it's zero tolerance expulsion."

"Where's the fun?" Ben asks.

"It's not as if we have to give up alcohol, Ben," Raffaela says. "We never had it in the first place."

"But if we're going to socialise and there's going to be live music. . . ."

"Hold on, hold on. What live music?" Santangelo asks.

"As if there isn't," one of the Mullet Brothers argues. "We've got a band . . . kind of."

"What you have is *not* a band. It's two guitarists," Santangelo says to them.

The Mullet Brothers are offended beyond words, staring at Santangelo as if he has betrayed them, and without even having to consult each other they turn and walk away towards the stage in a huff.

"Let's get back to the plan and work out the lack of entertainment later," Jonah Griggs says. "We might contemplate sharing the Club House, but it's them that control most of the space around it."

Then they're all looking at me. "Seventy foreigners on our land three nights a week? That's a lot to agree to."

"Plus access to the river," Jonah Griggs persists.

On the stage the Mullet Brothers are rehearsing and the amps are so loud we can hardly hear ourselves.

"I want to know one thing," I say. "What's in this for me? For us?" I say, pointing to Ben, hoping he likes the fact that I'm using his line. Except Ben is too wrapped up in what's happening on stage.

"Put the amps on two. It'll sound better," he calls out to them, as if they asked him.

"Ben?" I say, looking at him, reminding him why we're here. I can tell by the expression on his face that I've lost him for the afternoon.

"And put the electric guitar amps lower than the bass amps!" Choi shouts out. Jonah Griggs doesn't say anything to him. Just stares.

"Find us a venue where we don't have to put up with this crap," I say, standing and starting to leave.

"I know the perfect venue," Santangelo calls out. "It's called the Club House."

I swing around. "Once more with feeling. What's in it for me?"

I realise Ben isn't even following me. He's already close to the stage, arguing with Choi and the Mullet Brothers about the amps.

Instead, Jonah Griggs and Santangelo are standing there, almost side by side. Almost.

"Information," Santangelo says. He has that look again, as if he wants to tell me something but doesn't know how. He shakes his head, like he's changed his mind.

"Chaz? What?" Raffaela snaps.

"Nothing."

"Well, call me when you've got something," I say, walking away again.

"The Brigadier knew your mother," Jonah Griggs says, dropping what he knows is a bombshell.

I don't want to stop, but I do. Because I can't believe his audacity and I'm curious to see where he's going with this.

"Do you want me to let you in on a little secret?" I say. "Lots of men knew my mother. So don't go there."

"You wanted to go there three years ago," he says, walking towards me.

We are so close we're almost touching. My fists are clenched at my side, and I'm trying to find the right words.

"Oh, so you think I'm still that person I was on

the train?" I say, seething with anger. "My needs have moved on, thank you very much. It's what happens when you're betrayed."

He doesn't even flinch. "What I know is a whole lot more than I did back then and I can tell that this dickwit knows something about you, too," he says, glancing at Santangelo. "And I think it's pretty obvious that you're still an emotional mess looking for your mother and you know that if you find her, you'll find your father as well. So let's talk about river access and the Club House," he continues coolly, "and I'll tell you what you've been desperate to find out for most of your life."

I'm staring at him, so angry I can barely speak. "You know what I'm desperate to know, Griggs?" I spit at him. "What did you use on your father? Was it a gun or a knife?"

The room goes sickeningly silent except for the sound of Choi's footsteps hurrying towards us, like he knows what Griggs's next move is going to be. But he is too slow, because Griggs has me pinned against the wall, my feet dangling so that we're eye to eye.

Ben is on him and then Santangelo. Raffaela is

clutching onto me but I don't break eye contact with Griggs. Choi shakes a finger at me, like he's saying that my time will come and then pulls Griggs away and they walk out.

Ben, Santangelo, and Raffaela are looking at me in shock.

"Are you insane?"

I don't know who asks and I don't answer because I feel nothing but a need to get away from everyone. Instinct tells me to go to Hannah's, but she doesn't live there anymore and that's when I realise the major difference between my mother and Hannah. My mother deserted me at the 7-Eleven, hundred of kilometres away from home.

Hannah, however, did the unforgivable.

She deserted me in our own backyard.

As I walk back to the school on my own, I realise I'm crying. So I go back to the stories I've read about the five and I try to make sense of their lives because in making sense of theirs, I may understand mine. I say their names over and over again. Narnie, Webb, Tate, Fitz, Jude; Narnie, Webb, Tate, Fitz, Jude; Narnie, Webb, Tate, Fitz, Jude; Narnie, Narnie . . .

"Narnie! Open the door, Narnie, please!"

Webb's face had a sick pallor. Tate held on to him, crying, while Fitz paced the corridor outside Narnie's room.

"Get out of the way," Jude said, pushing Webb aside. He pounded on the door over and over again. "Fucking open it, Narnie."

After a while they heard the click of the lock and Jude yanked it open before she could change her mind.

"Narnie?" Webb said, holding her. "Don't do that to us. Please."

"What did you take?" Tate asked, shaking her gently.

"Panadol. I had a headache," she murmured.

"How many?"

"I need to sleep," she said. "If I sleep, everything will be better."

Webb led her to the bed and Tate sat down beside her.

Jude watched them fussing over her like they always seemed to. He remembered the story Webb had told him about Narnie in the car on the night *of the accident. It was after Fitz had come by to free them. How Narnie was stuck, frozen with fear, refusing to move. Narnie the fragile one who couldn't cope with living.*

"If you're going to kill yourself, don't do it until tomorrow night at ten," Tate said.

"Promise?" Webb begged.

"I had a headache and it wouldn't go away. That's why I rang you, Webb."

"Cross your heart, hope to die."

"But she does hope to die," Jude snapped.

"She knows what I mean," Tate said.

Narnie crossed her heart.

"That's not where her heart is," Jude said bitingly.

"Scano, leave it," Webb said tiredly.

"Well, it's not. She just crossed her shoulder blade. What kind of a suicide victim are you, Narnie, when you don't even know where the life force is that you're dying to squash? Right here." He poked her in the heart. "You want to do it properly, you make sure you get yourself right there."

Narnie looked at him and he felt a wave of self-hatred, but he didn't care.

"You're an arsehole, Jude. Big time," Tate said, almost in tears, putting an arm around Narnie.

"Yeah, I probably am. But I can't be a part of this deal-making. Screw you, Narnie. If you die, a big chunk of us dies with you."

He slammed out of the room and even Fitz seemed speechless.

Narnie curled up on the mattress and Tate lay beside her. "We'll see you guys tomorrow," she told them.

Webb leaned over, kissing Narnie and then Tate.

"You can keep Chairman Meow with you," he said, snuggling the cat in next to Narnie before leaving.

Tate smoothed her brow. "Maybe it's a good idea not to go to sleep for a while."

"I can't stay awake."

"I'll tell you about To Kill a Mockingbird. You might get in trouble if you don't read it for English by tomorrow," Tate said. "Do you remember what you're up to?"

Narnie thought for a moment and then nodded. "Atticus makes Jem read to the old woman."

Tate settled in next to her. "Well," she began,

"Mrs. Dubose is really nasty. She lives next door and calls out to them every single time they walk past the house about how disrespectful they are and blah blah blah. Anyway, every afternoon Jem has to read to her and sometimes he takes Scout along and what they discover is that Mrs. Dubose is dying. But there's a problem. You see, she's been addicted to morphine most of her life and because she's such a proud woman, she figures that she doesn't want to die beholden to anything or anyone."

"Even though the morphine would ease the pain of her dying?" Narnie asked.

"Uh-huh. So her pain-killer is actually Jem reading to her. It takes her mind off it. At the end of the chapter she dies, but she's free and Jem's respect for her is intense."

"My father . . . he would have made us do that as well." After a moment Narnie smiled. "Read to me, Jem."

"Sure thing, Mrs. Dubose."

So Tate read to Narnie all night and in the morning, when Tate could hardly keep her eyes open and Narnie could actually see some kind of light, they both closed their eyes.

"One day, if you need me to, I'll be Jem and you be Mrs. Dubose," Narnie promised sleepily.

"I'll hold you to that," Tate said softly, and they both slept.

Back in my room, the stand-off with the dying cat ends. It's listless as I hold it in my arms and suddenly I'm engulfed with a feeling of love for it and a need to set it free. I consider the best place and take it out to a spot in Hannah's garden, near the river.

For a long time I sit and watch it, but it doesn't move. It doesn't run away, like I expected. It doesn't hiss or snarl. It's like it wants to give up but doesn't know how.

"Go!" I tell it, but it's shivering, its misery so visible that for the second time today I find myself crying. I remember what Hannah said once, that it had been dying for years and should have been put out of its misery long ago. But she didn't have the guts. So I need to. I gather the cat in my arms, whispering soothingly in its ears, and take it to the river. I can't bear the idea of it being under the water on its own so I go down with it, clutching it, whispering, "I'm here, I'm here," over and over again until we are

underwater, eyes open, watching each other. I want to know its secrets and for a moment I sense something unexplainable. Peaceful. It makes me want to stay down there even after the cat stops moving. But above me I see the sun push its way through the branches of the oak tree and it's like a light beckoning me to something better. I swim us both to the surface, my lungs exploding, and suddenly I can breathe in a way I haven't been able to for a while.

Later, I lie on the sand bar in the river, my body shaking from the cold, but I feel a peace come over me. As I drift off to sleep, I sense that I'm not alone and I feel myself being carried and it's like I'm back in my childhood, on the shoulders of a giant again, happy.

When I wake up I'm in my room and Raffaela and Ms. Morris are there.

"Would you like something to eat?" Ms. Morris asks gently.

I nod. She walks out and Raffaela fusses with the blankets around me, avoiding my gaze. We don't talk for a moment or two and I take her hand to stop the fussing.

She clutches onto it and it's the safest I've felt since Hannah left. It's the power Raffaela has always had and maybe that's why I've spent most of our lives together pushing her away. Because being so dependent on people scares me. But I don't have the energy to keep Raffaela out anymore.

"I'm going to look for my mother," I tell her quietly.

"No," she says, and I can hear her frustration. "This is your home, Taylor, regardless of what you think it is. When school finishes next year, we'll go to uni in Bathurst and then you can come back here and stay with Hannah. Because this is where you belong. In this town."

But Raffy knows it's a lost cause.

"Raffy," I ask, "remember the dorms? I told you something about what happened in the city when I was young. You cried. Do you remember?"

She doesn't move for a moment. Her face is pinched and tense and then she nods.

"Well, I can't remember and I need you to tell me what it was."

She shakes her head emphatically.

"That's my memory," I say firmly. "*Mine*. You

need to give it back to me."

"What you told me," she begins, "won't lead to your mother. It'll just make you remember something that should be forgotten and never spoken about again. You're right. It is your memory and you have more right to it than me but I'm holding this one, Taylor."

"You need to ask Santangelo what he knows," I try instead.

"Santangelo knows nothing," she says, and she's crying. "He's an idiot. He thinks he's going to be a big-shot Fed and he thinks he's too good-looking and he feels too much and never forgives anything and I hate him because he's going to make you go crazy."

I hold on to her tightly. "Don't," I say. "I need you to help me run this House . . . this school and I can't do that if we're both crying."

"When the Brigadier carried you in here . . . I thought you were dead. . . . I always think you're going to do something to yourself, Taylor. . . ."

I let go of her and shake my head. "Not interested in dying just yet," I say, getting out of bed.

When I walk out of my room, I stop suddenly.

They all seem to be there. The seniors in my House. Some sitting on the steps, leaning on the railing, standing around. As if they've been waiting for me. I don't know what to say to them but as I make my way down the stairs, I realise they are all looking for something in my face to show that I'm okay. There's so much silence that it eats away at my skin and leaves me exposed.

Do I remember what Raffaela said in the car park of the Evangelical church?

"Who do you believe in?" she had repeated as if it was the dumbest question she'd ever heard. "I believe in you, Taylor Markham."

"Dinner is in an hour," I say to them all firmly. "Seniors are on duty. And we eat together tonight."

I walk into the dorm study towards Jessa and Chloe P. I sit down next to Chloe, take the protractor out of her trembling hand, and make a perfect circle. My hand is shaking, too, and when I look up, I see fear in Jessa's eyes. I feel like those psycho fathers in movies: one minute abusive, next minute human.

"I'll come and find you next time Hannah rings, Taylor," Chloe P. whispers. "I promise. Wherever you are."

I nod, swallowing hard. My hands are still shaking.

Jessa takes hold of both my scratched hands, pressing them until they stop. "That's what my dad used to do when I was scared," she tells me.

Later, I stand side by side with Ms. Morris and Raffaela and the other seniors preparing dinner while Jessa and Chloe P. and the rest of the juniors annoy us with ridiculous questionnaires from teen magazines and force us to listen to bizarre hypotheticals. But it calms down my heart rate and it makes me laugh and each time one of them walks by, I feel a hand on my shoulder or a squeeze of my arm and it makes me feel that tonight it will be safe for me to go to sleep.

Chapter 13

Three things happen in the next week that keep us tense and on edge.

First, we hear on the news that two girls have gone missing from the highway near a town named Rabine. It's nowhere near us but Jessa manages to convince everyone that we could be next. Second, Richard attempts a coup and sends out word to the Townies and Cadets that, due to unforeseen circumstances, he is taking control of the UC. And finally, the Cadets, true to form, exploit the situation and take three Darling House girls hostage.

"What are they playing at?" I say to Raffaela and Ben as we race towards the clearing.

"They sent a message back with Chloe P."

"Is she okay?"

"Kind of. She's halfway between total hysteria

and total excitement, so it could go either way."

"Richard thinks he's in charge," Raffaela says.

Like hell he is.

News has got around quickly and a mass exodus from the Houses takes place, with most people joining up in the valley outside Murrumbidgee House where Trini, the leader of Darling House, is being consoled. Ben gives a wave to two of the teachers who are looking at us suspiciously, and the sobbing from Trini is put on hold.

"Bushwalk!" he calls out to them. "You interested?"

They wave us off and walk away and once they are out of sight the sobbing re-commences.

"Let's go," I say, breaking into a run. We take the trail just behind Murray House, which is probably the densest and least cultivated.

"What kind of a deal are they looking at?" I ask Chloe P.

"He just said that negotiations for a possible release of hostages would take place at four thirty," she says, panting alongside me.

"Are you sure they weren't taken by the serial killer?" Jessa pipes up. She's torn between excitement and concern. I hear gasps of dismay from the younger kids. I stop to catch my breath and I'm amazed at just how large a crowd has gathered, squashed into almost single file on a track that hasn't seen too many walkers in its time.

"Get back to the Houses," I say firmly. "All juniors back to your Houses!"

There are complaints and pleading and the younger boys especially are begging me to let them come along.

"We need to have the Houses guarded as well," I tell the leaders standing around me. "I read about this happening in ninety-two. They kidnapped three students and while the leaders went to negotiate, they invaded the Houses and the teachers never found out because the students were kept hidden."

"Why would we hide them?" the leader of Hastings asks.

"No choice. The rules of invasion allow the invaders twenty-four hours of diplomatic immunity within enemy territory," Raffaela explains to them.

"Any point of entry in every House is to be locked and all juniors are to be confined indoors. Raffy, I want you back home."

It takes us a while to get to the boundary and I have to spend most of the time listening to the threats from some of the senior boys about what they'll do when they come across the Cadets. Which is slightly amusing because, knowing these guys, one look at Jonah Griggs and they'll be pushing me forward as a human shield.

We reach the clearing and Chloe P. is brought back up to me.

"Is this the place?" I ask patiently.

She nods solemnly. "See, there's Teresa's beret."

More sobbing from Trini, who clutches the beret tragically. Ben exchanges a long-suffering look with me and I push him towards her. While he methodically pats her on the back, I walk away and check the markings of the boundaries. I can't help thinking how petty the Cadets have been on this occasion. The girls would have taken no more than two steps into their territory before they were on them. I begin to wonder what Jonah Griggs is up to. I try to listen out for their approach, giving the others a silent *shush* gesture. But staying inconspicuous is not going to work. Trini is hyperventilating and some of the senior boys are continually swinging around in a paranoid attempt to see who's behind them. Even I have a sick feeling in the pit of my stomach.

Outside the dramatics of the Jellicoe students, there is a stillness around that makes it seem as if no one else exists, but the Cadets are cunning and knowing Jonah Griggs, he's probably watching us already.

"This means we're going to lose another trail or part of the property," Ben says to me quietly.

"Shhh." I take a few steps back. "Who knows," I whisper, "but we're running out of things to trade with them."

Four thirty comes, as does five o'clock, but nobody surfaces. I stay, standing the whole time, on guard, but by five twenty I'm exhausted and almost ready to give in to the suggestion of one of the guys that we invade.

"It's best that we stay put on our side of the boundaries," I tell them. "I don't know what Griggs's game is, but we need to know what we're up against and I'm betting that the moment we cross that line they'll be on us like a ton of bricks and trying to negotiate back seniors is going to be a lot harder."

"I don't think they're around, Taylor," the leader

of Murray tells me.

"Don't bet on it."

After sitting for almost an hour, Richard comes to stand alongside me. It's his way of making it seem that we're equal and of asserting some kind of power in this whole farce.

"If they want something from us," I tell him calmly, "I'm going to give them the trail closest to your House so that every time you see them loitering behind those trees you'll remember how your little coup attempt contributed to this."

"Why don't you just go and have a breakdown somewhere?" he says, walking away.

By five thirty I'm pissed off and bored and I have absolutely no idea whether these guys are going to jump out of the sky or walk straight out of the bushland in front of us.

"Jonah Griggs!" I call out.

"Taylor Markham!" he answers from the bushes right in front of me.

Ben looks at me, rolling his eyes, and I turn around and motion for the others to step back.

"Stay here," I say to Ben, stepping over the boundary lines.

Griggs comes out of hiding and approaches me as if he is on some Sunday afternoon walk, appreciating the nature around him.

"Where are they?" I ask, seething.

He peers closely at my face.

"Don't like these things," he says, pointing to what I'm presuming are the rings under my eyes. "You really need to get some sleep."

I slap his hand away. "Where are they?" I ask again, forcefully.

"You didn't warn them about the boundary lines. Those girls had absolutely no idea, whereas my juniors could point them out in their sleep."

"Why don't you just give yourself a pat on the back for being the world's best leader, then." He gives himself a pat on the back and I can tell he is enjoying himself at my expense.

"I can't believe how petty you are. They're in year seven!"

"Why is this a surprise to you?" he asks. "This has always happened. One of you ventures into our territory and there's payback. Do you remember that?" he calls out to Ben. "Payback for trespassing?"

"With alarming clarity," Ben calls back.

"Same with us. Happened to my friend Choi here, last year. Do you remember that, Choi?"

Behind him I notice at least one hundred Cadets either sitting in trees or coming out from behind shrubs and branches. I have to hand it to them. When it comes to camouflage, they certainly know what they're doing.

"He ventured into your territory and our leader had to go fight your leader to get him back."

Anson Choi nods solemnly. "Traumatic time. They put me into Murrumbidgee House. Very uptight bastards in there. They thought I'd be good at chess and they forced me to play all night."

"So you and I are going to have a punch-up?" I ask Griggs.

"What do you propose I do?"

"Hand back my year sevens."

"This is how the territory wars have always been fought," he says firmly. "It's in the handbook. Do you think they're just about threats and 'don't walk on our boundaries'? It's hand-to-hand combat. Someone is always going to lose. Sometimes it's just one to the jaw. Other times a few to the gut and, presto, we hand back the hostages. The only thing is that for the past four years the leaders have been male."

"Let's change the rules this year. Because just between you and me, you're scaring me."

He looks at me closely again. "You need to put all your shit behind you because we've had at least two meetings about the Club House without you there and Santangelo and I are about this close," he says, indicating a couple of centimetres with his fingers, "to breaking each other's necks."

"Jonah, hand over the kids," I say tiredly.

He turns around and gives a whistle. The three Darling kids are taken out of their hiding spot and I relax slightly, a bit grateful, a bit surprised. This is a good victory for me in front of my school. All done with not one drop of blood or petty skirmish.

"Are you in charge?" he calls over my shoulder.

I turn around and watch Richard nod smugly. "Technically," he says, walking towards us.

"Technicalities rarely interest me," Griggs says, and then he smashes Richard in the face.

"We don't really like scaring the kids," he says patiently, looking to where Richard has fallen. "So you need to warn them that for every one of them who enters our territory, their leader gets payback. You, of course, can distribute punishment to them for your troubles. I've found in the past if I have to be the punching bag for one of my juniors, I usually get him to polish my shoes, maybe do my washing— the petty things, you know. But it rarely happens. You see, my juniors know who's in charge. We try not to confuse them because it puts them in danger." Griggs feigns confusion. "So who is in charge around here?"

"I'm in charge," I say, staring at him, bristling with fury.

He looks down at Richard and extends a hand. Richard is still stunned and doesn't know whether to take it or not.

"You okay with that decision, Dick? Can I call you that? Her being in charge?"

Richard mumbles something unintelligable.

"Good to hear." Griggs walks away.

Richard sways slightly so I hold him up. He puts his sleeve to his nose. "Maybe we should meet tonight and discuss the boundaries," he says.

"Clear this area now," I tell him before turning to Trini, who is clutching the three kids to her breast.

"You okay?" I ask them, but they're too busy trying to disentangle themselves.

"Make sure you debrief them and that they're okay," I tell Trini. "I'll come and speak to them later."

"I don't want them hassled," she says, leading them away.

I walk back towards the disappearing Cadets. "Hey," I call out after Jonah Griggs. He stops with Anson Choi by a tree and leans against it, a ghost of a smile on his face. He looks pleased with himself and I give him that little moment of triumph before I get up close and slap him hard across the face.

"Don't you ever do that again," I say, furious.

"Ouch, that hurt!" he says, rubbing his cheek.

"I can fight my own battles."

"I wasn't fighting your battles," he argues.

"Yes you were. That's my business," I say, pointing to where the others, except for Ben, have retreated, "and your little patronising act could put me in a weak position with them."

"I don't think they realised he was protecting your interests, Tayls," Ben calls out. "They're too stupid."

"I wasn't protecting her," Griggs argues angrily over my shoulder at Ben.

"It kind of came across as if you were," Anson Choi explains to Griggs patiently.

"Did I ask your opinion, Choi?"

"No, but just from my perspective and what I know about your history," Anson Choi says calmly, "it came across like you were—"

Griggs gives him a look and Anson Choi puts up his hand and nods as if he understands that silence is required.

"Protect your boundaries and it won't happen again," Griggs tells us.

"If you think you're scaring us, think again, GI Jerk," Ben says.

I look at Ben, impressed with his wit and force. "Let's go," I say to him, and we walk away.

When we reach the bend and they no longer can see us, Ben gives a laugh. "How bloody impressive was that?"

"I thought you were very impressive," I say.

"No, I mean him giving Richard a biffo."

I stop and stare at him.

"He had it coming to him, Taylor. While you've

been so tragic for the past week with the whole death-by-eighties-music thing, Richard was an arsehole. I was bloody impressed with Griggs," he says to me. "He's gone from a zero in my eyes to a two."

"How does he get to a ten?"

"If he did to Richard what he did to me. I got the full enchilada, you see. One to the face and the two to the gut, plus the stepping on the fingers."

"So when it's happening to someone else it's all cool?"

"Any pain inflicted on Richard warms my heart and it warms yours as well. Go on, admit it. When he hit the ground and the blood went flying and you knew in your heart his nose was broken, didn't you just want to jump for joy and stomp on his ugly face?"

I look at him, shaking my head. "Actually, no, Ben. I didn't. I was thinking that I'd rather be in the common-room watching *Home and Away.*"

"You know what your problem is? You don't know how to enjoy yourself. That was fun. That was better than *Home and Away.*"

Later I go see the Darling girls and take Jessa and Chloe P. with me, only because they're convincing about their ability to ask questions of people their own age as opposed to my question-asking, which Jessa points out could be intimidating.

Darling House is a touchy-feely House. Everyone is really sweet and they even say grace before meals. It's interesting to see how other Houses work. The past leaders of my House were so hell-bent on being the best that there was no room for anything that didn't have to do with power. Here, every emotion and talent and opinion is nurtured and supported.

"I'm grateful for what you did," Trini says to me, offering me tea and jam tarts, which are served to me on what looks like their best china.

"I'm not really here for your gratitude," I say honestly. "I need your support and frankly it hasn't really come my way."

"Well, change is scary," she says, as if she's giving a lecture to her House. "The past leaders have always been despots. We feel safe that way. Richard is exactly like them and it's better the devil you know."

"But you don't run this House like a despot."

"Of course I don't. It's against our ideology. But outside this House we still need order. Just say you let the Cadets run around our property and I have to worry twenty-four-seven about the girls. It's bad enough keeping those Murray and Clarence guys away from them."

"I would never let the Cadets run around our property."

"Well, Richard said—"

"Screw Richard, Trini."

"Taylor, we don't use that type of language in our House," she says reprovingly.

She leans forward and stares at me intently. "I'm responsible for these kids, Taylor. Like you are for yours. When I leave for holidays, those who don't have a place to go, they come home with me. So if those Cadets ever come near my year sevens again, I will maim them."

I nod.

"Would you like to see them now?"

We walk into the junior dorms, where Jessa and Chloe P. are deep in conversation with a cluster of the juniors who are bombarding the hostages with questions.

"Tell me about the set-up," I say to them, sitting down on one of the beds where some of them are congregated.

The girls look at me blankly.

"What she actually means, girls, is what was it like out there? Kind of describe it to us," Jessa says, beaming at them and then at me. Trini beams at her and there's a lot of beaming happening.

The spokesperson for the three sits up. "They had us in a tent and they had two senior boys guarding us and all these boys wanted to come and look at us because they don't get to see many girls but the two boys guarding us wouldn't let anyone near us because someone told them that Jonah Griggs said that if anyone touched us they were to break their arms."

"Jonah Griggs is their leader," another one of them explains to me.

"Did they scare you?" I asked.

"When they first caught us, it was a bit scary."

"They have a barbecue every night. That's what the Cadet guarding us said."

"Wow," Jessa says. Chloe P. is equally impressed.

"So what was it like out there?" I say brightly, repeating Jessa's words. "Kind of describe it to us."

"There are six boys to each tent and about fifteen tents per form. The year-eleven tents are the closest to the bush trails and the teachers' tents are right in the middle of them all. They have this Brigadier from the real army staying with them and everyone thinks it's cool but they said he can be a bit scary. You should see his tent: it's massive and always locked up."

"And where is the Brigadier's tent?" I ask innocently.

The girls draw me a diagram and I'm impressed at just how much they took in.

"She's very impressed," Jessa tells them, beaming.

Everyone's still beaming and this time I beam back.

Chapter 14

The look on the constable's face said it all to Jude. Another fifteen minutes of their life would be wasted by indifference. But he could see the younger cop sitting at a desk behind him—the one who always stopped Fitz in the street to make sure everything was okay. The young constable caught Jude's eye and after a moment he wandered over casually.

"You want me to take care of this?" he said to the officer on duty.

"It's all yours."

Jude noticed that the constable didn't look much older than them. Up close, his olive skin was smooth and his dark eyes were questioning but kind.

"So you want to tell me what's going on?"

"You're kind of the fourth person and no one's really listening," Jude said.

"*I'm listening.*"

"*We're missing someone.*"

"*Not Fitz?*"

"*No, but he's gone AWOL. Our friend Webb— Narnie's brother—he's gone. You've probably received word from the school. We don't know where he is but it's been two days.*"

The young cop's stomach turned. He knew these kids—the girls, anyway. During his first week on the job five years ago he had been called out to an accident on the Jellicoe Road. It had been the first time he had ever seen dead bodies and he remembered how he had thrown up on the side of the road while his sergeant had told him to pull himself together. He remembered these faces. He remembered Fitz with them, a new look in the troubled kid's eyes.

"*I know what you're going to say,*" Jude said. "*Some shit about him being seventeen and probably taking a bit of 'time out.' But I bet if his parents were beating down your door, you'd be listening.*"

"*I said I'm listening,*" the constable said firmly. His gaze went from Jude to the girls. "*Who was the last to see him?*"

A muffled sound came from Tate but Jude could hardly look at her. It was as if she had disappeared in the last two days. Like the light had gone out of her eyes. He couldn't handle Tate like this. Narnie, he was used to but not Tate.

"Was he acting strange?" the cop asked. "Did he take anything with him?"

"Nothing's really missing," Jude said. "Probably what he would always have on him. Like his Felix cap and he always had his Walkman and that's gone. But nothing else."

"What about money?"

Jude looked at Narnie and she numbly shook her head. "There's no money until we're eighteen."

"But that's soon, isn't it?" he asked gently.

She gave the young constable the full force of her stare. "Why are you asking us this? He didn't leave. He would never leave. Something has happened to him. Something bad."

"Look," he said. "I'm not saying I don't believe that but we hear stories like this all the time. That there's no way someone would run away or just take off, but they do. Stuff happens that not even the closest person to them knows about."

"*You don't know my brother.*"

"*Tate, you were the last to see him,*" Jude said. "*Can you remember?*"

She looked at Jude, bewildered. "*Remember? I can remember everything I've ever said to him and every single thing he's ever said to me.*"

They looked at her, waiting. "*He told me about his university choices and that he was looking in the city papers for a place to live for me and him and how Narnie would come and join us next year when school was out. And how we'd stay in the city for just four years and then we'd come back here because he's going to build me a house. A house for me and Narnie and him. And that it was going to be hard leaving Fitz behind but maybe, just maybe, we could convince Fitz to come to the city with us and that Jude would be there, too, and then I told him . . . I told him we were going to have a baby.*"

"*Tate.*" Narnie breathed softly. "*Oh, Tate.*"

"*He was . . . I don't know, shocked. Like he couldn't believe it. I mean, we've been together . . . in that way . . . forever . . . because there was never going to be anyone but Webb. That night,*" she said, looking at Narnie. "*Remember that night? I heard* his voice and it was like . . . it was like God spoke and I knew, from that moment on, that I'd be with him for the rest of my life. That's the only reason I lived. To be with that boy with that voice. Remember, Narnie? He climbed through the window, through all that glass, just to hold my hand."

"No, Tate, you climbed through the window to hold our hands. You cut your arm, remember? Just to be with us."

Jude watched Narnie put her arm around Tate. He didn't know this Narnie. Her voice was stronger and he had spent the last two days not being able to look at her because her gaze was so sharp and focused that it pierced through him.

"Maybe he decided—" the cop started.

"No," Narnie said, staring at him as if warning him against saying anything that would upset Tate. "My brother would never in a million years leave us. You quote all your statistics and what you've seen on this job but you don't know Webb."

The constable picked up his pen and began to record details, adopting an air of professionalism but deep down he felt a sorrow for these kids that made his insides churn.

"I need a photo," he said, "and can I suggest a GP? My wife's having a baby as well, you see."

Narnie looked at Tate and nodded.

"Let's start with his name," the constable said.

We attend another meeting with the Townies and Cadets in the scout hall, ready to talk real issues and make intelligent demands. When Raffaela, Ben, and I arrive, some of the Townie girls are hanging around the entrance where Jonah Griggs and Anson Choi are just about to walk in. One of the girls approaches Jonah Griggs and just hands him her phone. No warm up, no "Hi, how are you, can I call you sometime?" She just hands over a mobile phone so he can record his number. I want to be petty and tell them we don't have coverage out off the Jellicoe Road but that would just mean I cared.

"Sorry, we don't have phone coverage off the Jellicoe Road," Jonah Griggs says, handing it back and disappearing beyond the doors.

As I walk past the girls, I hear one say, "That's his girlfriend," and I stop and face them.

"What did you say?"

They ignore me with that wide-eyed how-uncool-is-this-girl-for-responding look on their face.

"I'm not his girlfriend," I say forcefully.

"Well, good for us," one of them says snidely.

"Not really," Raffaela tells them. "He's got a girlfriend and he's madly in love with her. She lives next door back home."

I am surprised by this news. Even more surprised that Raffy knows but then again Raffy has this way of knowing everything. As we enter the room, I ask the burning question as indifferently as I can. "How did you find out all that stuff about Griggs and his girlfriend?"

"It was easy. I lied."

The meeting is a farce from the moment things get started. Santangelo is babysitting three of his sisters and they practise Beyoncé dance movements while the Mullet Brothers insist on playing their guitars.

"Your mother told my mother that she wants Jessa McKenzie for the holidays," Raffaela tells Santangelo above the noise. "Do you guys know her?"

It's the first I've heard of the plan and I feel an anxiety that I can't explain.

"Oh, bloody wonderful," he says bitterly. "Because

there just aren't enough women living in my house already."

The Mullet Brothers fight amongst themselves the whole time and at one stage Anson Choi and Ben are trying to keep them off each other while having an argument themselves about musical pitch and when Jonah Griggs yells, "This is ridiculous! I'm not coming back," I have to agree for once.

Outside, the Townie girls are still hanging around and while we wait for Ben, I notice them speaking to Griggs, who is very amused at what they have to say, which has to be fake because there is no way these girls would be witty.

We walk home, the Cadets behind us and, not really wanting the Cadets to listen to our conversation, Ben, Raffaela, and I walk in silence.

"You know what I'm going to do when I get back to camp, Choi?" Griggs says a bit too cheerfully.

"What, Griggs?"

"I'm going to write a letter to my next-door neighbour. She's my girlfriend. We're madly in love."

Raffaela gives me a sideways glance and I can tell she's trying not to laugh and I realise what Griggs found so amusing when he was talking to the Townie girls.

"I didn't know you had a girlfriend, Griggs." Anson Choi feigns surprise. "What's her name?"

"I didn't actually catch her name," Griggs continues.

"Lily," Raffaela says over her shoulder and this time I give her a sideways look.

"Great to know that I'm in love with a girl with a cool name."

"It's Taylor's middle name," Raffaela calls back again.

Placing Raffaela in the path of an oncoming car becomes one of the major priorities of the next ten seconds of my life.

"So apart from writing letters home to your fantasy girlfriends," Ben says, walking backwards, "what do you guys do out here without television and phones?"

"Men's business. Bit confidential," Griggs says patronisingly.

"Wow, wish I were you," Ben says, shaking his head with mock regret. "All I'll be doing tonight is hanging out in Taylor's bedroom, lying on her bed, sharing my earphones with her, hoping she won't hog all the room because it's such a tiny space."

He gives them a wave. "Now you have fun with your men's business and spare a thought for my plight."

Griggs and Ben compete in a who-can-outstare-each-other-longer competition until Anson Choi drags Griggs away to the other side of the road.

I look at Ben then Raffaela. "What was that all about?" I whisper angrily. "The Lily thing and the hanging out in Taylor's bedroom?"

They both have a what-did-we-do look on their faces.

"He just went from a zero to a two in my eyes for not smashing you, Ben!"

"How does he get to be a ten?"

I look over to the other side of the road and watch Griggs as he walks. It's a lazy walk but so full of confidence that you want to be standing behind him all the way.

How does Jonah Griggs get to be a ten? He sits on a train with me when we're fourteen and he weeps, tearing at his hair, bashing his head with the palm of his hand, self-hatred pouring out of him like blood from a gut wound in a war movie, and for the first time in my whole life I have a purpose. I am the holder of the grief and pain and guilt and passion of Jonah Griggs and as we sit huddled on the floor of the carriage, he allows me to hold him, to say, "Shhh, Jonah, it wasn't your fault." While his body still shakes from the convulsions, he takes hold of my hand and links my fingers with his and I feel someone else's pain for the first time that I can remember.

The knock at my window that night frightens the hell out of me. I've used the window for years as an exit point, but nobody has used it as an entry and for a crazy moment I convince myself that the boy in the tree in my dreams is coming after me.

I get up from my computer and peer out and there, crouching on the ledge, is Griggs. He doesn't ask to be let in. He just stands up, expecting me to step aside. Technically this could be considered against the rules of the territory wars but I open the window. He looks down at my singlet and underpants and stares for a long time as if it's the most natural thing in the world. Then he climbs in and looks around the room without commenting.

I walk to my drawers and put on my jumper, which hardly reaches my thighs.

"Hope you didn't do that on my account."

I don't say anything and he casually leans against my desk, picking up the novel that's sitting there.

"It's bullshit," he tells me, flicking through it. "There's no such thing as Atticus Finch."

I shrug. "It'd be good if there was, though. Why are you here?"

"Why else? The Club House," he says.

I nod. "If we agree on this, we need to explain the rules to the Townies," I tell him.

"Okay," he says. "No ridiculous dress codes concocted by irrational women."

It's like he's making things up off the top of his head.

"It's our men who are irrational," I explain to him. "We prefer to be labelled as pragmatic and long-suffering."

"So how do they get in here?"

"Who?"

"Your irrational men. Cassidy? The rest?"

For a moment I get a sense of why he's really here.

I feel my face flushing and see that his is, too.

I clear my throat and get back to business. "Ban for life on anyone who gets drunk."

"No boy-band music."

I don't know what to say to that one because I'm making all this up as well.

"No . . . Benny Rogers."

"Kenny," he corrects.

"We insist that the Mullet Brothers don't play every night."

"Mullet Brothers?" After a moment he works out who I'm talking about and he nods. "We call them Heckle and Jeckle."

"And you never step on my second-in-command's fingers ever again."

He nods once more. "My second-in-command? Choi? He DJs. He'll want to do that at least once."

I nod. Lots of nodding. It's all too awkward. A few days ago I had brought up one of the most taboo subjects of his life and he had me pinned against the wall and here we are pretending it never happened.

"If this backfires, there'll be a war," I say.

"There already is a war. I think you forget that at times."

"And you don't?"

"Never. And you can't afford to either."

"Is that a warning?"

"Maybe. But let's not make it complicated. Let's just make sure it doesn't backfire."

He holds out a hand and I shake it and as I do he stands up from where he's leaning against my desk and it's like he hovers over me, which is strange because I've always been at eye-level with the boys around here.

I feel his fingers on my collarbone, faintly tracing the marks where my buttons scratched my skin when he grabbed me days before.

"I shouldn't have said what I said," I say quietly. "I don't know why I did."

He shrugs. "I didn't come here to ask or give forgiveness."

And it's like a trigger word, making every pulse inside of me throb. "Forgive me," I whisper, dizzy from the sensation.

He leans forward and our foreheads are almost touching and for a moment, a tiny moment, a slight vulnerability appears on his face.

"Nothing to forgive," he says.

I shake my head. "No. That's what he said. 'Forgive me.' It's what the Hermit whispered in my ear before he shot himself."

"My father took one hundred and thirty-two minutes to die. I counted. It happened on the Jellicoe Road, the prettiest road I'd ever seen . . ."

Jude sat still, listening to a memory so sad that he wondered how Narnie could tell it so calmly, with so much clarity and detail. Over the years he'd had a fair idea of what had happened that night on the Jellicoe Road and sometimes he hated himself for wanting to be part of something so tragic. He wanted to be the hero riding by on a stolen bike. He wanted to be the one carrying their parents and Tate's sister out of the cars. He wanted to belong to them. With them he found solace.

They sat by the river and he wanted to take Narnie's hand but didn't dare.

"Do you know why I couldn't count how long it took my mother to die?"

As much as he knew that he didn't want to hear the answer, he shook his head.

"Because she flew out that window. I could see

her the whole time. From where I was sitting. And I knew she was dead straightaway because she didn't have a head, Jude, and I stayed in that spot, not moving a single inch and everyone thought I was scared but I wasn't. Because if I moved an inch, Webb would see her and you don't know how much Webb loved her, Jude, and I would have died right there if I knew that Webb saw her like that. I would have . . . I would have. . . ."

It was a despair he could not comprehend, spilling from her mouth. Not knowing any other way to stop her, he covered her mouth with his hand but she pulled it away.

"If he doesn't come back, there's no one left, Jude," she whispered, the horror of it all there on her face. "They're all gone. Everyone's dead."

He held her against him and for once he understood what she had felt every day that he had known her.

"Hold my hand," she said, sobbing against him. "Hold my hand because I might disappear."

Chapter 15

It's peaceful like this, on my back. A loving sun caresses my face and it wraps me in a blanket of fluffy clouds, like the feeling of my mother's hands when she first held me. For a moment I'm back there, in a place where I want to be.

But then somewhere up-river, a speedboat or Jet Ski causes a ripple effect and miniature waves slap water onto my face, like an angry hand of reprimand, and the shock of it almost causes me to go under. I fight hard to stay afloat and suddenly I remember the feeling of fear in my mother's touch. Some say it's impossible because you remember nothing when you're five seconds old but I promise you this: I remember the tremble in my mother's body when the midwife first placed me in her arms. I remember the feeling of slipping between those fingers. It's like she never really managed to grab hold of me with a firmness that spoke of never letting go. It's like she never got it right.

But that's my job.

My body becomes a raft and there's this part of me that wants just literally to go with the flow. To close my eyes and let it take me. But I know sooner or later I will have to get out, that I need to feel the earth beneath my feet, between my toes—the splinters, the bindi-eyes, the burning sensation of hot dirt, the sting of cuts, the twigs, the bites, the heat, the discomfort, the everything. I need desperately to feel it all, so when something wonderful happens, the contrast will be so massive that I will bottle the impact and keep it for the rest of my life.

For a moment I sense something flying menacingly low over me and I start with fright, losing my balance and this time I do go under. But the sky is a never-ending blue, no birds, no clouds. Just a stillness that tells me I'm the only person left in the world.

Until I see Jonah Griggs.

On my side of the river.

I breaststroke over and attempt to get out with as much dignity as possible. One is always at a disadvantage when standing dripping wet in one's bathing suit, no matter how modest it is.

I try to think of the rules and begin to say in a strong assertive voice, "The Little Purple Book . . ."

". . . states that any negotiated land must not be accessed by the enemy and, if caught, the handing over of territory is to take place with alacrity," he finishes for me.

"You know the water access belongs to us. You are tres—"

Before I can say another word, a body comes flying over the river and lands, expertly, just next to me. Griggs and Anson Choi shake hands, the enjoyment so evident in their faces. For a moment I'm reminded that Griggs is just a typical guy our age. There's a softness to his face that's almost painful to see because it makes him vulnerable and to think of Jonah Griggs as vulnerable is to imagine him as a ten-year-old boy at the mercy of his father.

"So who does the air belong to?" he asks me. "Can't recall that being in the Little Purple Book."

"This is private property."

"According to rule four-four-three of the Little Purple Book, private property is neutral ground."

Nodding. Like I know rule four-four-three well. We are standing approximately one kilometre away from the Jellicoe Houses. The leaders would have a fit if they knew the Cadets were this close. If they get inside our Houses, we have to trade. If we get inside their tents, they have to trade.

I'm shivering from the cold and he must read a little panic in my eyes.

"Don't worry," he says before his whistle pierces my eardrum. A rope comes flying across and he grabs it. "Today, we're just practising."

Ben and Raffy are dumbfounded.

"They're planning an invasion, aren't they?"

I nod.

"Pretty gutsy," Ben says with a whistle.

"How about the Townies?" Raffy asks. "We can ask for their help and finalise this deal."

I shake my head. The Townies would want something from us. We don't have much to give.

"Just say they get into the Houses?" she asks.

"Tell me the rule about invasion?" I say to her.

"You need six enemies in your territory to confirm it as an invasion. If they attempt twice and fail both times, we get to negotiate diplomatic immunity for the rest of their stay."

"Today's attempt was just two of them, so it doesn't count."

I look outside the window. Any movement sets me on edge. We're studying *Macbeth* in Drama and any moment I expect Birnam Wood to come to Dunsinane. That would be just their thing.

"I'm going to Hannah's," I say.

I see the disappointment on both their faces.

"Taylor, please. This isn't the time. We need to concentrate on the territory wars just for this week," Raffy says.

I begin walking out of the room and they're on my tail. "I want cows," I tell them.

"Cows?"

Outside the House they are still trying to keep up. "This isn't going to be like . . . that cat thing, is it?" Ben asks.

I see Raffy signal Ben to be quiet. Any talk of the drowning of the cat has been off-limits. Like an unwritten rule.

"Hannah wanted me to work on the garden and I never did."

"Hannah's house isn't the issue here, Taylor," Raffy says.

"Yes it is." I continue walking.

Ben grabs my arm. "Then I'm taking over," he says angrily. "Go work on Hannah's house but I'm working on those Cadets not getting within one metre of us. All you can think of is planting—"

"Manure," I tell them. "All over her front garden. Perfect for growing vegetables."

It's like he wants to hit me with frustration. "You're losing it!" he shouts. "No one wants to tell you that, but you . . ." I see the light go on. ". . . You are a genius."

Raffy looks at him confused. "She's a genius? I'm lost."

"What he means is that we're not giving in without a shit fight," I tell them. "Literally."

Strategies come in all shapes and sizes and as juvenile as this one is, it keeps me amused.

They come calling again late the next afternoon. Griggs is first. Territory war aside, he is a pleasure to observe, like he was built for flying through the air.

He picks himself up from his landing, inspecting

his fatigues. Then he looks up to where I'm sitting on Hannah's verandah, my legs dangling over the edge. He sloshes towards me and I can tell it's not easy.

A war cry is heard from the other side and before he has time to warn them, at least six Cadets come flying over the river and land around him. They looked shocked, and I actually feel like giggling at their horror.

"We're an Ag college," I explain to them. "Not as good as the one in Yanco but we have livestock."

"Cows?" Anson Choi asks, covering his nose.

"Pigs, too. And horses. Great for growing tomatoes."

The Cadets are wanna-be soldiers. City people. They may know how to street fight but they don't know how to wade through manure.

"I'm going to throw up," one of the guys says.

"Don't feel too bad," I explain. "Some of our lot did while they were laying out this stuff. Actually, right there where you're standing."

The Cadets look even more horrified, peering down, imagining the worst.

I point to the neutral path that is at least a forty-minute walk back to their camp. "It's manure-free,"

I offer. "And I do believe you have access to it."

Griggs stares at me.

"If you try to invade us again and fail, then we may have to talk. Rule three-two-one of the Little Purple Book."

"This is war," he says quietly.

"Well, thank God you're dressed for it, Griggs."

And so the war games continue and sometimes it's so much fun that Hannah and my mother disappear from my head for a minute or two. The Townies find out about it and are diligent about neither of us using their territory as neutral ground, so game plans are drawn up by Richard, who is in his element. Anytime now I expect him to start smoking a pipe and wearing a beret.

The plan is that we force the Cadets to invade, rather than wait for them to spring it on us. So on Saturday morning, when we know that Jonah Griggs's troops are on their morning drills, Ben, Raffy, and I stroll onto Cadet territory. Accidentally.

The Cadet in front sees us almost instantly and I watch his eyes narrow. He looks behind, to Griggs, I guess. I stand on the path not ten metres away and I allow a tiny bit of fear to enter my eyes before I turn and bolt.

We run for our lives. The heavy footsteps of the Cadets crash behind us. Raffy knows exactly where to lead us. My heart is pounding with the fear that they will grab us before we reach our lines. Our only advantage is that we know this bushland inside out. It's our playground for most of the year when they're not around. For them it becomes an obstacle course but we know what to roll under and jump over. We know what trees to grab for assistance and which ones will let us down, caving under the pressure of our grips. We know where the limbo-stick trees are and we shimmy under them like contestants on *Dancing with the Stars*, and what plants to avoid for fear of the sticky hidden thorns. But they have speed and discipline and sometimes I can feel the breath of the first Cadet on my neck.

Then, in the distance, I see the area we refer to as "no-man's land." It's the strangest area of the property. Exactly one hectare of land, devoid of trees but knee-high in wild grass on both sides of a path that looks like a dug-out trench. Our territory officially begins smack in the middle. My lungs are begging me for air but I know I can't stop, not until I get to our line. More importantly, not until the Cadets get to our line. The trenches are tricky, but we can do "tricky" any day of the week. We make it over the invisible line and a few seconds later, I know all eight Cadets have, too. I hear the roar coming from the wild grass on both sides and Richard's voice booms, "No prisoners! No prisoners!"—which is ridiculous, because it's not as if we're going to kill them, but he has this Lawrence of Arabia obsession—and all of a sudden our seniors come flying out from all directions.

Later, I'm reminded that Jonah Griggs is a rugby league player and if there's one thing he can do, it's tackle or dodge a bunch of those of us whose closest thing to a contact sport is a biffo that might take place after a chess game. So it's not surprising that when I look back for a moment, he's battling his way between our guys. It's like one of those scenes in slow-mo because our eyes make contact and I yell to Ben and Raffy to keep running. There's something about the look on Griggs's face that tells me our army is not going to keep him back. When we make our way out of no-man's land, Raffy takes a detour and I know she's heading towards the Prayer Tree because it's too early in the morning for the Townies to be out here.

The Prayer Tree is a kind of Jerusalem. It used to belong to us, the trail leading up to it belongs to the Cadets, and now it belongs to the Townies. When I see it in the distance, a sense of euphoria comes over me but when we reach the trunk, we notice that the rope ladder is nowhere to be seen.

We stare up at it, our sides pained with excruciating stitches. I look behind, waiting for Jonah Griggs to make an appearance.

Santangelo's head appears at the top. "If they get you, what's the worst thing they can do?" he yells down to us.

We are standing on Cadet territory. Santangelo knows exactly what they can do. He's our only hope.

"Let's make a deal," I say finally.

"Club House?"

I look at Raffy and she nods.

"Club House," I say between gasps.

The ladder comes down and we begin our climb. I'm halfway up when I see Griggs come out of the clearing and I try to go faster but my legs fall between the steps. Santangelo, Ben, and Raffy pull me up from almost the fourth step down and they grab the rope ladder and yank it up at the exact moment that Griggs reaches it. He's on his own but who knows how many Cadets have broken through and are about to join him.

"They can't get up here. No chance," Santangelo says behind me.

I can hardly breathe and I feel Raffy take the inhaler out of my pocket and put it in my hands.

When we all have our breaths back, I look over the side.

"It's not as if he's going to chop us down," Raffy says.

"We're stuck here until he goes," Ben says.

"They're sticklers for time. As soon as their bugle sounds, they're out of here," Santangelo says. "One goes off at ten."

Two and a half hours.

Griggs stands at the bottom and stares at the trunk and I can tell he's reading it. I wonder if he sees the names of the five or if he understands about nothing stopping them in the field in their day. I wonder which statement is his favourite. I wonder if he sees the blood of someone who cut themselves while carving out their soul. Or if he's imagining what he'd write if he had a knife in his hand.

But then he's gone and I panic more at the idea that I can't see him than when he was standing at the bottom. Knowing Griggs, he's lying in wait for us.

Surprisingly, the time passes pleasantly, apart from Santangelo going into specific detail about his plans for the Club House. Half an hour later, though, Griggs is back. Holding a bucket.

"Great tree," he calls up to us.

"What's he got?" Raffy asks, trying to peer over my shoulder.

"Whatever it is won't get him up here," Santangelo says.

Suddenly my heart goes cold. In his hand he holds a paint roller. Jonah Griggs is either going to tar or paint over the trunk.

"You can't do that!" I yell out.

"Then come down and stop me!"

A rage comes over me but I don't move. Because deep down I don't believe he'll wipe out those voices.

"Which one do you want me to go for first?" he calls out cockily.

"I don't give a shit!" I yell back, hoping he doesn't call my bluff.

"Really? Because according to my surveillance

team, you're here every night."

I feel Raffy and Ben looking at me. Santangelo goes to say something but, by the sound of his "ouch," is slammed in the ribs by Raffy.

From all the way up here I see Griggs place the roller in the bucket and it hits the trunk. The next minute I grab the rope ladder and throw it down. When it's securely in place, I begin my descent, sick at the thought of what I'm about to see.

I reach the bottom and smash into him with my fists as hard as I can. He falls and I can't believe he goes down so easy, caught off-balance.

"You care about nothing, you piece of shit!"

I'm on the verge of tears, like I always seem to be these days, and I hear the catch in my voice and I hate myself for it. He throws me off him and I can tell there is a fury in him.

"*Never*," he tells me in a tone full of ice, "underestimate who or what I care for."

I look over to where the bucket has tipped over and I notice that there's no tar, no paint, there's nothing. Just water. I look up at the trunk and everything is still intact, except for the glistening of the drops of water lodged inside the carvings.

He's lying next to me and I don't look at him but I hold out my hand to him.

"Truce?" I ask.

He takes my hand but doesn't shake. Just holds it and it flops onto his chest, where I can feel his heart pounding. I'm not sure how to break the moment or how long we're going to stay here, but there's something so awkwardly peaceful about it all, lying under the Prayer Tree.

"Coffee?" Santangelo calls down to us. We both look up. He, Ben, and Raffy are hanging over the side.

"Is it espresso?" Anson Choi asks behind us.

"Freshly percolated," Ben answers. "You should see the gadgets they have up here."

Anson Choi aims a begging look at Griggs.

"You want to sell out over a coffee?" Griggs asks him with disgust.

"They've got muffins as well," I tell them. "Double chocolate chip. His mum made them."

Griggs gets up and holds out a hand to me. "Truce."

Chapter 16

By the second day of the holidays everyone has left the House. I ignore Jessa's protests that she'd rather stay with me, first because I know she'll drive me insane and second because I know she's lying, which is confirmed when I see the look of excitement in her eyes when Santangelo's mum and his sisters come to pick her up.

For the first two days I relish the peace and quiet and lack of questions and drama, and not having to share the television or the internet or even the snacks in the kitchen. By the time Raffy approaches the front verandah on the Wednesday, though, the company of Taylor Lily Markham is beginning to wear a bit thin.

"I'm bored to death," she tells me. "Want to get out of town? Somewhere with a shopping centre?"

"It'll take us ages to get there. By the time we walk down to town and take the coach . . ."

"Just say we've got a car?"

I look at her, puzzled.

"Santangelo has one," she explains. "Keeps it in the old shed off the trail across the river."

"How do you know that?"

She shrugs. "I went to youth group on Saturday night."

"Santangelo belongs to youth group?"

"No, but his girlfriend does, and I swear to God, the stuff I can get out of this girl is incredible. You see, Santangelo has to keep the car a secret because his father caught him doing five Ks over the speed limit."

"Poor guy," I say, thinking what a bummer it would be to have the police sergeant as your dad. But the sympathy doesn't last long. "Keys?"

She scoffs at the idea. "No one in this town locks their doors, plus we can hotwire."

There must be another confused look on my face because she explains. "It's one of those Townie stories. Too long and insignificant, but being taught to hotwire has been pretty valuable."

I'm liking the idea. Having access to a car for the holidays might even take me as far as Sydney.

The old shed is at least a thirty-minute walk, so we take the trail bikes and trespass into Cadet territory, hoping we don't get caught. The Cadets are on a partial holiday. No school work, but plenty of hikes outside the area; so there's no time like the present to violate the treaty.

It's fun to be on the bikes again and I remember the times when I was in year nine, before we lost the trail to the Cadets, when we'd go flying over the twists and turns of the dirt road, racing one another across the most ridiculously dangerous terrain around. I broke my arm once by flying straight into a tree and Hannah didn't talk to me for a week. But Hannah's not around and Raffy and I race each other, both of us skidding off the bikes at least once. The scrape on my leg stings but I get there first and our adrenalin is so pumped that I'm ready to commit any felony, including breaking into the illegal car of the local sergeant's son.

There's something about the shabbiness of the dilapidated shed that makes me think that nothing could be driven into it without it falling apart. We park the bikes at the back and with great difficulty pull open the two wooden doors. By the time we get them open we are saturated with perspiration and exhausted. But once we step inside, our fatigue changes to a sense of triumph. In front of us is an old but incredible shiny dark blue Commodore. As Raffy promised, the doors are unlocked and we circle it for a moment, celebrating the audacity of what we are about to do.

Raffy climbs in and disappears under the dashboard. I lean on the windowsill looking in as she pulls out wires and connects them like someone out of those movies that I have always been so dubious about because it's always looked so easy.

"You are impressing me like crazy here," I say to her.

"I can't wait to tell him one day," she says with a giggle. "'Hey, Chaz, guess what? We knew where your precious car was all the time.' I'd like to take a photo of his face. What do you think?"

The car begins to purr and I hear her "Yesss" of victory.

"I reckon I'd smile really nicely in the photo," Santangelo says behind me, yanking me out of the way, "knowing that you'll be keeping it under your pillow for the rest of your life."

He opens the car door and pulls her out, bumping her head on the way. Jonah Griggs is standing behind him, equally unimpressed.

"Don't you *ever* touch my car again," Santangelo says with the same fury he had on his face when Jonah Griggs made comments about his mother.

Raffy touches the car with her finger in a very dramatic way.

"You've just made our hit list," he says, getting a hanky out of his pocket and cleaning off some imaginary mark. I haven't seen a hanky in ages and seeing Santangelo with one makes it really difficult to keep a straight face.

"Oh, scary, scary," Raffy says. "Let's go, Taylor."

"What are you guys up to?" I ask suspiciously. "Why are you hanging out together?"

"We're not," Santangelo says.

"Well, it looks like you are," I say.

"We're not," Jonah Griggs says. "Believe me. His father's made us paint half this town and if we stick around any longer he'll make us paint the rest of it."

"As a punishment for Gala Day?" Raffy asks.

"No. I think it was the Seven-Eleven thing," he mutters, looking away.

"It could be because of that thing outside Woolworths," Santangelo says. We didn't know about that one. "My nanna Faye saw it and told my mum and she told my dad."

"You guys have to stop the fighting," Raffy says. "It's passé. No one has punch-ups anymore."

"This whole bloody town is passé," Griggs says. "Can we just get out of here?"

"Are you going to smash him for that or will I?" Raffy asks Santangelo, glaring at Griggs.

I pull her away. "We're out of here."

We don't look back. The trail bikes are prohibited for town use, so we go back to a world with no wheels but at least I have company in my boredom. Our shopping gets downsized to the two or three dress shops in town. It takes us longer to get to the Jellicoe Road from the garage than it would from our House but when we get there, Santangelo's car is parked by the side of the trail.

"We can give you a lift," he says grudgingly. Griggs is looking straight ahead as if he doesn't give a shit.

"But just say we get finger marks on the seats?" I

ask. "Can we borrow your hanky?"

Raffy and I are both amused by my humour.

"Just don't touch anything."

Apart from the ride with Mr. Palmer on the night of my gaol visit, I haven't been in a car for ages, especially during the day. There's something so normal about it all, even if the guys in the front seat are your arch-enemies. Santangelo and Griggs have a massive argument about whose CD they put in first and Griggs wins, based on the logistics of Santangelo having his hands on the wheel. It's a New Order song and from the moment the opening strands are over and the full passion of the music begins, I feel as if I am a thousand miles away from the turmoil of the past week. With the window down and my head out, I feel like everything inside of me is switched on. Santangelo is a good driver and knows every inch of the road, handling its turns and potholes effortlessly. I drift into a dreamy mode, to the beat of the music, and the dual voices of the singers make me close my eyes but still the colours around me penetrate my eyelids and I let them in. Flashes of greens and browns and greens and browns and . . .

"Stop!" I yell out. "Santangelo, stop!"

He comes to a screeching halt and we're all thrown forward in our seats.

"What?" they're all asking me at once.

"Are you okay?" Raffy asks.

I unlatch my seatbelt, get out of the car, and begin walking back down the road. I hear the slamming of three doors behind me and feel them following.

In front of us, on the side of the road, among weeds and ferns and rocks and tangled bushes, are a group of poppies. Surrounding them is a pebbled border, which seems to convey the message to keep clear. I'm staring at the flowers in amazement and then I look at Griggs.

"Do you guys jog along here?"

He shakes his head. "We go the other way."

"What is it?" Raffy asks. "One of those roadside shrines or something?"

"Makes sense," Santangelo says. "There was supposed to be the world's worst accident here about twenty years ago."

I turn to him. "Who died?"

He shrugs. "My dad would know, obviously. I think two families got wiped out. But they weren't from here."

Griggs is watching me carefully. "You okay?" he asks quietly.

There's a part of me that doesn't want to tell them the story. It's like it belongs to me . . . and Hannah. I don't know what's true or not. Did Hannah know about those families?

"There's this story," I begin, "that they were planted by these kids who went to the Jellicoe School and one day they were destroyed by the Cadets while they were jogging. It was the first year the Cadets came. But the next day, one of the Cadets came back and he planted them again. With the kids, that is."

"Where did you hear that?" Griggs asks.

"From Hannah."

"The one who looks after you?"

I don't answer. There's just something about this spot. I turn around and look at the other side of the road where Jude first saw Narnie, thinking she was an apparition. They're not real, I keep on telling myself. Those people aren't real.

Griggs, Santangelo, and Raffy are looking at me closely and I walk back to the car.

Griggs convinces Santangelo that he should drive,

in case Santangelo's dad sees us. "So where to?" he asks.

Santangelo turns around in the seat, looking at me. "I'll show you the spot where they found something that belonged to the missing kid."

"That's morbid," Raffy says.

"What missing kid?" Griggs asks.

Santangelo turns back around but I catch his eye in the rear-view mirror and he looks away. Once again I get a sense that he knows something more than I do about my own life. I can't imagine what it is but I suspect as the son of a policeman, he comes across all sorts of information. Stuck out at the school in the middle of a territory war, I have never had access to any information from town. Then again, I've never searched for it, because Jellicoe never seemed like anything more than a weak link between my mother and Hannah. Over the years I'd wondered sometimes if they had met while Hannah was at university in the city or maybe working in a pub someplace. Or maybe Hannah was a neighbour who felt an affinity for a single mother her age who couldn't get through her day without a cocktail of alcohol, drugs, and pain-killers. Hannah could have worked at the methadone clinic one of the times my mother tried to quit. But every time I spoke to Hannah about the connection between her and my mother she'd just ask, "Do you feel safe?" I'd shrug because I didn't feel threatened and she'd say, "Then for the time being that has to be enough."

But it was never enough. And I resent her more for it now than I ever have.

But Santangelo seems to know something and, more than anything, he seems willing to tell.

"Take us there," I say quietly.

The spot is way on the other side of town. As we drive I follow the river, right through town and back out into the middle of nowhere again.

The place is almost as majestic as Hannah's property. Big weeping willows shade the area by the river. Ropes hang off branches ready for swimmers to throw themselves into the water.

We sit, the four of us, watching the river, not saying much because it's not as if we're friends who have things in common to discuss. But strangely enough, it's not awkward—just silent, apart from the typical nature soundtrack buzzing in the air. Once in a while some little flying insect stations itself right in front of my nose and then it's off doing a crazy three-sixty turn before flying away in a manic direction.

"You're not another one who's obsessed with that serial killer, are you?" I ask Santangelo.

"No."

"Then why mention a boy who disappeared almost twenty years ago?"

"How do you know it was almost twenty years ago?" Santangelo asks.

"You said."

"No he didn't," Griggs says, looking suddenly interested.

"And I didn't say it was a boy."

"Was it?" Griggs asks him.

Santangelo nods.

"I've probably been told about it before," I say. I didn't want to tell them about Hannah's manuscript. "You?"

He shrugs, but I keep my focus on him until he fidgets uncomfortably. "I saw a photo of him once," he says quietly. "It left an impression."

"Because he was our age?" Raffy asks.

Santangelo thinks for a moment, as if he needs to

figure something out himself while trying to explain it to other people.

"Do you ever wonder how someone our age can possibly be dead? There's just something really unnatural about it."

I watch his face as he tries to explain.

"If you saw the photo you'd understand. You'd want to say to the kid in it, "Why weren't you strong enough to resist death? Didn't that look in your eye stop anything bad from happening to you?"

"But you're not talking about someone's age; now you're talking about their spirit," Raffy says.

"Maybe I am. It's like when I was in year eight and we had to study *The Diary of Anne Frank*. I mean, she died of typhoid. Can you believe it? How could Anne Frank die of typhoid? The girl never kept her mouth shut, she was bloody annoying, and it was like nothing could kill what was inside of her. I thought, okay, maybe a gas chamber or a firing squad could kill her but not an illness that other people survived."

I'm very disturbed to find out that the leader of the Townies has a soul and I'm beginning to develop a bit of a crush on him.

"At the end of the day it's about heart beats and blood flow," Griggs says flatly. "People's spirits don't keep them alive."

Santangelo looks at me again. "The kid in the photo . . . his hair was kind of wavy, like a golden brown, and his eyes were that colour that's not blue or green and he was smiling, so he had this kind of cut in his face. Not a real one. As if the smile made cuts in his cheek, but they weren't dimples."

Raffy and Griggs look at me. I stare out at the river.

"I saw you once," Santangelo says, and I know he's speaking to me. "It was about two years ago and you were sitting next to Raf. There was this performer at the Jellicoe fair. You know, one of those travelling Shakespeare slapstick comedies and you were laughing and you kind of—well, not to be insulting or anything because you don't look like a boy anymore . . . the guys always say, 'That Taylor Markham, she's not too bad-looking,' so I don't want you to think that I think you look masculine because I swear to God you don't, you look—"

"Get to the point," Griggs interrupts.

"It was like I was looking at him," Santangelo

finishes. "The kid in the photo."

"This all based on one photo," Raffy says.

"You've got to see it to understand. Actually, there are two photos. The other is of the group."

"What group?" I ask. My heart is beating fast and my mouth is getting that churning sweet feeling of nausea.

"About five of them. One's a Cadet; I could tell by the uniform. My father had the file out on his desk once when I was in there. All I saw were the two photos and the cap, which was found out there," he says, pointing to the river.

"What was his name?"

"Xavier."

My stomach settles back down and I take a deep breath of relief. "Never heard of him."

"Xavier Webster Schroeder."

I feel faint and my breath seems to leave my body with a speed I can't control. I need it desperately to come back, because the feeling that I'm breathing through a straw frightens the hell out of me.

"Are you okay?" Griggs says, looking at me. He turns to Santangelo. "Why do you always do this?"

"Why do you always go berserk when she loses a bit of colour?" Santangelo asks back.

"Because she's an asthmatic, you moron, and every time you open your mouth and tell her something she forgets how to breathe."

I get this horrible feeling that while I'm in the middle of an asthma attack these two are going to thump the hell out of each other again.

Raffy fumbles through my backpack for my inhaler and I take a few puffs until I get my breathing back under control. She glares at both of them, a bit pale herself.

"What?" Santangelo asks again.

"Just drop us off at my place," she says, helping me up. "And if you guys have one more fight, I swear to God, Chaz, I will never speak to you again."

They stand staring at each other and I'm waiting for a comeback from him. But Santangelo just looks a bit gutted and I realise it's because Raffy looks just as bad and I get a glimpse of how things really are between them.

Without looking at Griggs he holds out a hand to him and Griggs shakes it, reluctantly.

We get into the car and I lean back, exhausted. Santangelo turns and looks at both of us. "So what's the story?"

I close my eyes and curl up on the seat.

"Our House guardian who lives by the river," Raffy says. "Her name is Hannah Schroeder."

We get dropped off at Raffy's place and her mother forces me to have a lie down and then refuses to drive me home that night. So I'm taken prisoner and made to wear a crisp white nightie for middle-aged people that has pink and white bows on the shoulders. Raffy looks apologetic because she left any nightwear she could have lent me back at the school. We sit watching television until late. I haven't said much since finding out about the missing boy's link to Hannah and my uncanny resemblance to him. I don't want to even think about it right now, so we lie in bed, pretending the conversation never came up, and just concentrate on trivial stuff, like the guys.

"Do you miss being friends with Santangelo?" I ask her after the lights are out and we're almost asleep.

"What makes you think we were friends?"

"Everything."

I hear her yawn.

"Being enemies with him is better," she tells me. There's a pause and I think she's going to say something more but she doesn't and it's just silence for a long while.

"My father . . ." I begin, realising that I have never said those words out loud. "If I look like that kid in the photo and he's disappeared . . ."

She turns to face me and although I can't see her in the dark, I sense her there. "Don't listen to Santangelo. Once he was convinced that a girl he was going out with looked exactly like Cameron Diaz and, I swear to God, my father looks more like Cameron Diaz."

I curl into the nightie, the crisp cotton cocooning me in a wave of security and I go to sleep thinking of the boy in Santangelo's photo.

Because thinking of him brings me solace.

We're still in our nightwear at eleven o'clock the next morning. Raffy's dad is making us breakfast. The doorbell rings and Raffy's mum calls out, "It's open." I just can't believe these people invite people into their home without asking who it is.

Santangelo and Griggs walk in and Raffy and I exchange looks of mini-mortification. They're surprised to see me but Raffy's mum is too busy kissing

Santangelo with such enthusiasm that it's like Jesus Christ has just walked in.

"And this is Gri—Jonah," Santangelo says, trying very hard to let the name roll off his tongue.

Jonah Griggs shakes hands with both Raffy's parents like they're in the military. As usual he is dressed in his fatigues and looks away the instant someone tries to make eye contact. Raffy's mum forces them to sit down and they get to see us up close and personal in our nighties. I think I felt less self-conscious in my undies and singlet the night Griggs came to my room.

I watch Raffy's mother standing behind her chair, holding on to Raffy's long hair as if putting it into a ponytail and there's this pride on her face while she's touching her, like she's saying, "Look at my beautiful girl." It makes my eyes fill with tears and I quickly brush them away but as usual Jonah Griggs is looking and I want to melt into the ground and have the nightie cover the insignificant puddle that is me. It's not that I miss my mother. It's just that I miss the idea of what one would be.

"We were just driving around . . . in Jonah's car and we thought maybe we'd pick Raffy up and then

Taylor at the school, but obviously she's here."

"What a pity. We've already made plans to go shopping," Raffy's mum says.

"Shame," Raffy says. "We'll see the guys out," she adds, standing up.

"Raffy, they might want some breakfast."

The boys speak over each other, explaining that they've already eaten, and I walk out with Griggs while Santangelo has a twenty-minute goodbye with Raffy's parents.

"What's with what you're wearing?" Griggs asks while we stand outside waiting for the others.

"It's pretty hideous, isn't it?" I say.

"Don't force me to look at it," he says. "It's see-through."

That kills conversation for a couple of seconds.

"Strange that you're hanging out with Santangelo," I say, trying to keep the silence from growing even more awkward. It's much easier dealing with him as an enemy in the territory wars than like this.

"Strange? I don't think that word comes anywhere near it. My troops are on an overnight camp three hundred kilometres away from here. I had to sleep at the Santangelo penitentiary for pre-pubescent girls.

There are hundreds of them, including that annoying pest that belongs to you. I have one brother and I live with four hundred guys. Girls under the age of fourteen are the most frightening creatures I have ever come across. They all insist on running around the house in their underwear. Then Nanna Faye comes over as well as Nonna Caterina and I have to drive them to Bingo in 'my car' and then they make us stay and we have to call out the numbers and they have these Bingo codes like, 'Tweak of the thumb . . . Stop and run . . . Two fat ladies . . . Clickety click,' and did you know Santangelo's black and Italian? Do you know how many cousins he has as a result? Well, I've met them all and they ask me a hundred questions and I rarely talk to anyone outside my immediate family or school so let's just say that the past twenty-four hours have been somewhat on the traumatic side. And to top it all off there's the sergeant who looks at me like I'm going to wipe out his family during the night."

"As if Santangelo's dad would ever have you in his house if he thought that," I say quietly.

He's not looking at me and suddenly I get why he doesn't look people in the eye. It's like he thinks he'll see the doubt or the distrust or the questions about his past.

"Okay, so it's not that bad," he says after a while. "So, like I asked, what's with the nightie?"

"It smells like what I always think mothers smell like," I tell him honestly, knowing I don't have to explain.

He nods. "My mum has one just the same and you have no idea how disturbing it is that it's turning me on."

Before I can even go red, Raffy and Santangelo walk towards us.

"Your nighties' see-through," Santangelo says, getting into the car. He rolls down the window. "I have a plan," he says.

I shake my head. "I can't do territory wars at the moment."

"It's not about that," he says. "It's about those photos."

"Do you have a death wish?" Griggs warns.

Santangelo ignores him. "I'm going to get them for you," he tells me.

"How?"

"Easy. I'm going to break into the police station."

I talk about going back to the school every day but I always end up staying. On Saturday night they take me to a twenty-first party. I have no idea who it's for but it's at the scout hall and I'm almost convinced that the whole town has been invited. Jonah Griggs is sitting at a table with Santangelo, Santangelo's girlfriend, and some of her friends. When he sees me, there's a look of surprise and something else.

I'm self-conscious about the skirt I bought with Raffy and the T-shirt that barely covers my midriff, and the fact that I let Raffy's mum brainwash me into believing that no woman should leave her house without wearing lipstick but I like the way it makes me feel.

Senior Cadets are allowed out on a Saturday night during the holidays and the place is packed with them. The music is loud but the people's voices are louder and every one of them looks happy. I haven't seen so many happy people all in one room, except on television, but these people don't look like they're acting.

It surprises me to see Ben in a huddle with the Mullet Brothers and Anson Choi and some of the Townies. I didn't know he was back from holidays.

He walks towards me doing this salsa cha-cha thing and it makes me laugh and I dance back towards him. He drags me over and introduces me to people he's just met. "They think you're a babe," he whispers in my ear, and because nobody has ever called me a babe before, I find myself charmed. Then Griggs and Santangelo are beside me and somehow Griggs has managed to shoulder his way between Ben and me. Although I don't look at him, I feel him at my shoulder for most of the night. The Townies poke fun at Griggs and Choi because they're in uniform but the banter is good-natured and I'm surprised how clever Griggs is in his response to it.

We're in a world full of people Raffy knows. People who bring her to life and it seems as if her feet hardly touch the ground because every second person picks her up and twirls her around. While she's speaking to her uncle, friends from her primary school introduce themselves to me.

"I married her in grade six," one named Joe Salvatore tells me, grinning.

"What did a wedding consist of in grade six?" I ask.

"An exchange of rings made of grass and a

reception of candy and sherbet," he explains. "Chaz refused to attend because she was his best friend since they were born and he thought she was his."

"As if," Santangelo says, scowling. Griggs doesn't look too impressed, either, and Joe Salvatore seems to enjoy their irritation. When Raffy finally reaches us, he lifts her off the ground and smothers her with noisy kisses and she's giggling in a way I've never heard before.

I talk local politics with Santangelo's mum and teacher shortages with Raffy's dad. I do the twist with Santangelo and politely decline an invitation to go for a drive with one of his friends. I do the Time Warp with Jessa and the Zorba with Raffy and, when I need to stop for air, Jonah Griggs is there and he takes my hand and leads me through the crowd until we're outside.

I take deep breaths, looking at the town stretched in front of me. When I turn around, he cups my face in his hands and he kisses me so deeply that I don't know who is breathing for who, but his mouth and tongue taste like warm honey. I don't know how long it lasts, but when I let go of him, I miss it instantly.

We end up with the Townies and Cadets at

McDonald's on the highway at two in the morning. I look around at everyone and I can't help thinking how normal we look and I don't think I've ever felt normal. I watch Raffy as she removes the pickles from her hamburger and hands them over to Santangelo without them exchanging a word and I realise again there is more to that relationship than spelling bees and being enemies. These people have history and I crave history. I crave someone knowing me so well that they can tell what I'm thinking. Jonah Griggs takes my hand under the table and links my fingers with his and I know that I would sacrifice almost anything just to keep this state of mind, for the rest of the week at least.

Chapter 17

On one of those days during the holidays when they were completely bored, Webb came up with a plan. The five of them sat by the river, at the very spot where Webb dreamed of building a house.

"We build a tunnel," Webb said. "It runs from my House to Tate and Narnie's and then we take a detour and it goes from their House, underneath the driveway and then to the clearing."

"Purpose?" Jude asked, practising his overarm with rocks against the tree.

"To get around after hours. It'll be tops."

"Tops, will it be?"

"The Great Escape. They built a tunnel," Fitz said, enthused.

"They needed to, morons. It was a matter of life and death," Jude said dryly.

"We're bored to death, Jude, so isn't that a matter of life and death?" Tate asked.

Webb was grinning. Tate, too. They always grinned in unison. Like they were thinking with the same mind, sharing the same heart. Ever since any of them could remember, Webb and Tate had been like that. Jude knew it was why he was drawn to them. They were like beacons for Narnie, who couldn't seem to operate without them and Fitz and Jude loved the three, unashamedly.

"They think I saved them but they saved me," Fitz once told him. "I didn't exist before I belonged to the Fucked-Up Four."

"Five," Jude had corrected.

He could hear Webb, Tate, and Fitz discussing the tunnel as if it already existed.

"Narnie, explain to the delusional trio why the POWs needed that tunnel more than we do," he said.

"Nazis," she muttered, sitting against the tree. Bad day for Narnie.

"Weren't your grandparents Nazis?" Fitz asked, lining up at least five imaginary enemies and, with his finger and popping sounds, eliminating them one by one.

"They were Germans," Narnie said. "Big difference."

"Although Oma Rose vas a Nazi vhen it came to eating za sauerkraut," Webb said in a bad German accent, and for the first time in a long time, Narnie laughed.

"I'm all for the tunnel. It could save our life one day," Tate said. "We could be chased by evil and have to hide down there."

"Evil out in Jellicoe? I wish," Fitz said.

"Think of how tunnels saved people from Hitler," Tate said.

"Yeah, but last I heard Hitler was dead. The bunker, a gun, Eva. Ring a bell?" Jude said.

"Cyanide," Narnie corrected.

"We'll pretend we're the East Germans trying to escape to West Germany. No Nazis."

"Just Communists."

"All we need is to be able to get from one House to the other and then from that House to the clearing," Webb said, slightly frustrated by the fact that nobody but Tate was taking him seriously.

Jude looked from Tate to Webb, shaking his head.

"You know what?" Webb asked. "I'm getting

another fantastic idea." The seven P.M. *call bell rang in the distance but Webb was in another world.*

"Skirmish," he said, impressed with himself. "Let's have a war."

There was a new plan every day, bigger and better than the day before. Each afternoon at four o'clock they would meet to discuss it.

On Jude's last day they met at midnight and camped under the oak by the river. Fitz handed them a bottle and Webb took a swig, spitting it out instantly.

"What the hell was that, Fitz?" he asked, trying to regain his breath.

"Grappa. Got it from the Italians next door. Burns your insides out."

"And the enjoyment is?" Jude said, taking a swig, his eyes instantly tearing up and his breath coming in gasps.

"I reckon if I put a match right here, you'd see fireworks," Fitz continued, taking out his matches and breathing heavily into the air.

Still trying to recover, Jude stared at him. "Why would you want to do that, dickhead?"

"Live on the edge, GI Jude. That's my motto."

Fitz took out a cigarette and Jude grabbed it out of his mouth. "You're going to set us all on fire, you homicidal feral fruitcake."

"Hand it over," Tate said, taking a few deep breaths before swigging from the bottle. She stared at Narnie in shock and started coughing out of control. Narnie fanned her down, patting her on the back until the coughing subsided.

"Can we stay focused?" Webb asked, taking out a purple leather book.

"Mate, no one is going to take you seriously with a book that looks like that," Jude said.

"Yeah, Chairman Mao and his little purple book," Fitz said, laughing at his own joke.

"It's Chairman Meow to you, and I've got a system set up that's going to blow your mind."

"I wouldn't mind other parts of me bl—"

"Fitz!" Tate said. "Grossed out. Majorly."

"Is anyone listening to me?" Webb asked, annoyed. "Is that too much to ask?"

"I am," Narnie replied.

Webb leaned over and grabbed her face. "Then I can die happy."

Narnie patted the space next to her and Fitz sat down obediently.

"Okay, we play skirmish," Webb said. "Cadets, Townies, us. We split this area into territories and anyone who tries to invade loses ground. We have rules of engagement, diplomatic immunity, and one or two fisticuffs."

"What part of this are we going to enjoy?" Tate asked, pointing to Narnie and herself.

"The part where we take you hostage and ravage you," Fitz said.

"You're an animal."

Fitz did gorilla impersonations and Narnie shushed him gently.

"Fitz, you head the Townies, Jude heads the Cadets, and I'll get the Houses together back here. We need to get the six Houses working, so we need rules."

"No fraternising with leaders of other Houses," Tate said. "Rule number one."

Webb looked taken aback.

"What happens if you do?" he asked, jumping on top of her and trapping her with his arms and legs.

"The two leaders get placed in exile . . . together.

For the rest of their lives."

"Okay," he said with enthusiasm, jumping off her. "I'm writing that rule in. 'No relationship between leaders of opposite Houses'."

"I've got one for the territory wars," Fitz said, his eyes bloodshot from the spirit. "If trespassing occurs, there's payback." He jabbed at thin air. "One to the jaw, two to the gut."

"So what does the winner get in the end?" Tate asked.

"They get to sit around with the losers and say, 'I am King Xavier of the world.' Repeat after me."

"And me?" Tate asked.

"You get to be my queen."

Tate looked pleased with the idea.

"How come you're the leader of the community?" Narnie asked, almost smiling. "Why can't Tate be?"

Webb looked at his sister, grinning. "Why can't you, Narnie?"

Fitz leaned his head on Narnie's shoulder. "And I'll be your queen?"

"You can be the eunuch," Jude said, shoving him out of the way, "and I'll be her prince." He bowed and took Narnie's hand, kissing it, and their eyes

met. It was awkward for a moment until Narnie looked away.

"So how long will it take to get your troops in gear?" Webb asked him. "We're serious here, you know."

"Mate, we've been ready for years."

"By the time you come back next year, we'll be ready—tunnel and all."

"If it's going to be like The Great Escape, *make sure there are trail bikes," Jude said.*

"So you're in?"

He shrugged. "As long as I get to play Steve McQueen."

Spending days with Santangelo and Griggs becomes a habit for the rest of the holidays. Most of the time the Mullet Brothers, Choi, Ben, Santangelo's sisters, and Jessa McKenzie come along as well. We end up either at Santangelo's place or Raffy's, but mostly the former because Raffy's mum and dad teach the Townies and keep on asking them for overdue homework.

The Santangelo home is like a madhouse. I'm not quite sure how his mum finds time to be the mayor of the town as well but she manages. She's the only person who gets away with calling Santangelo a "little shit" and once in a while she'll go for the collective and refer to both Griggs and Santangelo as those "two little shits." Most of the time the "two little shits" take it on the chin but sometimes Santangelo says, "I'm fucking out of here," and his mum warns, "Don't you dare swear, you little shit." The Santangelo sisters, Griggs, and Raffy ignore it all, but Jessa and I are fascinated and frightened at the same time. We wait for a showdown but it tends not to happen and then everything's all calm again and the only two left in a mess are Jessa and me. Sometimes we are very relieved to escape it all.

It's during those moments that I notice how similar we are. Both Jessa and I have spent almost half our lives brought up by people other than our parents and neither of us have siblings. She has no recollection of her mother, who died of cancer when Jessa was two years old, and I have too much recollection of mine. Jessa lived with her aunt but hero-worshipped her father, who died when she was nine in some apparent freak accident, and my only memory of my father is of being on his shoulders and touching the sky.

Though after Santangelo's revelation about the boy in the photo, I'm not too sure anymore. More than anything, we have Hannah in common, and somehow during these holidays I begin to see Jessa as a kind of link to whatever it is out there that I need to work out.

"Do you think of Hannah a lot?" she asks me when we move back to the House close to the end of the holidays. I'm letting her sleep in the spare bed in my room because everyone else isn't back until the weekend and there's no one else in the dorms.

All the time, I want to say.

"Sometimes."

"Do you think something's happened to her?" she asks quietly.

All the time, I want to say.

"Sometimes."

"Taylor, just say the seri—"

"Don't," I say, irritated, turning over, away from her. "Jessa, forget the serial killer. There are enough other things to worry about."

"She'd never leave us, so it can only be the serial killer."

I grit my teeth and count to ten so I won't yell at

her. "He only takes teenagers," I say, not so reassuringly. "She's in her thirties."

"But I read on this website that, in the townships stretching from the Sturt to the Hume Highways, there have been eleven attempted kidnaps and three actual kidnaps of women over twenty-five in the last ten years."

"Can I suggest another website? It's www-dot-shutupabouttheserialkiller-dot-com."

She is silent for a moment and I feel guilty about the aggression.

"If Hannah doesn't come back, I'll have no one," she says in the smallest voice I've heard her use.

I reluctantly turn to face her again but looking at Jessa's face always has this sledgehammer effect on me, so I lie on my back and stare at the ceiling.

"Hannah's coming back. Anyway, you've got whoever looked after you before you came here."

"My aunt. But she has my cousins and I know she likes me, even loves me, but it's not like I felt as if I belonged. Until Hannah turned up."

"She turned up one day? Just like that?"

"Uh-huh. I just thought she was so beautiful. She said, 'Let me look at you,' and then she cried and held me and said that if she had known about me, she would have come much sooner."

"Funny. She turned up just like that for me as well."

"Maybe she's like in that TV show where those angels moonlight as people and they come down to help others. You know. Like in *Touched by an Angel*."

"I don't think she's an angel, Jessa. She swears worse than Santangelo and Griggs." I turn and lean on my elbow, facing her. "So what did she say when she showed up?"

"That she was a friend of my dad's, but I don't really believe that. I couldn't imagine Hannah knowing my dad and she seemed much younger than him, anyway."

"I've never known my father," I tell her.

"My aunt said mine was a crazy man and that he lost his marbles years ago, but I don't think he was, you know. I think he was just really sad."

"Maybe because your mum died."

"I don't know but when he came to visit, he'd tell me the best stories about growing up around here. When Hannah told me I'd be coming here when I was twelve, I was ecstatic."

She looks at me intently. "She used to talk about you. She'd tell me that when I came to the school, I would have you and that she'd be the luckiest person in the world because she'd have both of us. I used to think she was your mum."

"I have a mother and she's not Hannah."

"But don't you ever wish she was? I do."

I don't answer. I just wish Hannah would come back and tell me off like she used to. Or even keep me a little at arm's-length, which she always seemed to do with me. Not like Jessa. I'd watch them together: Hannah would smother Jessa with kisses and cuddles and they'd giggle like kids. Maybe my guard was up all the time and she was reacting to that. But I wish she had seen through it and I wish that once, *just once*, I had told her how I feel. That I feel safer when she is around. Sometimes I had tested her, wanting so desperately for her to let me down so then I would have an excuse to walk away. But she never did. I wish I could tell her it breaks my heart that I miss her more than I ever missed my mother and that the thing that frightens me the most about next October when I graduate is not that I won't have a home, but that I won't have her.

"You know what?" Jessa says after a moment, yawning. "I reckon that Brigadier knows where she is."

My pulse does this thumping thing that happens every time I think of him.

"Why do you say that? Has he ever hassled you? Tell me!"

She frowns and I don't know whether it's because she remembers something or because of my aggression. "He looks at me all the time."

"Does it freak you out?" I ask, not wanting to put more fear in her head.

"No, but Chloe P. reckons he could be the serial killer."

"Oh, please," I say, even though I once thought the same.

"She reckons whoever it is lives between Sydney and Truscott."

"Which covers seven hundred kilometres, narrowing our suspects down to about one million people."

"And the kidnappings have always taken place between September and the end of the year and would probably be committed by someone who drives those seven hundred kilometres. The Brigadier would get to cover at least five hundred of them. He goes back and forth from Sydney to here all the time. Well, this year he has, anyway. Last year he wasn't around, or the year before, and there were no kidnappings."

"How do you know?"

"That he wasn't around last year? Because Teresa, one of the hostages, is going around with one of the Cadets and he told her and she told me."

"Can you point out to Teresa that the Cadets are our enemy and she's not allowed to 'go around' with one of them?"

"But you pashed Jonah Griggs and he's the leader of the enemy."

I stare at her in amazement with absolutely no comeback.

"We saw you at the party on Saturday night," she says, grinning, "We thought it was really romantic."

"Who's we?"

"Mary and Sarah and Elisha and Tilly Santangelo and their cousins and some of their friends from school. How can you breathe when his tongue—"

"Go to sleep," I say, turning over again.

I wanted to say that I didn't need to breathe on my own when Jonah Griggs was kissing me, but seeing he hasn't touched me since that night, I can't even bring myself to think of him. It's not like he's ignoring me, because that would be proactive. It's like I'm just anyone to him. Even when we were squashed in the back seat, our knees glued together and our shoulders touching and my insides full of butterflies, he was speaking over my head the whole time with Santangelo about some ridiculous AFL/Rugby League thing. Somewhere along the way, Jonah Griggs has become a priority in my life and his attitude this week has been crushing.

On the last Saturday of the holidays, Santangelo takes Griggs, Raffy, and me back to the place by the river on the other side of town. He's convinced that there is some other clue down there to do with the missing boy and if there is one thing I've noticed about Santangelo, it's that he has a touch of obsessive compulsive about him and won't let an idea go.

"Apparently the Hermit was obsessed with this river," he tells us. "Why do you think that is?" he persists.

I just shrug but I can tell Raffy and Griggs are trying to come up with something intelligent. When nobody answers he holds out his hands as if to say, "Go on, answer."

"Santangelo, you're dying to tell us, so just tell us," Griggs says, irritated.

"Because I think he knew that kid, Xavier."

"Webb," I say, and the three of them look at me. "That's what they called him."

"Webb." He nods. "Well, think of this river. There are so many bends where stuff going down the river gets lodged."

"Stuff?" I ask. "Wow. Hold back on the jargon."

"So let's go in," Griggs says.

"It's deep and by the time you get to the bottom and check out what's down there, you'll have to come back up again for breath."

"I'll go down," Raffy said. "I'm the fifteen-hundred-metre swimmer and can hold my breath the longest."

I watch the guys. It's as if she's stripped them of their masculinity.

"It's no big deal. It's just about better lungs," she reassures them, turning to face me and rolling her eyes as she takes off her shoes and socks. The guys are not coping and I sit back and hug my knees to watch the show.

"How do you know Griggs isn't a long-distance swimmer who has fantastic lungs?" Santangelo asks.

"Because he looks like a Rugby player, not a swimmer," Raffy tells him. "You look like an AFL player, not a swimmer. I look like a swimmer."

"What about me?" I ask.

The three of them look at me. Being tall has never meant I was labelled as athletic. Just lanky.

"You look like someone who can wipe out the opposition in a chess game," Raffy says.

"I won the table tennis title two years in a row," I remind her.

"But you're not a swimmer," she says.

"You only beat me in the fifteen-hundred that one time," Santangelo says.

I can tell this could go on forever and I'm not in the mood. "Look," I say, "he beat you in the spelling bee. She beat you in the fifteen-hundred metres. Let's just get this Fab Four adventure over and done with and go home."

"I think two of us should go in," Raffy says, taking off her top.

"Look the other way," Santangelo tells Griggs as she unzips her jeans.

"As if."

When Raffy is down to her undies and singlet, she dives in with ease. Her head emerges, her teeth chattering. Santangelo begins to strip as well and I certainly don't look the other way.

As soon as Santangelo and Raffy's heads go under, Griggs leans over and kisses me. It's a hungry kind of kiss, like he's been dying to do it for ages and he can't get enough but after a while I open my eyes and just stare at him.

"You're supposed to close your eyes," he says, a little unnerved.

"I'm not supposed to do anything," I say, moving away from him and looking into the river, waiting for Raffy and Santangelo to come back up.

"Is there a problem here?"

"There's nothing here."

"Really? Because that wasn't the message you were giving me last Saturday night."

"And between last Saturday and today there have

been at least six days, so let's just say that I'm going by the message that you've been giving me since then."

"We've been surrounded by the Santangelo circus and that little pest who is either attached to you surgically or me and then, when they're not around, Casanova Cassidy is hanging off every word you say or Raffy is giving me one of those 'girl zone only' looks," he says. "So if I haven't been giving you the attention—"

"So you're admitting it. That you can just switch this on and off?"

"Yeah, whatever you say. I'm over it."

"Good, because I was never into it!"

I feel like someone off Jerry Springer. Any moment now I'm going to be saying "boyfriend" with a bit of Afro-American attitude thrown in but I can't help it.

Santangelo emerges and I feel horrible because I've almost forgotten that they're down there. He swings around looking for Raffy and I move closer to the river until her head appears.

"Anything?" I ask, as if there was a likelihood that they would find something constructive, just because we were looking for it.

"No," Santangelo says, dragging himself out. "But there are heaps of tree trunks lying on the bottom and anything could be stuck in or under them."

Santangelo comes up with yet another idea about getting some diving material for a better search, but I'm not listening anymore and neither is Griggs.

Santangelo and Raffy drop us off on the Jellicoe Road and I get out without saying a word and walk away, but Griggs is right behind me.

"So explain to me again what I did wrong."

I don't stop. "You know what? You didn't do anything wrong. I did. It's this dumb thing I do. I look into things and see more than I'm supposed to."

"You're implying that last week meant nothing to me."

This time I do stop, staring at him. "It's not an implication. It's a fact. Just like when we ran away. No big deal, Griggs."

"It was a big deal, so why are you pretending that it isn't?"

"No. It wasn't. It was just a coincidence. We were waiting for the same train, for the same reason—to go see our mothers—and maybe being together meant more to me than it did to you. Maybe I've got to stop believing that everyone feels the same way I do about things."

Like my mother, I want to say to him. Like Hannah. Like you.

"I wrote to you for a year and you never wrote back," he says. "I rang you over and over again and you would never come to the phone. What part of that gives the impression that I didn't care?"

"You know what I think," I tell him. "You thought I was too much baggage. Or maybe you got bored. Like she would have. She'd get bored being good. She'd get bored trying to go clean. She got bored being my mother. And I wanted to ask her why, but you switched off and you rang the Brigadier to come and get you when I was so close to where I wanted to be and I can't believe that you preferred to miss out on seeing your mum and brother just so you wouldn't have to spend another moment with me."

He shakes his head like he can't believe what he's hearing. "I didn't ring the Brigadier," he snaps. "I didn't even know him at the time and one day, when you're interested, I might tell you why I rang my school. But for the time being why don't you just continue feeling sorry for yourself and comparing the rest of the world with your mother. That will make you popular." He crosses the road, but not without a parting look of such hostility that it makes me ill.

"There will be no 'one day,'" I yell. "Because holidays are over, Griggs, and you and I are never going to cross paths again. Not in the next ten days. Not ever! Have a fantastic life."

He walks back towards me and I take a step back, not because I'm scared but because he doesn't give me much room and this is Griggs without control. Apart from the train and that time in the scout hall, I've never seen him like this. I've seen measured Griggs who provokes the fight, who is never taken by surprise, who walks at his own pace to the beat of life. But not Griggs like he is now.

"Be careful what you wish for," he says with quiet menace, "because I'm about this close to telling you to get the fuck out of my life."

I stare at him.

"What do you want from me?" he asks.

What I want from every person in my life, I want to tell him.

More.

But I don't say anything and neither of us move.

"What if I told you that I lied that day on the platform?" he says after a moment.

"You're lying now," I say angrily. "Don't you dare try to get out of the fact that you were missing your mother and brother and you wanted to see them. You were a mess. I was there, remember?"

He shakes his head. "I lied."

"Am I supposed to think you're all tough because you don't need people, Griggs? Is that what you're trying to do here?"

"No, that's your thing."

"Then stop lying, and admit you were there because you missed your family."

"I've missed my mother and brother every day that I've been out here this time round. But not that day."

There is something in his eyes that frightens the hell out of me and I want to walk away. I don't want to hear another word because I know that whatever he has to say is going to destroy a part of me.

"I knew who you were before that day," he says. "Some morbid prick pointed you out to me in the street when I arrived here that first year. Told me how some Hermit had whispered something in your ear and then blown his brains out."

The words are brutal. I've never really heard it described that way. I block my ears for a moment but when you block your ears you tend to close your eyes and when I close my eyes I see blood and brain-matter and I smell the sickly scent of blood.

"So you were at the train station and saw me come along and you thought I'd be a fun person to hang out with for a weekend?" I say snidely. "And you made up some story about wanting to see your mother and brother?"

"No, I was waiting for the train. The three forty-seven to Yass. Comes every afternoon and, according to the station master, it's never late and I knew that. And then you came along and you spoke to me and nobody had looked me in the eye for years. My mum wouldn't. She told me later that she couldn't, because she was scared to see that I might hate her. She feels like she didn't protect me from him. But I remember you that day and you looked at peace with yourself and it made me reconsider everything I had planned to do. Because I thought to myself, you can't do this to her, not after the Hermit thing."

"Do what to me? I don't think that leaving me on that platform would have changed my life, Griggs," I lie.

"You being on that platform changed mine."

This isn't romance. This isn't a declaration of love or affirmation of friendship. This is something more.

"I wasn't there that day to get on the three forty-seven to Yass," he says. "I was there to throw myself in front of it."

Chapter 18

On the last day of the holidays, Santangelo sends word through the Cadets that he has something I want. Which makes me wonder: how the hell does Santangelo know what I want when I don't even know? And does getting what I want just mean more confusion?

"It's a trick," Raffy says. "He just wants to talk Club House and he thinks the territory wars are over because you and Griggs pashed. Let's not go."

But she doesn't look me in the eye and I know that Raffy is scared that whatever we find out about Webb will change everything for me.

"I'm going," I tell her flatly and firmly. But I think I hear a pleading in my voice when I ask, "Are you coming?"

Santangelo organises to meet us at the scout hall,

except the scouts are meeting there, so it ends up being on the steps of the water tower in the middle of town. I begin to understand his desperate need for the Club House and the Townies' need for a place to go.

Raffy and I take Jessa with us because not everyone's back yet from holidays. While we wait for him, I tell them the story of the kids in Hannah's manuscript. I try to tell it in sequence and at times it gets hard, but they are mesmerised. Jessa makes me repeat the story of the boy who came riding by on the stolen bike at least twice.

"He crawls in through the back passenger's window of the car on top," I explain to them, "and the first person he finds is Narnie. Except Narnie won't move. She's petrified and he begs her to come out with him but she won't. The other two, Tate and Webb, are pleading with her, 'Come on Narnie. Please.' They had begun to smell petrol and were terrified the cars would blow. Then Narnie leans over and she whispers something into the ear of the boy who came by on the stolen bike. Tate and Webb say later that the look on his face was one of horror and they just cried. They think that Narnie has asked him to let her stay there and die. So he begins with them. First Tate and then Webb. He takes them out and places them under a tree and he makes them promise not to move. He tells them that if they don't move, he just might be able to convince Narnie to come out. Five minutes later, Narnie comes out with him and he lays her down beside her brother and tells Webb not to let her out of his sight. They ask him where he's going but he doesn't answer. Then he goes back into those cars four more times and he carries out the bodies of Tate's mum and then Tate's dad and then Tate's sister and then Webb and Narnie's father. He places them on the other side of the road."

"What about Narnie and Webb's mum?" Jessa asks.

I shake my head. It's the part of the story I do not want to tell.

"Anyway," I continue, "not even two minutes later, the cars blow up."

"He could have died," Jessa says in a hushed voice.

I nod. "And he knew that, but all his life he'd been treated like crap to the point that he believed he was crap. He'd never done anything good and nobody had ever said anything positive about him. But that night, on the Jellicoe Road, it was like he was reborn. The lives he saved gave him purpose and he loved those kids more than anything."

"So where's the rest of the story?" Raffy asks.

"I left the manuscript on the floor in Hannah's house and the Brigadier stole it."

"Why?"

I shrug but Jessa can't contain herself. "Because he's the serial killer."

Raffy is irritated. "Don't say that in front of Chaz. The Santangelo household is in a state of fear because of you, Jessa. Enough about the serial killer," she says firmly.

"Do you think they're real? Those people in Hannah's story?" Jessa asks.

"Yes I do," I say. And it's the first time I've said out loud that Hannah's story is real.

"Why can't we just get the rest of the manuscript?" Jessa asks.

"How? Knock on his tent and say, 'Yoo-hoo, remember me? I threw a stretcher bed at you. Can I have the manuscript back?'"

"According to Teresa and the boy she's going

around with, the Brigadier hasn't been there during the holidays. He doesn't get back until tomorrow."

"How does Teresa know that?" Raffy asks.

"Teresa's in a relationship with one of the Cadets. They're going 'around' with each other," I explain patiently.

"The Cadets are the enemy," Raffy says. "We're not supposed to be conducting relationships with them."

I nod in agreement.

"Although the whole town is talking about the snog you and Griggs—"

"Enough about that," I snap. "It was a one-off."

"What's a one-off?" Santangelo asks as he arrives.

Raffy looks at me, knowing I'll lose it if she mentions it again. "Nothing," she mutters.

Jessa has already run off with Santangelo's sister, Tilly, and the three of us are left beating around the bush until Raffy holds out her hand.

"What have you got?" she says to him.

"It's not about the territory wars."

Her hand is still out and he looks at me because mine isn't. Then he reluctantly hands over an envelope.

"It's a photo," he says. "I got it from the file at the station."

A photo that I am dying to see, although I'm sure something inside of me will die from seeing it.

"What's the worst thing that can happen?" he asks.

I watch Jessa and Tilly swing off the stairs of the water tower like monkeys without a care in the world. "Be careful," Santangelo calls out to them.

It takes me a moment to find my voice. "If I look at the photo and whoever it is looks exactly like me, that only means he can be my father, and if he's the boy who's been missing for eighteen years, it means that my father is dead and I've never thought that. *Ever.*"

"Then don't look at it," Raffy says. "You know you had a father, Taylor. You were on his shoulders and you lay between him and your mother. It was the first thing you told me in year seven. Remember?"

I nod. "And then I told you something else."

She looks at me. "But the shoulders of the giant is a better story."

I remember love. It's what I have to keep on reminding myself. It's funny how you can forget everything except people loving you. Maybe that's why humans find it so hard getting over love affairs. It's not the pain they're getting over, it's the love.

"Then I'll take it back," Santangelo says. "Maybe memories should be left the way they are."

I can feel Raffy's eyes on me and I lean over and take the envelope gently out of her hands. "Thanks, Raf, but I think this belong to me."

I do the count to ten that always reaches eleven and then begin again. Until I find the guts to look.

He's the most beautiful creature I have ever seen and it's not about his face but the life force I can see in him. It's the smile and the pure promise of everything he has to offer. Like he's saying, "Here I am, world; are you ready for so much passion and beauty and goodness and love and every other word that should be in the dictionary under the word *life*?" Except this boy is dead and the unnaturalness of it makes me want to pull my hair out with Tate's and Narnie's and Fitz's and Jude's grief all combined. It makes me want to yell at the God that I wish I didn't believe in. For hogging him all to himself. I want to say, You greedy God. Give him back. I needed him here.

There is total silence around me and I'm not sure

if I have said all this out loud or shouted it in my heart.

I hand the photo to Raffy and she does what I can't. She bursts into tears.

This is what I know. I look like my father. My father disappeared when he was seventeen years old. Hannah once told me that there is something unnatural about being older than your father ever got to be. When you can say that at the age of seventeen, it's a different kind of devastating.

Later we walk to the police station to ask Santangelo's dad if his sister can stay at the school for the night. I feel numb with a sort of anger at no one in particular but I feel it brew inside me and I want to lash out at anyone.

Santangelo's dad comes outside. I watch his daughter jump onto him and he piggybacks her to us and I see the look on her face that says that nothing can happen to her if she is holding on to her dad. It kills me to hate them so much for having that.

"She can stay with us for the night," Raffy says. "There are spare beds in the dorm."

Tilly and Jessa are crazy with excitement.

"Take care of my little girl," Santangelo's dad says to me and for a moment my blood runs cold.

"*What*? What did you say?"

He is confused. "Tilly. Take care of her."

And then the moment is gone but the words still ring in my ears.

"I think he's worried about the serial killer," Jessa tells me.

"No mention of the serial killer," Santangelo's dad says warningly as he takes both girls inside to ring Santangelo's mum.

The three of us sit on the footpath and I can tell they want to say something. *Anything*.

"At least it means that your father wasn't weak and didn't leave you," Santangelo says.

I stare at him. "Dead or weak? Are they my options? I think I just might say yes to a weak father rather than a dead one, if you don't mind."

He tries to find something else to talk about and I want to make it easier for him because it's not his fault, but all I can think of is Hannah's story. My aunt's story. How strange it is to use those words for the first time. I have an aunt and I don't even know where she is. But I do know that I yearn for her in a way I never thought possible, and that she's somehow written the story of my family's life. And part of that story is sitting in the Brigadier's tent. Halfway through Santangelo's spiel about Club House stuff, Raffy looks at me and she knows exactly what I'm thinking.

"We're going into Cadet territory," she interrupts him. "Tonight. And you're coming with us."

"I'm sorry?"

"I need to get something out of the Brigadier's tent," I explain to him. "He's not there and I'm breaking in."

"Are you nuts?" he says, as though we couldn't possibly be serious. "Both of you?"

"He has something of mine . . . well, kind of mine."

"I'm not breaking into the Brigadier's tent and neither are you!"

"Come on, Chaz," Raffy says. "You and Joe Salvatore are experts on locks." She looks at me. "Joe's father's a locksmith and Chaz worked there part-time for a while. He broke into the high school once for my mum when she left her teacher's chronicle there."

"Wow."

"Breaking and entering is a crime," he reminds us, not falling for the feigned enthusiasm. "Can we just get back to what I was saying? Stevie reckons he's got hold of an espresso machine and—"

"You broke into your father's police station," I remind him. "That's a crime."

"To help you," he says forcefully, giving up on telling us about the Club House.

"Santangelo, I promise you," I say, "somewhere deep down I have a feeling that the thing in the Brigadier's tent is going to help me. Please."

"I'm going home," Santangelo says. "You're going back to your House and no one is invading Cadet territory."

"What are you going to do? Arrest us?" Raffy asks.

Santangelo is irritated. "We're not supposed to be collaborating. It's supposed to be a war and you're supposed to stick to the boundaries."

"We've seen you in your jocks," she reminds him. "Taylor and Griggs have pashed. You've broken into your father's police station for us. Don't you think the war has lost a bit of its tension?"

"Yeah, well, it doesn't seem to have lost the tension between them," he says, presumably referring to Griggs and me.

"Why? What has he said to you?" I ask.

"I'm going home," he says, ignoring my question. "Count me out."

Raffy dismisses him with a shrug. "We'll do it on our own, Taylor. Joe Salvatore said he was hopeless under pressure, anyway."

It doesn't take Santangelo long to get the lock open. I am very impressed by Raffy's and Santangelo's abilities to commit crimes with such finesse.

"You keep watch," I whisper, looking at the rows of tents around us. Once or twice I see a flashlight on in one of them, but the chances of anyone going for a walk at this time of night should be low. I find myself wondering which one is Jonah Griggs's tent. There's a part of me that desperately wants to see him, to make him promise two trillion times over that he will never do anything to hurt himself. But I'm a coward and I know that he will never realise how much he means to me.

"Griggs will kill us," Santangelo whispers back.

"You don't owe Griggs anything," I say as I open the flap. I walk into the tent, taking out the small flashlight and trying to be as discreet as possible. I'm surprised at how big the tent actually is—almost the size of an office, with a bed in one corner and a desk and cabinet in the other, as well as tea- and coffee making facilities alongside it. When I approach the desk, I look for locks, ready to call Santangelo in, but there doesn't seem to be any and there's no mystery about where anything is. In the largest drawer I find the manuscript and alongside it is something else that belongs to Hannah. It's a stationery box that she has always kept in her bedroom in the Lachlan House cottage, and I realise that not only has the Brigadier been in the unfinished house by the river but on school territory as well. I've never been curious about the stationery box but I am now that the Brigadier thinks it's important enough to steal.

I open it slowly and shine the torch on the contents: Hannah's passport and birth certificate and those of Xavier Webster Schroeder, a tape cassette, a couple of newspaper clippings, and a few photos. My heart begins to beat hard as I touch the photographs. I am about to see my first images of the five. I wonder if they will live up to my expectations and answer my questions. But the first few photos are of a child, about three years old, with eyes that are big and wide and a mullet that the Townies would envy. Although I have never seen a photograph of myself as a child, I know it is me. Whoever I was back then, I looked happy and whoever I was looking at was the very person who made me happy. How can someone who made me look this happy no longer be in my life?

I turn my attention to the two newspaper articles. One is small and looks older than the other. It's about the disappearance of Xavier Webster Schroeder. Just fifty words or so. Is that all he was worth? When I think of the screaming headlines of the teenagers who have gone missing over the years, I can't help wondering how many words they would spend on me if I disappeared. It mentions the Jellicoe School and calls for any information to be forwarded to the police station and I'm not surprised to see the Santangelo name there, back when Chaz's dad was a constable. I pick up the second article but can hardly read the print. It's as if the words have faded with too much sun, but the photo and the headline are clear and they send a chill right through me. Because looking straight at me, thinner in the face, younger by almost ten years, is the Brigadier. But it's not the photograph that shatters me the most. It's the headline above it. KIDNAPPING CHARGES DROPPED. I feel woozy and nauseous and for the first time in four weeks I accept the fact that Chloe P. and Jessa might be right about the Brigadier and that I may never *ever* see Hannah again. I feel a sob rising in my throat, but suddenly a hand is placed over my mouth.

"Are you insane?" Griggs whispers in my ear. When he feels me relax, he lets go and I pull away. I put everything back in the box and pick it up, ignoring him.

"You can't take that," he whispers loudly, turning me to face him. It's the first time I've seen him in clothes other than his fatigues. He's wearing boxer shorts and a long-sleeved South Sydney football T-shirt. He looks exactly how I feel. Like shit.

"It's mine," I manage to say.

"Why would the Brigadier have what's yours?"

"Because it's Hannah's."

"Then it's not yours."

"Well, it's not his," I say as forcefully as I can but I feel sick at heart. I take a few deep breaths, still clutching the box and the manuscript. "I need to go," I say, turning off the flashlight. He tries to take my hand.

"Don't," he says.

But I pull free again. "I need to go, Jonah."

"They must have a history, Taylor. It has nothing to do with you."

I switch the flashlight back on angrily and thrust the box in his hand, pulling out a photo and holding it up to his face.

"Would you say this has something to do with me?"

He puts down the box and takes the photograph out of my hand, looking at it carefully. All of a sudden I see the look on his face that says it's not so simple anymore.

"What if I told you that I think the Brigadier is the serial killer and Hannah knew and he's done something to her?"

"Jesus, Taylor! Please don't be crazy."

"Maybe I am," I say, nodding, and I'm trying so hard not to cry but my voice keeps cracking. "What if I told you that some kid who looks exactly like me is probably my father and probably dead and I think he comes visiting me at night and I'm going crazy because he's trying to tell me that something bad is going to happen."

I grab the photo out of his hand. "What if I told you that from when this photo was taken until I was ten years old I didn't exist? There is no proof of my existence. I didn't even go to school, so no school records, no school friends."

"You have a mother."

"Just say I made her up? Just say she doesn't exist, either? Where's the proof? Where's my birth certificate? Where's my father? Where's Hannah?"

I try to control myself, attempting to concentrate on something else. A thought occurs to me and I move away, yanking open the other drawers of the desk. "I bet I know his writing," I say, throwing things out of the way. Griggs grabs hold of me and I pull away but I fall back against the chair and it tumbles, making a crashing sound and the manuscript and the box go flying. He grabs me again, pushing me against the table, trying to keep me still and I try to break free, but his grip is hurting me and his face is so close to mine that it's like he can see inside my soul.

"What if I told you that if you took me to that train right now, I'd throw myself in front of it without a moment's hesitation?" I whisper. "I swear to God I would, Jonah."

Santangelo pokes his head through the flaps.

"Get out!" Griggs says forcefully, not looking away from me.

"Let go of her, Griggs."

"I said get the fuck out!"

"You've got one minute and I'm taking her with me," Santangelo says just as forcefully.

I'm shaking so hard and it feels like I'll never be able to stop.

"Please don't be crazy, Taylor," Griggs whispers, leaning his head against mine. "Please don't be crazy." He kisses me, holding my face between his hands, whispering over and over again, "*Please.*"

It's the pleading in his voice that calms my heart rate.

"Will you listen to me?" I whisper.

He gently pushes the hair out of my face, tucking it behind my ears and then he nods.

"I think he did something to my father and Hannah knew stuff about him and now she's gone,"

I try to explain. "Remember when he picked us up in Yass and the same day those kids disappeared? Do you think it's a coincidence he was in that town on the same day?"

"I was with him all night after we dropped you off. He drove me back to Sydney."

"They could have been taken in the morning. Who knows how long he was out there before he caught up with us in the mailman's van?"

"Taylor, he's sat at my table and eaten with my family, in my home."

"Your father was in your home and he ate at your table and he was your biggest threat."

He is silent for a moment. "There are no similarities between my father and the Brigadier," he says at last.

"I bet if I found his handwriting in this room it would be the same as the writing on Hannah's note."

"That only proves he's a friend of Hannah's."

"No," I say, shaking my head. "He's not. I remember the one time he was around her. She couldn't even look him in the eye. He was all rigid and something else, like he knew that she was on to him."

"Maybe they've got a . . . thing going. You've only seen them together once. Maybe they see each other when you're not around. Sometimes he's come to my house after being 'out bush' as he calls it. He's more relaxed. Like someone's calmed him down. Just say this place is 'out bush'?"

"Is he relaxed out here with you guys?"

"No. Do you know who he reminds me of? You. Distracted and lost and whatever else. Has it occurred to you that the reason you both keep on meeting each other around Hannah's house might be because you are both desperately missing the same person?"

I shake my head. "Why wouldn't she have told me?"

"The same reason she hasn't told you anything else. Maybe she promised someone she wouldn't. I was there when they returned you to her that day, Taylor. She was crazy. I've seen that craziness on my mother's face when she thinks something's happened to me or my brother. You and Hannah are connected big-time in some way."

"I've just found out that she's my father's sister. I think I'm all she has left. But I'll never understand why she wouldn't tell me."

"Knowing what you've told me about her, there would have to be a good explanation."

I show him the newspaper article about the Brigadier. "Can you explain this?"

He takes a moment to read it. "No, but if I told you what the headlines were the day after my father died, would you think I was a murderer?"

Santangelo looks in again. "Let's go, Taylor."

I look at him and nod and he doesn't move.

"Can we have a bit of privacy?" Griggs asks him, seething.

"Why? So you can make her go crazy?"

"Who was the dickhead who let her break in here tonight? Don't think for one moment that I've forgotten that!"

Raffy pushes Santangelo out of the way and pokes her head in. "Someone is out here," she hisses, "so can you both tone down the testosterone levels."

I look up at Griggs and disentangle myself from his grip. "I've got to go," I say, picking up the manuscript and the box from the floor and trying to grab as much of the stuff that fell out as possible. Under the table in the corner, out of my reach, I can see some photos and I stretch to get them but Raffy is urgently beckoning to me and I can't quite reach.

As I turn to leave, Griggs catches me by the arm. "You've always had it wrong about that day," he whispers. "I had never seen the Brigadier before. He didn't come looking for me, Taylor. He came looking for you."

The next morning, Jessa comes into my room and climbs into bed next to me.

"It was on the news," she whispers. "Two kids from Mittagong have gone missing." She's shaking hard so I hold on to her until I feel her heart stop racing and tell her the story of the boy on the stolen bike who saved the lives of those kids on the Jellicoe Road and became our hero.

Chapter 19

I go to see Santangelo's dad at the police station. He's working with his head down and when he looks up, he is startled for a moment, like he's seen a ghost.

"Who do I remind you of?" I ask quietly.

He grimaces, as though he regrets me seeing that look.

"Narnie Schroeder," he says with a sigh.

"Why did they call her Narnie?"

He walks to the counter and leans forward. I like his face. I trust it.

"She told me once it was what her brother called her when they were toddlers. Couldn't say Hannah; somehow it ended up being Narnie."

I nod.

"What can I do for you, Taylor?" he asks, like he's dreading the answer.

What can he do for me? He can tell me everything he knows.

"I know you're not going to tell me where Hannah is because she's probably made you promise not to, so I'm going to make this easy for you. I want to make contact with Fitz and I know you would know where he is."

He's shaking his head. The grimace is back but there is even more emotion.

"Please," I say. "I just want to see him. I need to. Because I've worked out that my father is dead and Fitz knew him and Fitz would be here because he was a Townie and I want to know someone who knew my father. Is that so much to ask?"

"I can't do that, Taylor."

"*Why*?" I say, and I realise that I'm close to tears. "Just give me *one* reason."

He pauses for a moment and I realise that the tears aren't just in my eyes.

"Because Fitz is dead." Nothing comes out of my mouth but a shaky breath. I feel gutted, but these days that's pretty normal.

"How?" I ask when I find my voice.

He shakes his head. "I can't tell you that."

"Can't because you don't know?"

"Why don't I call Raffy's mum and she'll come and get you?" he says, and I know he's not going to give me the answers I need.

"Because I don't want you to call Raffy's mum. I want you to call my mum and I know you can do that through Hannah. But you can't, or won't, or would love to but not today, thank you very much. Not a good day to hand out information."

He reaches over and touches my hand and I recoil. I'm embarrassed by my reaction but I keep my distance all the same.

"I promise you this, Taylor. Hannah's coming back. Hannah will always come back for you. You are everything to her and Jude."

Jude. Jude's alive. I feel relief for the first time in ages. Narnie's alive as well.

"And Tate?"

He hesitates for a moment and then nods and for the time being that has to be enough.

I hear him dial the phone and I know he's calling someone to come and get me so I turn to leave but then I see a poster on the wall. It's old—I can tell by the edges—and it's drawn by a child. Or children. There are two names at the bottom. CHAZ AND RAFFY, 5 YEARS OLD, ST. FRANCIS PRIMARY, JELLICOE. They drew trees, big ones, filled with animals and bird life. So full of colour and imagination and love for this place. I've seen this drawing before. My memory is like Hannah's manuscript—distorted and out of sequence—but instantly I know that years before my mother dumped me on the Jellicoe Road, I had been in this police station.

Narnie and Jude sat side by side watching the police divers.

It was a week since Webb had disappeared and suddenly the focus was on dragging the river. Even the press were there and throughout the day Jude tried to get close to the action, if only to catch a word or glimpse of something constructive he could bring back to Narnie.

"Keep her away," the young constable advised quietly. "You don't want her around if we find him."

"What makes you think you're going to find him here?"

"Take her home, Jude."

But Narnie wouldn't budge. She watched the divers move gradually down the river with a creased concentration on her face, like she was trying to work out a puzzle.

Most of the time, though, they watched Fitz. He kept climbing a tree to the very top branch and throwing himself into the river. Then he'd swim to the surface and make his way up the tree again.

Once Jude thought he saw Fitz watching them from behind the branches and for the first time all day, he left Narnie and made his way up. Climbing had always been Webb's forte, and both Webb and Fitz could do it with an agility that Jude lacked. By the time he heaved himself onto the branch at the top, the sound of his breathing was only surpassed by the sound of Fitz's sobbing.

"Fitz? Mate, come out. Narnie and Tate need you."

There was no answer, just a muffled sound like Fitz was forcing a fist into his mouth to stop himself crying.

"Come on, Fitz." Jude straddled the branch and moved in closer until he was able to see through to where Fitz was crouched.

But the Fitz in front of him was almost a stranger—caked in mud, his hair matted with debris, his face streaked with dirt and grime.

"Fitz," Jude whispered. "Where have you been? Why are you doing this to yourself?"

Fitz stood up on the branch and looked at Jude through bloodshot eyes. Barely balancing, he leaned towards him.

"Listen to the sound, Jude," he said in a hushed voice. "Listen."

And he threw himself over the side. Jude watched as Narnie waited below, like she did every time, for Fitz's head to emerge from the water. When Fitz reached the bank, he looked up to where Jude still sat.

"Did you hear that, Jude? Did you?" he called out.

Jude looked down at Narnie again, who was now standing, waiting for what would come next.

"Did I hear what, Fitz?" he called back, confused. To his dismay Fitz began climbing the tree again.

"No. Stay down there, Fitz!"

But Fitz was back up on the branch with Jude. There was blood on his forehead from where he had hit the riverbed.

"I went back," Fitz whispered. "I went back, Jude."

"Back where?"

"For the fifth tin," he answered. "The one I missed. Ping Ping Ping Ping. Remember I missed the fifth tin?" Fitz laughed. His normal crazy laugh. "That's almost a rhyme."

Jude's blood went cold. "What are you saying, Fitz?"

"And when I walked away, I heard something hit the water and I thought I must have killed a fucker of a bird. I looked but I couldn't see anything."

"Fitz? What are you saying?"

"Do you want to hear the sound it made?"

Jude lunged, trying to grab him before he went over again, but it was too late. He looked at Narnie, still staring up at him, and started to make his way down the tree.

"When is he going to stop?" Narnie asked quietly after he had sat with her for a while.

Jude didn't answer.

"Fix things, Jude. Tell him to stop," Narnie implored.

"I can't. Let's go home, Narnie."

But Narnie shook her head. "I don't have a home."

So they stayed. Long after the police divers had gone. Long after the photographers had packed up and disappeared. Long after the Cadets and Townies and Jellicoe kids had headed home.

Watching Fitz. Jump from the top branch. Wade to the bank. Climb up the tree. Jump from the branch. Over and over again. Ten times, fifteen times, his grunts and sobs as he pulled himself out of the water were unbearable. Then Jude realised that he was himself crying and the pain of it was like nothing he had ever experienced. But then Narnie stood and made her way into the river, wading towards Fitz lying exhausted in the shallows. She pulled at his wet clothing with all her strength, the bulk of him hard for her to manage. Then Jude was beside her, dragging them both onto the bank, where Narnie cradled Fitz in her arms, rocking.

"Shhh, Fitz. Shhh."

He shivered uncontrollably, but Narnie held him close.

"Narnie," he sobbed. "I'm sorry. I'm sorry."

"Shhh, Fitz."

"Forgive me, please. Please. Please. Please. Please." The words were pouring out of him, soaked with tears and phlegm and spit and blood, as she continued rocking him, while Jude held onto them both.

And at that moment Jude thought something that he would never forgive himself for.

He wished that he had never met any of them.

When I was fourteen years old, I met the Hermit who lived at the edge of the property at the end of the Jellicoe Road. Before I met him, I sensed him, watching. Sometimes I'd call out, but nobody would answer. But on this day, there he was. When I looked into his eyes I saw genuine love. Not guarded love like Hannah's or crazy erratic love like my mother's. I saw the real thing. I don't know why I felt no fear. Maybe he reminded me of the illustrations of Jesus Christ from Raffy's bible.

I sat with him and he showed me how to make a placemat out of thistles. We let the thistles prick our fingers to make them bleed because they made us feel alive.

Then we spoke about our dreams and how we

always felt safe in them, no matter how bad every-thing else seemed. He told me it was one of the best days of his life and then he took out his gun. A .22 rifle. And he leaned forward and whispered, "Forgive me, Taylor Markham." Before I could ask him how he knew my name and what I was to forgive him for he said, "Take care of my little girl."

And then he told me to close my eyes.

And I think I've been frightened to do just that ever since.

Chapter 20

Finally we came to an agreement about the Club House and a week before the Cadets are due to leave, we have the opening. My heart's not really in it and the only people who seem enthusiastic are Ben and Anson Choi and the Mullet Brothers, who have spent every possible moment with each other pretending they are a band.

It amazes me that we've got this far, so I suppose that's something to celebrate. But the thing is we don't know how to. Thirty people from each faction, ninety people all up, stand around staring at one another with absolutely nothing to say. There's a stage, a drink machine, and a few tables and chairs but apart from that, there's nothing else. No personality. No conversation. No atmosphere. Nicht. Nix.

Raffy stands next to me, commiserating, and

for once I wish someone would start a fight just to introduce noise to the place. On the other side of the room, Griggs is standing against the wall with that stony look on his face while the rest of the Cadets are huddled in his corner. One of the guys next to him is even clutching a chessboard, like he was forced here in the middle of a game. In another corner Santangelo looks slightly bored, even with his girlfriend hanging off him, and behind me I can feel Richard's eyes drilling into me as if I am the creator of this hell.

But then I catch Griggs's eye and he looks at me in a way that tells me exactly what he's feeling and I love that look. Suddenly I want to yell out to everyone, "*It's a game, these territory wars. They loved each other.*"

Instead I turn to Raffy. "See the guy standing next to Jonah Griggs?" I say. "Their chess champ. Apparently no one can beat him."

She looks at me as if to say, *Who cares*?

"As if," I hear Richard say.

"It's true. Jonah Griggs reckons he's a freak and that they've beaten every GPS School in Sydney."

"You know what I heard," Raffy says, catching

on. "That he thinks that no one in this area could possibly beat anyone from the city."

Richard glares at the guy, and I see the challenge in his eye.

"It'd be great if someone took him down a peg or two," I say, walking away. I approach Griggs, watching as he lifts himself off the wall, not quite sure what he has to prepare himself for, but with a look of relief on his face.

"What?" he asks. There's vulnerability in his face and I sense that our last session together affected him just as badly as it did me. There are a million things I want to say to him but in the end it seems safer talking about this debacle.

I lean in, trying not to seem too friendly to the rest of the world. "This is a disaster," I whisper.

"Seen bigger and better ones." He makes room between him and the chess guy and I feel our fingers touch slightly but neither of us moves away.

"See the guy you punched out the other day?" I say a bit louder. "He's our chess champ. He thinks no one can beat him."

He looks at me as if to say, *Who cares?*

"As if," I hear the guy with the chessboard say.

"It's true. He's a freak and his team has beaten every school in the country comp."

"He's up himself," Griggs says, catching on. "Choi reckons he heard him say that no GPS School from the city is ever going to beat him and his team."

The guy with the chessboard glares at Richard and I see that challenge in his eye. He moves away from us and stands huddled with some other guys, who follow his gaze towards Richard.

"I reckon I could take them all on," I tell Griggs quietly.

"You play chess?"

"I can beat him with my eyes closed. Why do you think Richard hates me so much?"

"Because you turn him on and it kills him that he doesn't turn you on," he says, looking at me.

"How do you know?" I grin. "That he doesn't turn me on, that is?"

He laughs and I see that people are watching us. "What do you think would happen if we kissed right here, right now?" he asks, digging his hands into the pockets of his khaki pants, grinning right back at me.

"I think it would cause a riot."

"Well, you know me," he says, lowering his head

towards me. "Causing a riot is what I do best."

Santangelo approaches before Griggs gets any closer and pulls him away. "Are you guys insane?" he says, irritated.

"It's called peaceful coexistence, Santangelo. You should try it and if it works we may sell the idea to the Israelis and Palestinians," I say, throwing his own words back at him.

"This isn't peaceful coexistence. This is the worst idea I've ever come up with. Everyone's miserable."

"I'm not," Griggs says. "It's easy." He beckons over some of the Cadets and introduces me to the first two. "They guarded the hostages," he tells me. Santangelo already seems to know them. Some of the Townies, who I recognise from the night at the party, come over and shake hands with Griggs and his guys.

I see Trini from Darling House in the crowd and wave her over. She looks hesitant so I drag two Cadets over to her. "These are the guys who looked after our year-seven trio," I say, looking at them with slightly exaggerated gratitude. "Guarded them with their lives."

The boys blush in unison.

"Griggs was telling me how it keeps him awake

at night thinking of the fear he put in the hearts of those girls," I say, looking at Griggs.

Trini and her friend look shocked at this news and Griggs gives a shrug. "I presume you are the one responsible for how brilliantly they composed themselves in such a harrowing situation," he says with such charm. He even accompanies it with a disarming smile.

The girls beam. "We are very strict but fair. Would you like to come and meet the other House seniors?" Trini asks the two Cadets. They nod and another five or six guys follow them across the room.

"We are so sick of each other's company," Griggs tells us, watching his guys being introduced to the Darling House girls. "Everyone's hanging to go home."

I look at him and feel a sick twist in my stomach. In ten days' time I will never see Jonah Griggs again. Ever. He looks at me as if he knows what I'm thinking.

Even Santangelo seems flat. "I regret the no-alcohol rule," he says as we make our way to where some guy is making espressos.

By the time we've had our second coffee, the

chess game between the Murrumbidgee guys and the Cadets is well and truly underway in one corner. On the other side of the room the Darling girls are surrounded by Cadets while the girls from Hastings House look on in total envy. Then the band comes on and I hate to admit it but they kind of make everything worthwhile. It's hard to explain what happens when jazz and punk fuse with a violin twist but it works. Probably because Anson Choi takes off his shirt while he's playing the saxophone. Whoever's not chatting up a Cadet or a girl from Darling House or playing chess with the guys is watching the band. I turn into a groupie.

Ben plays his violin like a madman and even the Mullet Brothers look cool, having grown sideburns for the occasion. One stares into space in that vacuous way most bass guitarists do and the other does these pirouettes in the air every time he jumps. Unfortunately they only have three songs but the music helps break the ice.

The drummer waves at Raffy and she walks over to the side of the stage to chat with him.

"Who's that?" Santangelo asks, offering me some chips.

"The arsonist from Clarence House," I say with my mouth half full.

From the stage Ben catches my eye. "This is for them, Taylor," he calls out as they begin to play. It's a song by the Waterboys and, like each time I hear the music played by the boy in the tree in my dreams, I experience a bittersweet sense of nostalgia I have no right to own. When it's time for Ben to play his solo—his eyes closed, his mind anywhere but here, his fingers so taut and precise that it almost looks painful—my eyes well with tears. Because you know from the look on Ben's face that he's somewhere you want to be. Somewhere the five would be each time they were together. The place goes off. I can feel Griggs's shoulder against mine and I hear him mutter something under his breath.

"What?" I say, irritated. "He's fantastic."

There's a look on his face that I don't recognise and I don't quite get it until Ben jumps off the stage, surrounded by Townie girls.

"Hey!" Griggs calls out to him. "Violin guy!"

Ben points to himself with that *who me?* look, walking towards us.

Griggs doesn't say anything for a moment, but

then he clears his throat. "If I had known . . . I wouldn't have gone for your fingers that time."

"You would have just chosen another body part?" Ben says.

"Probably. But not the fingers."

Ben nods. "Cheers." He looks pleased with himself. "I have numbers in this phone that I didn't have at the beginning of the night," he says, waving it around.

"No coverage," Griggs reminds him.

"And mobile numbers are blocked on our landlines," I add.

"Thanks for the optimism."

Ben sees Santangelo still staring at Raffy and the drummer and pats him on the back.

"Nothing to worry about. He set fire to her hair once in science and I think that killed the romance for her."

"Why would I be worried?" Santangelo asks, irritated, as Raffy walks back towards us.

"You should be worried," Ben says. "Because you're going out with that chick and Raff will go out with some guy and you'll spend the whole time with this 'thing' hovering between you and then you'll get married to other people and one day when you're middle-aged in your thirties, while both your kids are going to the same school, you're going to have this affair because of all the pent-up attraction and ruin the lives of everyone in the P and F."

"Your friends are freaks," Santangelo tells Raffy when she re-joins us.

"Chaz, I've always had freaks for friends. You should know that."

I look over at Richard, who is clearly dominating the chess game and I nudge Griggs. "Want me to teach you how to play speed chess?" I ask.

I spend the next half hour annihilating Richard and then we play doubles. The head nerd of the Cadets is my partner and when it's over he asks me for my number. I'm very flattered and he looks a bit crestfallen when I say no.

"It's because they don't have coverage out here," Griggs tells him.

"No," I say, looking up at Griggs. "It's actually because my heart belongs to someone else." And if I could bottle the look on his face, I'd keep it by my bedside for the rest of my life.

Chapter 21

One day Tate was there, a ghost of Tate, sitting
by the river where Webb had planned to build
a house—a dead look in her eye, a thin grimace
to her lips, a sick pallor to her skin that spoke of
despair. The next day she was gone—bags packed,
no note. And for Narnie, hours without them went
by, and then days, and then weeks. And in between
those seconds and minutes and hours and days and
weeks was the most acute sense of loneliness she'd
ever experienced. Sometimes she knew that Fitz
was watching her and she would call out, "Fitzee.
Please! Don't leave me!"

But no one came back.

Except Jude.

As predicted, the Club House is profitable and
after three nights we split the money between the

three factions and then we split it again between the Houses. The leaders have a meeting about what their Houses are going to do with the funds and I nod with great approval as everyone is united in their maturity and pragmatism.

Richard has made plans for a maths computer tutor for his house while Ben buys a guitar for his. Trini organises a year's subscription with Greenpeace and I mumble about some books and DVDs for our library or maybe some software for the computer.

"Let's get something we can have the bestest fun we've ever had with," Jessa begs one night when we're on washing-up duty.

"We're not here to have fun," I say.

"Who said?" one of the year tens asks me. I think about it for a moment and then shrug.

"I actually don't know. It's not that effective when you don't know, is it?"

So we get a karaoke machine.

On the first night, the year tens stage a competition, insisting that every member of the House has to be involved, so we clear the year-seven and -eight dorms and wait for our turn. Raffy is on second and does an impressive job of "I Can't Live, If Living

Means Without You" but then one of the seniors points out to her that she's chosen a dependency song and Raffy spends the whole night neuroticising about it.

"I just worked out that I don't have ambition," she says while one of the year eights sings tearfully, "Am I Not Pretty Enough?" I start compiling a list of all the kids I should be recommending to the school counsellor, based on their song choices.

"I think she's reading a little too much into it, Raf."

"No she isn't. Because do you know what my second and third choices were? 'Don't Leave Me This Way' and 'I Just Don't Know What to Do with Myself.'"

"Mary Grace chose 'Brown-eyed Girl' and she's got blue eyes and Serina sang 'It's Raining Men' and she's a lesbian. You're taking this way too seriously. Let it go."

"What have you chosen?"

"I'm doing something with Jessa. Apparently her father was a Lenny Rogers fan."

"Kenny," she corrects. "'Coward of the County'?"

I look at her suspiciously. "Why that one? Are

—— 300 ——

you implying I'm a coward?"

"Don't be ridiculous. It's just one of his well-known ones."

"Why didn't you say 'The Gambler'? That's pretty well known, according to Jessa. I'd rather be a gambler than a coward."

"It's just a song," she insists. But I'm not convinced.

I get up and sing "Islands in the Stream" with Jessa. As usual, she takes it all very seriously and she does these hands expressions as if she's clutching her heart and then giving it out to the audience. I refuse to follow but I do enjoy it. We have knockout rounds throughout the week after dinner and it's during this time that I truly get to know my House. Their choices make me laugh so much at times that I have tears running down my face and other times they are so poignant that they make me love them so much without even trying.

Raffy and I spend every other night in the Prayer Tree with Santangelo and Griggs. Each time we set out an agenda, which lists the Club House and the territory boundaries as items for discussion, but it never quite happens. We just end up talking about stuff, like the meaning of life or the importance of karaoke choices.

"Do you think they define you?" Raffy asks them.

"Hope not. I always end up singing some Michael Jackson song," Santangelo says.

"What did you pick?" Griggs asks me.

"Kenny Rogers."

"'Coward of the County'?"

I sit back and don't say a word. I am wounded. Griggs looks at me and then at Raffy. "I said the wrong thing, didn't I?" he asks.

She doesn't say anything out loud, but I know she's mouthing something to him because next minute he says, "I meant 'The Gambler.'"

I still don't say anything.

"At the end he saves Becky." Santangelo tries to help. "Remember? Everyone considered him the coward of the county but he actually wasn't one."

"It's frightening that you've put so much analysis into it," Griggs says.

"It's not me," Santangelo says. "You know what fathers with bad taste in music are like."

Except Griggs doesn't, and I can tell Santangelo feels like shit for saying it.

"My mum's boyfriend listens to Cold Chisel," Griggs says, trying to make Santangelo feel better. "He's taught my brother all the words to 'Khe San.' They sing it all the time."

Santangelo doesn't say anything and I can tell he's angry with himself.

For a while there is silence. Outside, the first cicadas of the season are humming and it's like there's no one else in the world but the four of us. It's Griggs who breaks the silence.

"I loved him, you know," he says quietly. The admission doesn't surprise me as much as the fact that he's speaking about it. "That would probably shock people. But I did. I look exactly like him. Same build, same face. I know every part of my personality that I got from my father. He was a prick, except even pricks don't deserve to be smashed over the head with a cricket bat."

"That's debatable," Raffy says.

"Do you want to know the worst part?" he asks. I can tell this is so hard for him because he won't look at us. "Sometimes I forget just how bad he was, so all I can remember is that he's dead because of me. It's unnatural, what I did. Sometimes I'm thinking about it in the middle of class and I'll walk out and ring my mum and say, 'I remember that he took us to the circus, and that we were laughing, so why did I do what I did?' She always has an answer. 'And that night he smashed my head against the glass cabinet, Jonah. Do you remember that? And when he burnt your brother with the cigarettes, Jonah?'

"Other times I'll wake her in the middle of the night and say, 'He told me that no one loved us as much as he did.' And she'll say, 'And then he walked around the house holding a gun, threatening to kill us all, because he wanted us to be together forever.'"

Griggs looks up at us. "What happens when she's not my memory anymore? What happens when she's not around to tell me about his belt leaving scars across my two-year-old brother's face or when he whacked her so hard that she lost her hearing for a week? Who'll be my memory?"

Santangelo doesn't miss a beat. "I will. Ring me."

"Same," Raffy says.

I look at him. I can't even speak because if I do

I know I'll cry but I smile and he knows what I'm thinking.

"So, getting back to the karaoke thing," says Griggs, not wanting to deal with too much emotion. "I'd have to go with . . ." He thinks for a moment. "Guns n' Roses, 'Paradise City.'"

"Oh, please," I say. "I'd rather be the coward of the county."

"Guns n' Roses have such skanky hos in their film clips," Raffy says.

"And the problem being?" Santangelo asks.

It's after midnight when Griggs takes something out of his pocket and puts it in front of me.

"You dropped them in the Brigadier's tent."

I stare at the photos in front of me. I'm not ready for more photos. Not after we've been talking about Jonah's father and unprofound lyrics and skanky hos.

"You can take them home with you," he says, "and look at them there."

I still don't say anything. I want to but I can't. I want to explain everything that's going on in my head but I can't find the words.

"Who are they of?" Raffy asks quietly.

"Just a bunch of kids our age," Jonah says.

I reach over with a shaking hand and put the pictures face up on the ground between us. So I can introduce them to the original five.

They are everything I imagined and more.

"Hannah," I say, pointing to one. She's much younger but I'd know her anywhere. "This is the Cadet," I say to them. "He helped them plant their poppies at the spot where their families died."

"Is that Fitz?" Raffy asks, pointing to the tallest of them.

I nod, swallowing hard. "Who came by on the stolen bike and saved their lives." My voice cracks, just a bit.

I look at Fitz for a long time. He is as wild as I knew he would be but so cheeky-looking. I almost expect him to leap out of the photograph and tap me on the face.

"I feel like I know him and I don't know why," Raffy says.

"He was a Townie," I say.

Santangelo looks at the photo and then at me, slightly puzzled. "Is he . . ."

I nod.

"Who?" Raffy asks.

Santangelo holds the photo in his hand and I see a blurry tear that he, embarrassed, quickly dashes away.

"The Hermit," I say, and I hear a sound come from Raffy but before I react, I see something else. Standing next to him in the picture, with an arm around his neck, is Webb. A smile from ear to ear, a look in his eyes so joyous that a second wave of grief comes over me. To be that boy, I think. To feel whatever he was feeling. It makes me feel sick and overwhelmed at the same time.

"Webb," I say. "He began the territory wars," I tell them. "But it was a joke. I mean, his best friends were Cadets and Townies and the only reason the boundaries came about was because they were bored and just wanted to hang out with each other."

"Who's that?" Griggs says, pointing.

It's like my heart stops beating. All because of the person standing at the edge. Tate. Looking up at Webb with a mixture of love and exasperation, as if they are the only two in the world. She is so beautiful that it makes me ache and I can hardly breathe. The others look at me questioningly because there are tears in my eyes and I'm just shaking my head.

"She's so beautiful," I whisper.

I look up at them. "See how beautiful she was."

"Was? Who is she?" Griggs asked, confused by my reaction.

I pick up the photo and study it closely. But her eyes refuse to meet mine because, for her, there was never anyone but Webb.

"Her name's Tate," I tell them. "She's my mother."

I lie in my bed, still clutching the photos. It's one in the morning and I know what I have to do. All this time I thought the answers were here. But now I know that Tate took those answers with her and that somehow Hannah's caught up in it. If I had to wish for something, just one thing, it would be that Hannah would never see Tate the way I did. Never see Tate's beautiful lush hair turn brittle, her skin sallow, her teeth ruined by anything she could get her hands on that would make her forget. That Hannah would never count how many men there were and how vile humans can be to one another. That she would never see the moments in my life that were full of neglect and fear and revulsion, moments I can never go back to because I know they will slow me down for the rest of my life if I let myself remember them for one moment. Tate, who had kept Hannah alive that night, reading her the story of Jem and Mrs. Dubose. And suddenly I know I have to go but this time without being chased by a Brigadier, without experiencing the kindness of a postman from Yass, and without taking along a Cadet who will change the way I breathe for the rest of my life.

When I get to the end of the clearing that leads to the Jellicoe Road, a part of me is not surprised to see Griggs standing there. Even though it's two in the morning and pitch black, I know it's Griggs. We stand looking at each other, not able to see much in the darkness, but I can feel his presence.

I ask the inevitable. "What are you doing here?"

"What are you?"

"I asked first."

"Does it matter who asked first?"

I begin to walk away. "Don't follow me, Jonah."

"I've got a car," he calls out after me. "And you've

got somewhere to go."

"How do you know that?"

"Because I have this amazing ability to read your mind, that's why."

I stop for a moment. "Do you want me to remind you what happened last time? I don't ever want to be that angry with you again, Jonah. I just want to get past Yass this time and find her."

"Maybe she doesn't want to be found."

"Oh, so you were reading her mind back then, too, were you? Is that why you called your school?"

"No, but just say I was reading yours and it was kind of saying, 'Whatever I find out there is going to kill me a bit inside.' And I know what you're thinking now. That if you can find Hannah, you can find your mother."

"You're wrong," I say, but I walk back to him and we take the track that leads to the garage.

And he *is* wrong. Because I was thinking the exact opposite. If I find my mother, it will lead me to Hannah.

Once we get off the Jellicoe Road, we stop at Santangelo's and text him to meet us outside. He comes out, barefoot and bleary-eyed, holding something in his hands, and Griggs gets out of the car to greet him. They talk for a while but I don't want to join in. I'm scared that everyone's going to try to talk me out of this. Santangelo comes to my window and pokes his head in.

"Soon as I got home I burnt you a CD," he says, handing it to me.

I nod.

"Take this," he says, putting some notes in my hand. "It's the Club House share. GI Joe won't take it."

"No."

"*Yes*. Pay me back later. The petrol alone will cost you a fortune and I can't promise this car will last."

Griggs opens the car door. "We've got to go."

Santangelo leans through the window and hugs me. "Raffy will kill me," he whispers.

He goes around to Griggs's side and they do that awkward thing where they can't acknowledge that they actually have a friendship. After standing around for a moment or two, they shake hands.

"You know shit's going to hit the fan, all in your direction," Griggs says to him as he gets into the car.

"I'll deal with the sergeant. But I'll tell you this. I'm giving you three days. If you aren't back in three days, I'm going to tell them exactly where you are."

"Fair enough," Griggs says, and I nod.

Chapter 22

Somewhere on the highway to Sydney I begin to cry and it's like I can't stop. Griggs reaches over and touches my face, then reaches down and takes hold of my hand. We stay like that for a while in silence. Like that time on the train, I feel whole and again it surprises me that I can feel so together when I am revisiting the most fragmented time of my life.

We listen to the CD that Santangelo burnt for us. A bit of Guns n' Roses and Kenny Rogers and the Waterboys and at least three or four of the most tragically dependent love songs of all times. I see a smile on Griggs's face and I am smiling myself.

We don't have much of a plan. An easy option would be to stay at his house but he knows his mother will call the Brigadier as soon as we arrive and he has promised me three days without voices of reason or authority. So the next seventy-two hours are in my territory with my rules. But remembering is difficult. Living with my mother meant we moved at least eight times, because she was obsessed with the idea that someone was after us. Once, I remember falling asleep in a squat in Melbourne and next morning I woke up in Adelaide. Another time I stayed with a foster family. I'm not sure how old I was but I remember kindness. I remember another time, waking up in a police station when I was about seven years old. I don't know how I got there, except that the trip back to my mother seemed a long way and now, when I think of it, I realise that police station was the one in Jellicoe.

My first clear memory of time and place was being in a hospital when I was four because of my asthma. The walls were painted with animals and trees and as I stared at one of the trees, I could swear there was a boy hiding in the branches. I didn't see that boy again until I got to Hannah's. Except I was never frightened of him or thought it strange, because I thought all people lived the way we did. Then my mother taught me to read during one of her more lucid times and I realised that there was something a bit dysfunctional about our existence. When I think back to it now, it amazes me that even when my mother left me at the 7-Eleven off the Jellicoe Road she was only about twenty-eight years old. Stranger still, that Hannah was even younger.

I sleep, one of those crazy sleeps where you think you're awake but it ends up being like you're in a time machine and you look at the clock and it's three hours later. The morning sun is blinding and there's a foul taste in my mouth.

"You were dribbling," Griggs says. He looks tired, but content.

"Thanks for mentioning it."

"Anson Choi dribbled on my shoulder the whole way down," he says. He looks at me for a moment and I know he wants to say something.

"What?" I ask.

"We passed Yass about half an hour ago."

I smile. Three years on and we've moved forward, past the town where the Brigadier found us.

"If you weren't driving, I'd kiss you senseless," I tell him.

He swerves to the side of the road and stops the car abruptly. "Not driving any more."

———

All I remember about the Sydney of my past is the last place we lived in near the Cross. At one stage we're on a road with four lanes of traffic on each side, in the middle of morning peak-hour traffic. I see a Coca-Cola sign in the distance and I'm amazed at what comes flooding back.

"We lived somewhere around here, to the left. Once we lived just behind that sign."

I'm impressed with Griggs's ability to drive in the city. I feel claustrophobic and caged in. Drivers beep their horns impatiently and there are so many signs and arrows. We drive around for ages, trying to work out where to park the car. Everywhere we go there are parking meters. Griggs decides that we need to park the car in a quieter street just outside the city.

"Do you know where?" I ask.

He shrugs. "I don't want to be seen too close to home. Everyone knows everyone."

"Where's home?"

"Waterloo. About five minutes from here."

"Waterloo. Is it a tough place?"

"No, but some people have tough lives. I'll take

you there one day."

"Turn left," I tell him. "There have to be some streets down here without parking meters."

The car isn't doing so well and I feel bad for Santangelo because he probably knew that a seven-hour trip would wipe it out but he let us have it all the same. Just thinking of him makes me think of Raffy and of how they would all be getting ready for school at the moment. I wonder what they're thinking. I left a note saying that I'd be back in a couple of days and for a moment I miss them all: Raffy and Jessa and Ben, and even Mr. Palmer and poor Chloe P., and the other seniors of the House and the year tens, whose energy I love. I even miss Richard.

After we finally find a car park, Griggs is pragmatic and goes into sergeant-major mode. I can tell that he's already wound up tight. This is a world he can't control the way he does the territory wars or the guys at his school.

"We begin with people you remember, places you remember. Houses you lived in, corner shops. Restaurants."

But I have no idea where to start because I recognise nothing. Even when we come across a playground that looks familiar, I see that the units and terraces around it have been renovated. They look expensive and trendy and I feel as if there is no way that we could ever have lived here and it begins to confuse me. The redevelopment around here is mind-blowing. Restaurants and cafes and a massive international hotel.

"Where did the other people go?" I ask Griggs. "The people with nothing but their plastic bags and shopping trolleys filled with everything they own? What did people say to them? 'You can't afford to be homeless here?'"

"Let's get something to eat. You haven't had anything since last night."

I don't answer and I realise that this was all a big mistake. He takes my hand but I pull away. I'm beginning to feel an anxiety attack coming on and it makes me irritable and narky.

"Did you ever eat at a regular restaurant around here?" he asks.

"Jonah, who eats at restaurants?" I snap. "I've never eaten in a restaurant in my life. So stop asking such stupid questions."

"I'm only asking because maybe someone might

recognise you and be able to help," he says patiently.

All of a sudden, everything about him annoys me. His pragmatism, his patience, his Levis, and his navy long-sleeved T-shirt. I want him back in his fatigues. I know how to deal with that Jonah Griggs. Out of uniform he's not playing a role anymore and the real Jonah Griggs is scarier than the Cadet leader. His emotions are a thousand times more real.

I stare at him and he has that look on his face that asks, *What?*

"Wherever we go or whoever we meet, promise me you won't judge my mother."

He doesn't say anything.

"Promise."

"I can't," he says, not only irritated but dismissive. "Don't ask me to do that."

"That's cold."

"Fine. Call it cold. But you've told me too many things that I'll never forgive her for."

"Then I wish I hadn't told you," I snap.

"But you did," he snaps back, "so find someone else who will love and forgive her, because it won't be me."

"Then why are you here?" I'm shouting now and

I don't know why, because the last thing I want to do is fight with him in the middle of a Sydney street.

He stops and looks at me. "I'm here because of you. You're my priority. Your happiness, in some fucked way, is tuned in to mine. Get that through your thick skull. Would I like it any other way? Hell, yes, but I don't think that will be happening in my lifetime."

"Wow," I say sarcastically. "That's way too much romance for me today."

"If you want romance, go be with Ben Cassidy. Maybe he'll fawn all over you or play a beautiful piece of violin music. I never promised you romance. And stop finding a reason to be angry with me. I didn't redevelop this place. I just asked if you ate at restaurants."

For a while we walk in silence, and it's uncomfortable and angry. We come across a café on a corner where business people are waiting in line to order coffee and two cheerful guys behind the counter are fast and efficient. Sometimes they look up at one of the customers and say, "Flat white and ham-and-cheese croissant?" before the person has even opened their mouth, and I wish they'd do the same with me. Just look up and recognise me and know exactly what I order every day.

But they don't, because this is a whole other world to the one I lived in seven years ago. Griggs orders coffee and bacon and eggs for himself then looks at me. I shrug.

"White toast and marmalade and a hot chocolate," he says, and it doesn't surprise me just how much he's taken in about me.

We eat in silence and then he buys some fruit and puts it in my backpack and we set off towards Kings Cross.

"Do you eat at restaurants?" I ask him quietly, wondering if he regrets coming with me.

"Yeah. With my mum and Daniel, my brother. Or sometimes with Jack, my mum's boyfriend. At least once a week."

"Do you like Jack?"

"He's a great guy. He's fantastic with Daniel and he takes care of my mum without trying to take over."

"Your brother sounds like he's your friend."

"My brother is my god," he says. "I can't begin to tell you how decent that kid is."

"I can't imagine him being more decent than his brother."

He looks at me and I can see his body relax a bit. He puts his arm around me and kisses the top of my head as we walk.

"Jonah," I say quietly, never wanting him to let go. "Just say I didn't exist?"

It's the longest day of my life. The lack of familiarity gets worse. The main drag of Kings Cross gives me snippets of memory but not enough. I feel like it's a foreign land. It's cleaner and the people look different: better dressed, better looking, comfortable. It's not as if there is something wrong about an area being cleaned up and gentrified, especially when it was famous for prostitution and drugs and corruption, but it has wiped out my history. Everything smells different and everyone walks at a different pace.

"When we lived here her name was Annie," I tell Griggs. "She used to change it all the time. She said that people were after us and she'd say, 'Your name is Tessa today.' But I'd lie in bed at night and I'd say to myself over and over again, 'My name is Taylor

Markham.' I never wanted to be anyone else. She used to say that I named myself. Like she didn't care enough to name me."

"It's probably a better reason than that. Did you hang out with any kids around here?"

"Not really. There was one kid, Simon. His father was a transvestite and he'd let us wear his clothes. We'd go to video arcades and games rooms. He was addicted to all the games. Sometimes we'd just hang out in the parks. It's how I learnt to play chess, you know."

"We can start there," Griggs says.

"I don't think I'd remember what he looked like," I say. "And I doubt he'd still be around."

"Where else would he go aside from the park?"

We go to a Time Zone. It's the closest reminder of my former life so far. A couple of kids are off their faces and someone has spewed right near the entrance. Some are in uniform and I can imagine them having left that morning pretending they were going to school. But the ones who leave the biggest impression are those in casual clothes. They don't have to answer to anyone. I ask the guy at the register if he knows Simon and he shrugs and carries on reading his magazine. "It's a common name," is all he says when I bug him again.

"If he comes in, can you tell him that Taylor Markham is looking for him? That I'll be at McDonald's across the road at six thirty tonight?"

It's like talking to a brick wall, actually even worse because at least I could lean on a brick wall. I talk to a few other people around and I give them the same information but by the time I walk out, I accept that Simon is not an option.

We go to one of the homeless hostels in East Sydney. One minute we're walking down a street that Griggs reckons has million-dollar properties and the next we're turning into a lane where old men lie on the road on filthy mattresses, garbage everywhere. When I look at them closely, though, I realise they aren't so old. The hostel caters only to men and after we ask around, we're directed to another one on the other side of the main road. For the first time in what feels like ages, I find myself thinking of the Hermit. In my memory he was old, but now I realise that he wasn't at all. He was like these men, who dirt and grime and neglect have made seem a thousand years older than they are.

When we get to the top of the queue at the second soup kitchen, I take out the photo of the five and show the girl serving. "Do you recognise this person?" I ask, pointing to Tate. "It's very dated but she may look familiar."

"Sorry, love," she says, shaking her head.

"I really need to find her," I say. "Could you ask the other people in there?"

What are the odds of anyone recognising my mother? What are the odds that these people have actually looked in the faces of the people who walk into this place? I glance at Griggs, who is looking around the room at everyone. I can tell he's a bit shell-shocked. He tries to muster up a smile but there's not really enough to keep it there.

When we're not asking people questions or roaming the streets for any type of recognition, we sit in McDonald's because it's the only place where they don't bug you to order or leave. By late afternoon I'm tired and I want to go back to my room at school and just lie down. I can sense that Griggs is exhausted, especially after driving all night. We make plans to book into one of the youth hostels in the street behind the main drag, careful of how we spend the money. We find out where the food vans are, in case I recognise someone there who might know my mother or even Simon, but my mind is a blank and I feel like there's no way I'll ever know anyone. Each time I check my watch I think of what Raffy and everyone else are doing back home. I have been away for not even twenty-four hours and I am homesick beyond comprehension.

At night the place begins to look a bit more like I remember it, and Griggs suggests that we stick around because this could be the time when people I might recognise come out of hibernation.

We stand by the fountain on Darlinghurst Road and for a moment I get a glimpse of who I was back then. Tagging along behind my mother on these streets, our feet dirty, but our dresses so pretty. I wore a white one, once, someone's old communion dress that we had found in an op-shop and I thought I was a princess. Suddenly, for one incredible moment, I remember something. That my mother smiled at me in wonder that day and said, "Look at my beautiful girl."

He had been away from the Jellicoe Road for a year and, when he finished his final exams, he came

back because he had promised Narnie he would.
Along the way he saw their ghosts—planting
the poppies, waiting for him at the general store,
planning their tunnel, grieving for their dead. But
living in the heart of Narnie was the only home
he had ever had. Deep down he knew he wasn't
enough to keep Narnie alive for the rest of her life.
But he could try.

"Promise me . . ." he said to her at her door, his
heart aching when he saw Webb's soul in her eyes.
But then he stopped himself. No promises about
death or keeping alive. That had been Tate's job
when Narnie seemed so fragile over the years. It
sounded weak coming from him.

"Promise me that you'll never go looking for
Tate. Whatever you do, don't go looking for Tate."

"Promise me that you'll never ask me that
again," she'd replied, her voice strong and clear.

He shook his head. "She's not Tate anymore,
Narnie. She's someone else and that baby . . ."

"Promise me that one day we'll bring them back
here, Jude."

He could tell her now what she'd find, because he
had gone looking himself. In the city, the Tate they
knew was gone. Lost to them. Lost to herself. But

Narnie stared deep inside him and he remembered what brought him to this place now. This girl, standing on the side of the Jellicoe Road like an apparition, promising him a richer life than he ever dreamed of. And he couldn't help himself, couldn't hold it back until they were in her room, tugging at each other's clothing, breathing each other's breath, tasting each other's grief.

"Promise me . . . promise me . . ." he said between gasps, bunching up her skirt, removing anything that got in their way. The need to be inside her, connected to her, made his body shudder just at the thought of it. She clutched him, her fingers digging in like she needed to gather parts of him to act as her own second skin for the rest of her life. He had never heard emotion from Narnie before and now . . . now it was so loud, so gut-wrenching that he wanted to cover her mouth with his hand. To hold everything within her. But Narnie had held it in for too long and her rage, or pain or grief or love, pierced his ears and he knew that, no matter what, he'd never be able to block it out. That he'd never want to.

Then when it was over, she gathered him into her arms. And told him the terrible irony of her life.

That she had wanted to be dead all those years while her brother was alive. That had been her sin.

And this was her penance.

Wanting to live when everyone else seemed dead.

Chapter 23

"Taylor Markham?"

I look up at the boy standing in front of me. One or two of his teeth are chipped and his skin looks rough with broken capillaries. It's not acne but it looks raw and painful. He is small and wiry and his eyes have that intense wild look that I've seen on many of the faces at the soup kitchens and food vans. This kid, younger than me by at least two years, looks like some kind of Charles Manson copycat. I stare at him for a moment, totally at a loss because I know it's not Simon. But then it hits me and my heart picks up a beat of excitement.

Not because he means something to me but because he is proof that I existed. He lived in the room next door to us. Him and his mum. She'd leave him with me sometimes and the rest is a blank.

He knows I can hardly remember him. He has that disgusted look on his face you get when someone forgets your name. "You're supposed to be dead," he says flatly.

The shock of his words makes my blood run cold and I can feel Griggs tensing up next to me. The kid is fidgety, like he's either on something or just coming off it. I look at his arm and see the bruising from the needle marks and he catches me looking but there's no expression on his face. He's numb to the world.

I stare at him. How can you just forget a person completely until the moment you see his face again? Who else is back there lurking in my head?

"My mother? Have you seen her?" I ask.

"Around. But not for a while."

"How long a while?"

"Don't care. I've got to be someplace," he says, and just like that he walks away.

I stand staring, my mind full of a thousand thoughts that I am so used to shoving into locked drawers. But this time I let those thoughts stay no matter how bad they may be.

Sam. I don't quite know where the name has come

from but it appears on my lips like a sob and I run after him. "Sam!" The sound of his name stops him and for a moment I see a flash of something like vulnerability.

"Go," I say. "Wherever you have to be. But meet us later. At the McDonald's."

He knows which McDonald's because we've been there before.

"My shout."

We wait for hours and then he's there. He totally ignores Griggs and sits down opposite me.

I don't know what to say to him and I don't really get the sense that he actually wants to talk to me but he doesn't move.

"Do you want something to eat?" I ask.

He shrugs. "Maybe a Big Mac."

I look at Griggs who keeps on staring at the kid like he doesn't trust him for a moment.

"Jonah?" I say. He gives me one of those looks that say, *I'm not going anywhere,* but after a moment he reluctantly stands up.

"Would you like fries with that?" he asks Sam sarcastically.

"Large Coke."

"Same," I say.

We're left alone.

"How come you thought I was dead?" I ask, staring at him the whole time, not really wanting to hear the answer.

The kid shrugs. He scratches a scab on his finger and the crust falls on the table in front of us. "Do you have cigarettes?" he asks.

"You can't smoke in here."

"For later."

I shake my head.

"Have you got ten dollars?"

I nod and we don't speak for a while.

Griggs returns and sits down again. Under the table, I squeeze his hand.

"Sam's mother worked with mine," I tell Griggs, almost conversationally. "I used to look after him."

Griggs nods.

"I don't think he actually understands what you mean by 'work,'" Sam says. "Do you, dickhead?"

"Maybe we can go outside and you can explain it to me," Griggs says to him quietly.

Not now, Griggs, I want to say. I can tell it is

going to kill him to keep his mouth shut.

Sam concentrates on the food and wolfs it down almost in three mouthfuls. I take small bites of mine.

"I need to find her, Sam," I say when he seems to be finished. "It's really important. Maybe your mum will know."

"Eve? She's a fruitcake. It's like everything's fried up there, do you know what I mean? Every time I ring her it's like, 'Sam, can you lend me twenty dollars?'" He puts on a whining voice. "'Can you buy me a case of beer? Can you buy me some ciggies?'" He looks at me intensely. As if a thought has just occurred to him. "And she never pays me back. She's a waste of space and she keeps on having these fucking kids."

I remember Eve now. She lived totally for the guy she was with and Sam was the number twelve priority in her life. Sam was a pathetic kid, so tiny and needy. His nose was continually running and he was always getting bashed up by older kids in the area. The one thing about my mother was that she never formed emotional attachments to men, so I never had to suffer the consequences of her relationships. Sometimes when we were walking along, I'd see her looking in the distance as if she was searching for someone. I think now that she believed that Webb could have been out here and it's what kept her around this place for so long.

"Do you remember the last time you saw me?" he asks.

I don't answer and he continues. "Eve had left us at home with Les, that arsehole she was going out with."

I shudder and I sense Griggs looking at me.

"The cops got him, you know. Part of the kid porn thing a couple of months ago. Remember your mum came after her shift and went berserk and she was belting Les with everything she could find and she was screaming, 'What the fuck have you done to them?'"

I shake my head. But I do remember now and I know it's the story I told Raffy that she'll never forget. The one she wouldn't let me remember.

"And we were just standing there in our knickers crying because we didn't get why she was going apeshit and she grabbed you and dragged you out of there and Eve was shouting at her and calling her a crazy bitch and the neighbours went nuts."

"Whose mother was the bigger fruitcake? Yours or mine?"

Next to me I sense the change in Griggs's breathing.

"And I never saw you again. Two days later she came back without you. She was so off her face. Eve asked, 'Where's the kid?' and your mum said, 'She's in heaven,' and she just killed herself laughing for ages. Fuck, I cried for a week, you know."

I'm staring at him with my mouth open. "Why would my mother say something like that?"

Sam doesn't respond to questions and doesn't wait for answers. He just speaks and I can't even block him out because it takes too much effort.

"You had a Spiderman outfit," he continues.

"Saving the neighbourhood from evil," I say weakly, remembering my line.

He stands up. "Got to be somewhere," he says. "You said you had money."

I look at Griggs, pleadingly, but Griggs is staring at me like he's been hit by a truck.

I glance back at Sam and there's a look on his face. Like he hates me. "You're angry with me," I say as he begins to walk away.

"Let him go," Griggs says quietly.

But I can't. I jump out of the booth and go after him. "I didn't ask her to take me out to a Seven-Eleven six hundred kilometres from here and leave me there, Sam. At least your mother didn't do that to you," I say angrily. Griggs tries to pull me away.

"Mine went to Canberra for two weeks," Sam says, looking at me with massive cold eyes. "But she didn't leave me there. She left me with Les."

I stare at him. Griggs is standing next to me, rubbing his eyes, like he'd love to just disappear. After a couple of minutes I take some of Santangelo's money from Griggs and stuff it into Sam's hand. Our fingers touch for a moment.

"You didn't even know who I was," he says. "I knew you straightaway." And that little hurt boy is back and I let myself remember things that I've been blocking for years.

"What do you want me to remember, Sam? That I taught you to read? And we read the first Harry Potter book and when I finished you said . . . you said . . ." I can hardly speak because I'm crying again.

"I said, 'I wish I was a wizard,'" he whispers.

We stare at each other for a moment and he pockets the money.

"Do you know where Oxford Street is?" he asks after a moment.

I look at Griggs and he nods.

"Meet me there tonight at about ten thirty. At the lights outside the Court House Hotel."

I nod again.

"I'll find out what I can from Eve."

Griggs and I walk in total silence. We're in a laneway where rubbish is strewn and bins are overflowing. Suddenly he kicks one of the bins with full force and it goes flying. I stand and watch him. His back is to me. I walk up and put my arms around him, leaning against him.

I feel his heart thumping hard and his hands take mine and they are shaking.

"You okay now?" I ask him after a while.

He doesn't say anything, but just turns around and holds me.

"Jonah, regardless of what happened, I've spent the last six years living in . . ."

I think for a moment and a little touch of hope makes itself felt.

"What?" he asks.

"I was going to say, 'I've spent the last six years living in paradise.' Do you get it? It's like heaven. That's what she meant."

"Except the kid thought you were dead."

"She took me out there and rang up Hannah because if there was one place Tate loved, it was Jellicoe and she knew it would be the safest place for me."

"And when she came back, the kid said she was absolutely off her face because you were gone from her life," he said.

I'm looking at him in wonder. "I never thought she loved me, you know."

It's a quarter to eleven before Sam shows. He has that edgy look about him, unable to keep still, his eyes like a crazed rabbit about to be caught.

"She's in a hos—hospice? Up the road. St. Vincent's."

"Hospital," I correct.

"Whatever."

"What's wrong with her?"

He shrugs. He looks around, edging away, but I catch a glimpse of some need in his eyes. Like he hasn't given up completely.

Griggs takes my hand and pulls me away, but I don't want to let go.

"Sam!" I call out and he turns around. "I live on the Jellicoe Road. Where trees make canopies over-head and where you can sit at the top of them and see forever. My aunt built me a house there. Remember that."

He's staring at me but it's better than him walking away.

"Promise me you'll remember," I say forcefully.

He nods and we walk away but like Lot's wife I turn back. He's talking to this middle-aged guy who has his hand on his shoulder. The next minute they both get into a taxi and then they're gone.

"Let's go," Griggs says quietly.

At the hostel we get our own room. It's tiny with double bunks but we climb into the same bed and Griggs holds on to me like he's never going to let go.

"Do you want to know why I called my school

that time?" he asks in the dark.

"You don't have to explain."

"No, I want to. I had this dream. That someone—actually it was my father—spoke to me and he said, 'Jonah, if you go any farther, you will never come back,' and although I've been told a million times during counselling that I don't need his forgiveness, I just thought it was the closest thing to it. That maybe he was protecting me from something out there and that the warning was his way of saying that he forgave me. Then I thought, if I'm not coming back, then you probably won't be either so I called the school and next thing the Brigadier and Santangelo's dad turn up."

He sounds so sad that it breaks my heart.

"But now that we're out here, as bad as everything seems, I don't think my life or yours was at risk. So I must have imagined it all. There was no message. There was no forgiveness. Nothing."

"You don't know that. We were younger then, Jonah. Maybe something would have happened to us if we had reached the city. And, as Jessa would say, there is always that serial killer. Maybe your dad was warning you because he cared."

He shakes his head and, although it's dark, I can tell he's crying.

"What are you thinking?" I whisper after a while.

"That you deserve romance," he says.

I trace his face with my fingers. "Let me see. A guy tells me that he would have thrown himself in front of a train if it wasn't for me and then drives seven hours straight, without whingeing once, on a wild-goose chase in search of my mother with absolutely no clue where to start. He is, in all probability, going to get court-martialled because of me, has put up with my moodiness all day long, and knows exactly what to order me for breakfast. It doesn't get any more romantic than that, Jonah."

"I'm in year eleven, Taylor. I'm not going to get court-martialled."

"Just say you get expelled?"

"Then so be it. I still would have driven for seven hours and ordered you hot chocolate and white toast and marmalade."

"And you don't call that romantic? God, you've got a lot to learn."

I sit up in the dark and after a moment I take off

my singlet and I hear him taking off his T-shirt and we sit there, holding each other, kissing until our mouths are aching, and then we're pulling off the rest of our clothes and I'm under him and I feel as if I'm imprinted onto his body. Everything hurts, every single thing including the weight of him and I'm crying because it hurts and he's telling me he's sorry over and over again, and I figure that somewhere down the track we'll work out the right way of doing this but I don't want to let go, because tonight I'm not looking for anything more than being part of him. Because being part of him isn't just anything. It's kind of everything.

Chapter 24

During this time I start to get to know my mother again by piecing together fragments of our lives, snippets of Hannah's story and Sam's miserable memories. What kills me most is my inability to remember much of that journey when she drove me to the Jellicoe Road. And I want to. I want to remember the look in her eyes when she realised that she had to let go of the person who was her closest link to Webb. Did she look at me and tell me she loved me? Or did she not speak at all because the words would slice her throat, leaving her to bleed to death all the way back?

While I sit in the foyer of St. Vincent's hospital, waiting for the receptionist to finish on the phone, I think of everything I have always wanted to say to my mother and how in the past twenty-four hours all of it has changed.

"You ready?" Griggs asks, coming back from ringing Santangelo.

I shake my head.

"How about I go up and ask?"

I look at him, trying to manage a smile.

"What are you thinking?" he asks. I've been piecing together tiny details about him as well. That he always asks that question because he has to see a counsellor every week at home and that's what his counsellor asks him. And that sometimes he's a bit shy, like he is at the moment and has been all morning. It makes me feel shy back. I wonder if everyone else is shy the morning after or whether they chat and laugh as if it's the most natural thing in the world. I wonder if we're unnatural.

"I'm thinking that after last night you shouldn't have to spend your morning in a hospital finding out if my mother has tried to OD."

"And I'm thinking that after last night I want to be anywhere you are and if that means being in a hospital asking about your mother, then so be it."

But we know that we're both thinking about much more than what we're doing here now.

"Just say after Wednesday we never see each—"

"Don't," he says, angry.

"Jonah, you live six hundred kilometres away from me," I argue.

"Between now and when we graduate next year there are at least ten weeks' holiday and five random public holidays. There's email and if you manage to get down to the town, there's text messaging and mobile phone calls. If not, the five minutes you get to speak to me on your communal phone is better than nothing. There are the chess nerds who want to invite you to our school for the chess comp next March and there's this town in the middle, planned by Walter Burley Griffin, where we can meet up and protest against our government's refusal to sign the Kyoto treaty."

"Gees, Jonah," I say in mock indignation. "I wish you'd put more thought into our relationship."

"And then we make plans."

"As long as you don't have an affair with Lily, the girl next door."

"Her name's actually Gerty. She's bigger than me and can beat me in an arm-wrestle. There is no way in this world that I will ever, *ever* go out with someone called Gerty because if I married her and she wanted to take my name, she'd be called Gerty Griggs."

I laugh for the first time in days and then I take a deep breath and stand up. "I'm ready."

We walk to the counter and I ask politely for Tate Markham, hoping she's under that name. The receptionist looks on a written list in front of her and shakes her head.

"Are you sure she's here?" she asks.

"No, but we were told she was."

She taps her keyboard and I'm beginning to feel sick. Don't let me have to start again, I pray. She shakes her head and I hear Griggs clear his throat.

"Is there a St. Vincent's hospice around?"

"Next door."

I breathe a sigh of relief and thank her before walking away.

"What's the diff?" I ask him.

He shrugs.

When we walk into the hospice, I go through the same routine again. After a moment I can see the receptionist has come across the name and she peers at it closely. "She was here," she says.

I feel Griggs's arm around me. *Was*. What does *was* actually mean? The verb *to be*. Past tense of *is*. Does it mean that someone is no longer *being*?

"She checked out."

The relief almost sends me over the counter to hug her. "Checked out? Like not a euphemism 'checked out' but a real one?"

The woman looks confused. "She checked out six weeks ago."

Six weeks ago everything changed in my world. Hannah left. Griggs arrived. The boy in the tree in my dreams began to bring a sobbing creature to our nightly tête-à-tête.

"What was the date?"

She looks at us and I can see the shutter go down. "We have privacy laws and we can't just give out information. . . ."

"Please," I beg her, taking out my wallet and showing her my student card. "Our names are the same. I can show you a photo of her. She's my mother and I haven't seen her for six years."

She looks at me and then at Griggs and I feel as if she's going to get emotional as well but then she taps on her keyboard again.

"She was signed out on the sixteenth of September."

I look at Griggs. "Last time I saw Hannah was on the fifteenth."

"Are you sure?"

"We have the Leadership Council on the fifteenth of September every year and I saw her the morning after. We had an argument."

I turn back to the receptionist. "Did she sign herself out?" I ask.

"No," she says, reading the screen.

"Did Hannah Schroeder sign her out?"

"No," the receptionist peers closer at her screen. "Jude Scanlon did."

"Jude," I whisper, excited. "Oh my God, Jonah. I'm going to meet Jude."

"Jude Scanlon?" Griggs says. "You never mentioned a Jude Scanlon."

"Yeah I did," I look up at the woman and smile. "Thanks."

"Good luck," she says.

"He's the Cadet," I explain as we walk away. "The one I told you about who planted the poppies."

"Taylor," he says, and I can tell by the look on his

face that something is not right. "Jude Scanlon is not just the Cadet. He's the Brigadier."

I'm in shock but everything is starting to make sense. We go back to where we parked the car and it doesn't start. While Griggs attempts to fix it, I sit on the kerb and use his phone to ring home. One of the year nines answers and she puts me through a mini third-degree, questioning me about where I am and when I'm coming back and if I'm coming back and something about Mr. Palmer and the Army man taking Jessa that morning. I ask her to give the phone to Raffy and a few seconds later I hear her familiar voice.

"Where are you?" she asks, and there are five different tones in her voice, including shittiness and concern and relief.

"What's happening there?" I ask.

"I don't know," she sighs. "Mr. Palmer and the Brigadier took Jessa this morning and they haven't returned her. Please tell me they aren't the serial killers."

"No, they're not. Promise me that you'll never repeat that theory."

"Promise me that you're coming back."

"Of course I am. Why have they taken Jessa? Can't you find out through Chaz's dad?"

"Chaz's dad is furious. I mean big-time furious with a big fat F."

"Did he find out that Chaz broke into the police station?"

I can see Griggs looking up from what he's doing and waiting for the answer.

"Chaz is in so much trouble," she says.

"What? In gaol or painting the town," I try to joke.

"Taylor, his dad won't talk to him." I can tell that Raffy is in no mood for any kind of humour.

I look at Griggs and cover the mouthpiece. "Chaz's dad isn't talking to him. Did he tell you that?"

"Shit, no," he says, shocked. "He's not going to cope with that."

I get back to Raffy who is still talking. ". . . and Chaz is really cut about it and worse still, he won't tell them where you guys are so it's like the Cold War over there. He says his father reckons he'll never trust him again. Are you sure you're okay?"

"Are you?"

"Well, how can I be? You've run away, Jessa's been taken by someone you've both told me is a serial killer, Ben's reading the Old Testament and keeps quoting vengeance scenes and Jonah Griggs in the same breath, and Chaz is so down that he didn't speak for half the time I was with him last night."

"What did you do for the other half?" I ask.

"Very funny, Taylor. Come home and stop making things complicated," she says angrily.

"I can't find my mother and things *are* complicated."

"Then make them simple and come home."

"Just get Jessa back. I'll be there soon."

Griggs sits on the kerb with me, holding something that he's yanked out of the engine. I can tell he has absolutely no idea what to do with cars and the more he looks at it, the more confused he is. I don't know what to concentrate on and in what order. Should I begin with my mother, who checked out of a hospice for God knows what reason? Or with the Brigadier, who I've just discovered is one of her beloved childhood friends? Or maybe with Raffy, who is worried about Chaz? Or Jessa, who is being questioned as we speak? Or should I begin with

Griggs, who I . . . who I what? I don't even know what terminology to use. Did we have sex? Did we make love? Did we sleep together? Is he my boyfriend? And Hannah? Where's Hannah in all this?

"We're going to have to take the train to Yass and then make our way from there," Griggs says. "We'll have to leave the car here."

I look at him and shake my head. "You've officially given me an aversion to trains leading to Yass," I say. I dial directory assistance. "The Jellicoe Police Station," I say.

Griggs is looking at me as if I'm insane. They connect me and I wait for someone to answer. I say who I am and then I ask for Santangelo's dad. I wait less than three seconds and he's on the line.

"Taylor? Where are you?" Shitty tone.

"In Sydney. Is Jude Scanlon there?"

"No. Is Jonah with you?"

"Yes."

I hear the first sigh of relief. Two missing kids located. Tick.

"Can we expect you back soon?" He's now using a measured tone.

"Depends on the Brigadier. Can you give him a

message? Tell him that we'll be at the hospice. The one he signed my mother out of six weeks ago. He can ring us there or he can ring us on Jonah's phone. Tell him I want to know where my mother is and where Hannah is and I want Jessa McKenzie back in the dorms ASAP."

"Anything else?" Now it's a dry tone.

I'm about to say 'No' and hang up but I change my mind. "Yes, actually there is something else," I say. "I met this boy here who I knew as a kid and his mum left him with a pedophile for two weeks when he was eight years old and I'm presuming you know everything there is to know about Jonah's father, and that my father is dead, and my mother hasn't been around for years, and God knows Jessa's real story. So what I'm saying here, Sergeant, is that we're just a tad low on the reliable adult quota so you have no right to be all self-righteous about what Chaz did and if you're going to go around not talking to him when his only crime was wanting me to have what he has, then I think you're going to turn out to be a bit of a dud and you know something? I'm just a bit over life's little disappointments right now. Do you understand what I'm saying?"

He's silent for a moment.

"We just want you back here." The caring tone in his voice makes me want to cry but I need to keep my anger focused or I'll stop moving forward.

"Why?"

"Because it's what your mother wants and if she knew you were somewhere out there meeting up with God knows who, it would—"

"No lectures," I say. "Just answers. *Please.*"

I hear him sigh.

"I'll talk to Chaz and I'll give Jude your message. He'll have the answers, Taylor."

I hang up, and Griggs looks at me, stunned.

"You are very scary sometimes."

I give him back the phone and lean my head on his shoulder.

"Do you think the Brigadier will come and get us?" I ask.

"It's eleven thirty," he says. "It's a six- to seven-hour trip, tops. I'll bet you two trillion dollars that he'll be here by six P.M. on the dot."

When he wins the bet, I tell Griggs that it will take me a lifetime to save up two trillion dollars and he tells me that he's only giving me seventy years.

The Brigadier pulls up in front of the hospice and as he gets out of the car, it's very clear that he's not happy. Like Griggs, it's the first time I've seen him out of uniform and it's really the first time I've got a proper look at him. I must shiver because Griggs leans over and whispers to me not to worry. The Brigadier notices the exchange and I can tell he's unimpressed. There's a look in his eyes that says *I know what you did last night.*

"Hannah's out of her mind with worry."

"Really?" I say. "Well, now she must know how I've felt for the past six weeks."

He dismisses me with a look and turns to Griggs. "I'll drop you off at your home, Jonah. We'll be back in two days, anyway, so there's no point you coming all the way back."

I can't move. I'm stuck to Griggs, not wanting to let go. I hate this man for even suggesting it but Griggs gently pushes me to the front passenger seat.

"I'd prefer to return, sir."

"It's not really an option, Jonah," he says quietly.

"Sir, whether you drive me there or whether I hitch, I'll be returning to camp." Griggs doesn't even raise a sweat, which is amazing because I know how he feels about the Brigadier. He gets into the back seat and calmly puts on his seatbelt. The Brigadier looks at him through the rear-view mirror.

"It would have been better to have left this where it was three years ago."

"This," I presume, is my relationship with Griggs.

"Like you and Narnie did?" I ask. "You had a choice. You could have kept away but you came back."

He sits, staring ahead.

"Where's my mother?" I ask.

The Brigadier starts the car and pulls out of the narrow street.

"Where are they? My mum and Hannah?"

"We can't see them for now."

"Stop the car!" I say angrily.

He continues driving.

"I want to see them *now*." I take off my seatbelt. "Stop the car."

He doesn't stop and I hit him hard. The car swerves and Griggs comes over the back of my seat and grabs hold of me.

"Taylor, calm down," he says firmly, not letting go. The Brigadier slows down and pulls over to the side of the road. I'm so furious with him I want to hurt him more than anyone I have ever known.

"Soon," he says, and I realise that I've winded him. "It's what Tate wants, Taylor, and it might seem like the most unfair thing in the world to you but we have to go by what she wants."

I relax a little and Griggs lets go.

"Sir," he says, and there's something different in his voice. "Tell her the truth. Please."

I don't understand what he's talking about until Griggs leans forward.

"Her mum was in a hospice. My nan was in a hospice. I know what that means."

The Brigadier looks at me and I see him swallow hard. Slowly things start falling into place. "She doesn't have long."

I hear a sound. Like some kind of animal in pain and I realise that it has come from my throat. The next minute I'm out of the car and I'm running hard. I hear the pounding of heavy boots behind me and feel a hand snake out to grab me. It stops me but I wriggle out of the Brigadier's grasp and smash him hard over and over again. My hand is a fist and I'm yelling with rage and it hurts to be feeling this much. For a while he lets me pound into him, like he's resigned himself to this. Then he grabs my arms painfully and holds me tight, muffling my face against him and I hear the beating of his heart against my cheek.

Suddenly, I'm somewhere else, in another time. On the shoulders of a giant. I had wanted them to be my father's shoulders and all this time they were Jude's. But he holds on to me in a way that Hannah never has. I feel his relief, like he hasn't held someone in a long, long time. And he's wanted to.

We don't say much as we walk back to the car but he has his hand on my shoulder and I can feel it shaking. When we're settled inside, he clears his throat and starts up the engine.

"She thought you were the serial killer," Griggs tells him.

"I heard. From Jessa McKenzie."

I don't want to talk just yet but I'm curious. "What were you doing with her?" I ask quietly.

"Apart from questioning her about your whereabouts, I was listening to the most intriguing story about my life moonlighting as a kidnapper."

"Based on incriminating evidence," Griggs adds. "Apparently you're always around or away when someone disappears."

"Yes, well, kidnapping's my thing," he says dryly.

"According to the newspapers, it is."

"That wasn't kidnapping. That was taking you to a safer place."

"Me?" I ask.

"You."

No information comes easily. It's like he's spent a lifetime censoring himself. I can understand, having known Hannah so long myself.

"How come?"

"You were seven. Tate rang Hannah, wasted, with absolutely no idea where she had left you. By the time I drove down, you, being so resourceful, had been found in one of the luggage carts at Central."

My mother leaving me places was nothing new. That it actually meant something to her, however, surprises me.

"She was on a blinder for the next couple of days, so I stayed," he continues. "One day when she was out, I decided to take you back to Narnie's. Except by the time I got to Jellicoe, Tate had called the police and they had to charge me with kidnapping."

I bring out the photograph of me when I was three and show it to him. He takes it from me, glancing down at it for a moment before he looks back to the road.

"You took this photo?" I ask.

"Narnie did. You came to live with us. It was a bad time for Tate. She made us promise not to give you back to her until she was totally clean."

"Then why did you give me back?"

"Because she did get clean. If there was anyone who could make Tate feel anything it was you, Taylor, but then somehow she'd slip up and go downhill fast. Sometimes she'd disappear with you. We lost track of you both for a few years and then, one day, when you were eleven, she rang up Narnie, crazy mad, and said that she was to take you. She signed the papers and told us that under no condition were we to allow her ever to have you again. That she was poison. Her self-loathing was . . . I can't explain. She wouldn't even meet Narnie. She told her that you'd be at the Seven-Eleven at twelve fifteen. But she made Narnie promise one more thing. That Narnie was never to be a mother to you. You had a mother, she insisted."

And Narnie honoured that. Keeping me at a distance for as long as I can remember.

"We still have no idea what made her react that way," he said.

"It doesn't matter," I say quietly, thinking of Sam.

He looks at me carefully. "Oh, it does, believe me. Everything that's happened to you matters."

"But not today, sir," Griggs says firmly.

We're silent for a while and I want to ask one thousand questions but I don't know how. I watch him as he drives. There's a hollowness to his cheeks and a bit of a sadness in his eyes and although he is all muscle and no fat, he looks underweight and unhealthy.

He senses me staring and looks my way for a moment. Then he smiles and it's so lovely that it brings tears to my eyes.

"I look like Narnie," I say like I can read his mind.

"A bit. But you look a lot like Webb."

When the silence gets too much, I put on Santangelo's CD and he looks at me bemused.

"Kenny Rogers?"

"Jessa's a fan. I'm relating to some of the music," I tell him.

"'Coward of the County'?"

I glare at him and he looks uncomfortable and for a moment I see his eyes glance in the rear-view mirror at Griggs. "I meant 'The Gambler.'"

"Liar."

But my tone is softer. We've reached some kind of truce and as he starts speaking again, I begin to remember his voice. I've known it all my life. I realise that it is between this man and Hannah that I once slept as a child. I remember waking up from nightmares, my heart thumping so bad, and how his voice, reading me stories of dragons and wild things would calm me. Every time the character in the book, Max, would make the journey back home I'd point to the page and say, "He's going home to his mum."

While Griggs sleeps, he tells me stories I've never heard. About all the films they shot on Super 8, of dancing among the trees like pagans, of Fitz's .22 rifle and the pot shots he'd take at anything that moved, of sitting in a tree with Webb and philosophising about the meaning of life. And of their plans to build a bomb shelter in case the Russians and Americans blew each other up with nuclear weapons and the marathon scissor-paper-rock competitions and the card games that went all night.

I fall in love with these kids over and over again and my heart aches for their tragedies and marvels at their friendship. And it's like we've been talking for five minutes instead of five hours.

The days they loved best were spent in the clearing, talking about where they would go from there. Jude especially enjoyed these days because it meant he had something to offer them. The city was a whole new landscape, one that Jude knew better than any of them.

Fitz was in the tree, strategically positioning the five tins. "As long as we don't live in some wanky suburb where people drink coffee and talk shit," he called out.

"The gun has to stay behind," Jude said. "People in the city don't walk around with rifles, shooting tins out of trees."

Fitz swung off one branch to another and climbed

down the trunk a third of the way before diving off and landing in a commando-style roll at their feet.

"Reckon I can be in the Cadets, Jude?" he mocked.

"You have psycho tattooed on your face, Fitz. Of course they'll let you in."

Fitz picked up the gun and aimed and then fired, hitting two of the unseen tins in a row.

"What happens to Narnie?" Tate asked. "If we leave in a year's time, she'll be here on her own for the year after."

"You can't stay here," Narnie said quietly. "There's nowhere to live and there are no jobs. You have to go to the city."

"But we've got money when we turn eighteen," Webb explained. "And we're buying the one-acre block near the river on this side of the Jellicoe Road. The house is going to be three split levels, the one on top like an attic. It'll have a skylight so you can see every star in the galaxy. From the front window downstairs you'll be able to see the river and when all of us are old and grey, we'll sit by the window and die peacefully there, smoking our pipes, talking bullshit, bringing up our kinfolk—" His accent turned American and Narnie giggled.

A bullet hit the third tin and a few seconds later another one hit the fourth.

"Hey, GI Jude, can you beat that?"

"Hey, Fucked-up Fitz, don't want to."

"Good call." Tate laughed.

"When do we come back to build the house?" Jude asked.

"When we finish our degrees. We come back here and build for a year and then we scatter. But the house is always here to come back to."

"Scatter?" Tate said. "Why? We stay here. Why go anywhere else?"

"Because we'll never know how great this place is until we leave it," Narnie said.

"I miss it more every time I go," Jude said.

"And you're not even from here," Fitz said.

Jude stared at him. "What?" he asked angrily. "Do you have to be born here? Or do your parents have to be buried here? Or do you have to be related?"

Fitz aimed again and fired and for a moment everyone stopped, waiting for the sound of bullet on tin. But it never came. He looked at Jude and shrugged.

"Naw. You just have to belong. Long to be."

"By blood?"

"By love," Narnie said, not looking up.

"Good call," Webb said to her, proudly.

"Then you're in, Jude," Fitz said jumping on him. "Because I love you. I love you, Jude; you're my hero. Kiss kiss kiss kiss."

"You wish." Jude threw him off and they wrestled amongst the leaves good-naturedly. Webb threw himself in and Narnie did, too, her giggling turning into a gurgling laugh as they tickled her.

And Tate just watched and listened and took it all in. "Can you hear that?" she said softly, touching her belly. "Because you belong too."

Later, they walked back to the road to see Fitz and Jude off. As usual, their goodbyes took longer than the time they had spent together at the clearing. And when the sun had gone down and the trees swayed in the canopy overhead, they parted.

"You never got that fifth tin," Webb called to Fitz just before they disappeared through the trees.

"Not to worry," he said with a wave. "I'll go back for a shot on another day."

———

"How come you and Hannah aren't together anymore?" I ask drowsily as we reach the outskirts of town.

"Hannah and I will always be together in a way. It's just hard, that's all. By the time we lost Fitz . . ."

Then there's silence again. Always silence.

"I know who he is, you know. But that's all I know. And that Webb is dead and that Tate is dying. But there's more."

"What else do you need to know, Taylor? I'm your guardian. So is Hannah. We brought you up every second that Tate let you out of her sight. If Hannah had you, she was happy."

"And if you had Hannah you were happy?"

He takes his eyes off the road. "Without you she felt guilt and remorse and despair and she'd look at me and I knew what she was thinking. That she wished I was her brother or Fitz or Tate. We weren't supposed to survive, Hannah and me. We had the least hope."

We drive onto the Jellicoe Road and I feel the presence of the five all around me but more than anything I want to tell Jude Scanlon that he is wrong about what's going through Hannah's head.

I want to tell him that deep down each time Hannah looked at him she was grateful it was him because Jude did something that the others didn't. He came back for her.

"What happened to him?" Griggs asks quietly. "Fitz?"

"He went a bit crazy, on and off," the Brigadier says after a while. "Met a sweet girl, had a kid, and then the girl died. Cancer. And I think Fitz thought that everything he touched died, so he went into self-imposed exile, like he wanted to remove himself from his kid in case he cursed her in some way. But the thing about Fitz, and Tate, too, is that they loved their baby girls and they couldn't let go. But one day when he couldn't take the demons in his head any longer . . ."

He doesn't finish the sentence. He doesn't have to.

"What about his kid?" I ask. "We should find her."

But suddenly a fire truck whizzes past us and then another and then another.

"What the hell was that?" I ask, straining my eyes to see. The Brigadier puts on his high beams but turns them off instantly. Coming our way are two more sets of headlights.

"What's happening?" Griggs says. "Why would people be on the road at this time of the night?"

A third car drives by as we pass the only light on the Jellicoe Road. I see a face pressed up against one of the back windows, a face so small and frightened that it sends a wave of shock through me that almost paralyses me. It's the face of one of my year sevens.

"The school," I whisper. "I think it's burning down."

Chapter 25

There is a sick feeling in my stomach when we reach the driveway of the school. I know my world is about to come apart and it renders me so weak I can barely breathe. At another time I would have marvelled at the colour. The blaze is spectacular; and there are slivers of light coming from trucks and cars and floodlights and spinning red sirens. But the worst thing about the slivers of light is that you get to catch people's expressions for only a split second; then they disappear again, and in between you are forced to think about what it is that could make a person look so devastated.

The Brigadier brings the car to a sudden halt. I yank open the door and hit the ground running. I have no idea who or what I'm heading for but I'm flying and I follow the light, closer and closer to the blaze. My House is burning down. *My House*. Fire trucks are parked on the lawn, pumping water into the bottom floor. Around me there is bedlam. People are everywhere, holding on to any pyjama-clad girl they can find. House leaders and teachers are keeping the students back, shouting orders for everyone to return to their Houses. The police are here, ambulance officers, fire fighters. I have never seen this many strangers at the school in my life. I want everyone to leave so that I can find my people. I get glimpses of them and I take in their faces, knowing that I need to tick off forty-nine names in my head. When the girls from Lachlan House see me, they call out or come racing over, some holding on to me with all their might. Over their heads I meet the eyes of one of the teachers, who looks shattered.

I help the girls into any of the jackets or jumpers given to us by the other houses. Three of the year sevens don't move and I kneel in front of them.

"I want you to go with these people. They'll take care of you. Tomorrow I'll come and get you. Every one of you. I promise. I swear on the holy bible."

They look at me and nod, clutching my hand, their mouths quivering, tears spilling, sobs bursting out, like machine guns of grief, creating their own carnage of despair.

"We couldn't get to them," one of them whispers. "They were in the back room where all our junk is. One of them ran there when everything started going up. But I saw them. I saw them both and they couldn't get to us and we couldn't get to them and then the whole thing just—"

"Who?" I ask, trying to keep the horror out of my voice.

"... and she was saying, 'Don't worry' ... and then everything collapsed and she was repeating, 'Don't worry, my father ... my father ... my father ...' What did she always used to say about her father, Taylor? I can't remember anymore."

I feel someone put a blanket around me but I don't turn around to see who it is. I hold on to these three kids until one of the Townie parents comes to take them away. Then I see Raffy standing next to Ms. Morris, who is looking completely bewildered. For one moment my life goes back to the way it was half an hour ago. My heart beats at a regular pace. I make my way towards them, watching Raffy's manic movements as she scribbles stuff down on a sheet of paper. When she looks up, I almost don't recognise her. It's like I've been away for one million years and the world has changed.

"I've got all their names down," she says to me and Ms. Morris in that practical tone of hers. "I've written down T if they've gone to the town or the House name if they've gone there. See. So we can keep count and we'll know where to find them all later."

I can't read the list because her hand is shaking so much. We look at each other and I nod because I can't speak.

"I've got all the phone numbers as well," she says.

"How many are missing?" I manage to ask.

"Two."

I hear my gasping and I think, Not now, Taylor. Not everything is about your inability to breathe under pressure.

"Show me the list." I wheeze.

But she shakes her head over and over again. "Wait until everyone's here, Taylor. Just two more names and everyone will be here. *Everyone.*"

I look over at the House as it continues to burn. I

look at the fire fighters hovering outside.

I take the list out of Raffy's trembling hands and I see all the names of every person in my House, except for two. A wave of nausea comes over me. Please, not these two. Please, not any of them.

"Let's get you out of here," I hear Ms. Morris say. "It won't do your breathing any good with all this smoke."

But she's just one of the voices and one of the faces I see.

Raffy busies herself, chatting incessantly, ushering the year sevens and eights into the trail of cars that have come from the town. I see Santangelo's mum arrive. I want to go back to two weeks ago when she was calling Santangelo a little shit and Jessa and I were giggling at the organised turmoil of their household, wishing we belonged to it but relieved that we were able to walk away.

Raffy continues with her instructions. "Georgina's a diabetic, no sugar, insulin first thing in the morning. . . . Sarah, put in your plate before you lose it. . . ."

I see Trini of Darling House. No hysterics from her. Just a practical business-like ordering around and then we look at each other and she touches me, but I pull away because I'm a block of ice. I don't want to feel anything. I don't want to think.

"We'll take the seniors and the tens. Hastings will take the year nines," she tells me.

I just nod at her and she nods back and gets down to business.

Behind me Raffy is still giving instructions. ". . . she's allergic to penicillin . . . and they've got an assessment task. It's about Me, Myself, and I, and they have to collect at least five examples of . . ."

Everything is up close and then it swings away and the swaying of it plays with my stomach. Then Chaz is there, looking at me with such sadness, and then he sees Raffy.

". . . no peanuts. Peanuts will kill her so don't even breathe peanuts on her. . . ."

"Raf," he says in a tired voice. That's all. Just "Raf."

Then he holds her and for a moment I hear silence— that totally silent part of a cry that announces that the most horrible grief is going to follow. And it does and he's muffling it but I can hear and I want someone to come over and jab her with a sedative because its pitch pierces my soul.

I sway, watching Santangelo's father walk towards us. How come everyone looks a thousand years older in just a couple of hours?

He kneels next to Raffy. "Are you sure you haven't seen them?" he asks gently, trying to make himself heard over the noise. "They could have been taken by one of the parents into town."

She's shaking her head over and over again. "Sal," she whispers, horrified. "They're in the House."

I begin walking towards it, the blanket falling off my shoulders.

Jessa. Chloe P. Jessa. Chloe P. I'm walking towards the House. Jessa and Chloe P. are in the back room of the dorm. I'm running. Their names are in my mind then I realise that I'm not thinking them: I'm grunting their names and it hurts. Jessa and Chloe P. Then I'm there, next to the fire trucks a few metres away from the front verandah.

"Jessa!" I yell so hoarsely that it's like the sound rings through my ears and makes them pop. "Chloe!" Someone's hands are holding me back. The Brigadier's hands. Jude Scanlon's hands. And then I see the fire fighters pour out of the house, racing towards us, just as a crashing sound deafens our ears. Everyone stands back, helplessly watching. Windows are smashing under the pressure and the fire roars at us, like some ogre refusing to let us in.

I look around and the world becomes a hazy black blizzard. I sink lower and lower. I hear "someone grab her" and "get a bloody ambulance" and a claw-like hand finds its way into my mouth, down my throat, and into my lungs and it grabs my breath and squeezes the life out of it and I let it and let it and let it. . . .

I am with the boy in the tree in my dreams. I can breathe up here and I'm happy and I tell him that I had this dream where I went to a school off the Jellicoe Road and we fought a war with the Cadets and Townies and how I had lost because I had surrendered myself to the leader of the enemy years before.

Then I hear the sobbing and we both look in the direction of the sound.

"Where does he come from?" I ask.

The boy looks at me, confused. "You brought him to me, Taylor. Weeks ago."

"Me?"

"He won't come out," he tells me, "and I can't find my way in."

I crawl towards the sound, closer and closer, and when I'm a breath away from it, I put my hand through the branches and I leave it there and although it seems to take ages, he takes hold of my hand and drags me in. Then I'm sitting face to face with the Hermit and he's crying, "Forgive me, forgive me."

I realise that it's not me he's speaking to and I know what I have to do. I hold his hand firmly and convince him to come out with me onto the branch where the boy is waiting.

We sit there, the boy, the Hermit, and I, for a while. Sometimes I think I can hear people calling my name but I block it out because at the moment there is no other place I want to be. The boy leans over and tells me to explain to the Hermit that there is nothing to forgive and I do, and the look on the Hermit's face is one of pure joy.

They reminisce about Tate and Narnie and Jude. They talk about the Prayer Tree and of the messages they wrote on the trunk. They tell me about the tunnel and how once they timed themselves getting from one end to the other and how Webb fainted because he had never seen the world that dark. "We saw the devil down there," the Hermit tells me, and they laugh so hard that I'm jealous that I can't join in.

I stand up because from here everything looks fantastic and the boy smiles a smile that creases his cheeks and I will never see anything more beautiful. Then he takes my hand and walks me over to the edge.

I look at Webb and I say, "It was me you were coming for all along."

But he shakes his head and throws me over the side. . . .

I open my eyes. The faces around me look shocked and ashen. The Brigadier, Santangelo's dad, the fire chief. Raffaela is holding my inhaler to my lips. A second later, Griggs and Santangelo skid to a halt in front of me, staring. Griggs looks like he's seen a ghost. Does he know something that I don't know? He tries to talk to me, tries to take hold of me, but Santangelo's dad pushes him away gently. "Give her room."

"We heard . . ." Santangelo begins, his breathing is

so heavy he can hardly speak.

I'm back in reality now and suddenly I remember everything. But there's too much noise in my ears and too many people talking at the same time. I look beyond everyone to the House. Back there, everything seems to be under control but I know something is strange and I stare at the men in front of me. "You can't find them, can you? You can't find their bodies?"

I can tell the guy from the rural fire brigade is surprised because he exchanges a look with Santangelo's dad.

"And there's no other way out of that dorm."

"They wouldn't have been able to get out," Santangelo's dad says, "They're two little girls."

But I'm looking at the Brigadier and I see something in his eyes. "Except through the ground. 'My father said there's a tunnel somewhere down there,'" I whisper. "It's what Jessa used to say and Fitz would know, wouldn't he, Jude? You knew who she was, didn't you?" I say, turning to Santangelo's dad. "It's why you guys took her in for the holidays. You knew she belonged to Fitz."

"Let's get you to the hospital," Santangelo's dad

says, standing up and whistling over some of the emergency crew.

"She's in the tunnel, Jude. It's under Lachlan House, isn't it? It begins in the storeroom. Isn't that where they got stuck? Chloe P. ran to the storeroom when the fire started and Jessa went after her and that's where they got trapped."

Jude stands up, staring back at the house and then at me and then he turns in the direction of Murrumbidgee House.

"What's going on?" Santangelo's dad asks him quietly.

Jude shakes his head, confused. "Let's go," he says, holding out his hand to me.

The guy from the rural fire brigade looks irritated. "You're trying to tell me that you believe there's a tunnel that runs under those Houses?" he asks as Jude breaks into a run and everyone follows.

"I should know," Jude says as I try hard to keep up. "I helped build it."

We tear into Murrumbidgee House and Jude leads us straight through the dorms into the laundry. The kids in the dorm are shaken and still in a state of shock and I notice Richard with them, as if he hasn't left their side all night. We throw everything out of the way and there, under five tiles in the corner of the laundry, is a hole in the ground.

"Jesus Christ," Santangelo's dad says, shaking his head.

There's a shit fight about who goes under. The guy from the rural fire brigade volunteers but Santangelo's dad tells him that he's built like a brick shit house and can hardly get through the laundry door, let alone a hole in the floor, so he's eliminated instantly. Even Mr. Palmer offers but he's a heart attack waiting to happen, although no one says it to him in those words.

"I'm going," Jude says firmly.

"Sir, you've been driving for almost thirteen hours straight," Griggs says. "I'll go."

"I'm the fittest," Santangelo argues.

"I'm in the Cadets, you dick. Do you know how many times I've had to crawl on my stomach?"

"You're not going down there," Santangelo's dad says forcefully. "Neither of you are."

"Are you?" Santangelo asks. "You've got high blood pressure and mum will kill me if I let you go down."

"I'm going," Jude says. "I built it."

Griggs is already poking his head down the hole. He looks at Jude. "I'm presuming it's head first because there doesn't seem to be any room to move your body around."

"Jonah . . ."

"Let me do this," Griggs says. He looks at me. "I need to do this."

Jude knows he has no choice and reluctantly agrees. "You'll be on your stomach for most of the time."

"Hold on a minute," the rural brigade guy says, having watched the whole exchange. "Chances are they might . . ."

. . . be dead. Jessa and Chloe P. could be dead. Worse still is the fact that Griggs might come across the bodies. That's what the fire chief doesn't want to say.

I want to say one thousand things to Griggs but Jude has already taken hold of his boots, ready to hold him upside down.

"We can't waste any more time. If you find the girls, you won't be able to turn around. There's absolutely no room. You'll have to travel backwards.

We'll try to get as much light as possible in there but for the time being you'll have our torches. It's darker than anyplace you've been in on drills, Jonah."

Griggs nods and he goes down before anyone says another word.

Looking at Santangelo's dad's face makes me realise that he doesn't believe that anything good is going to come of this. That's the worst thing about cops. They see so many bad things and they rarely get a happy ending. Santangelo is the same. He spends the whole time with his head in the hole, shining the torch into the tunnel so Griggs can have a bit of light.

"When I fainted," I begin telling Jude, "I saw my father and I saw the Hermit but it was really Fitz. I always remember him looking old but it's only per-spective. Like that time I saw him when he had the gun and he kept saying, 'Forgive me, Forgive me,' but he was never speaking to me. It was Webb he was speaking to. All this time, I thought that Webb was bringing him along into my dream but now I realise that I was bringing him along to Webb's. All he wanted was forgiveness and Webb said, 'Tell him, nothing to forgive.'"

Santangelo's dad stares at me and then at Jude. I know they think I'm crazy but I know I'm not.

"It was such a good dream," I tell Jude, wanting him to believe me, "and I wanted to stay but he threw me off the tree and then I woke up."

"You weren't asleep, Taylor," Mr. Palmer says flatly, "and you didn't faint."

Someone comes in with floodlights and they put them down the hole. Richard crouches next to me and we wait.

"You think Jessa and Chloe P. are down there?" he asks.

"I know they are."

He moves as close to the hole as possible and then crawls back to where I am. "Who built it?" he asks.

"Hannah, the Brigadier, Jessa's dad, and my mum and dad. My dad was the leader of Murrumbidgee House, you know," I explain, and for the first time in my whole life I feel a sense of pride. "He was the one who came up with the idea."

"That explains your psychotic personality," he mutters before leaving.

I watch the rural brigade guy because he looks like he's going to be our number one prophet of doom.

"Jude? Can I have a word?" he asks. There's this look between them that I don't trust.

"You're going to ask him how long they can stay down there, aren't you?" I say, looking to Jude for the answer. "How long they have left."

There is silence for a moment and even Santangelo pulls his head out of the hole just to hear the answer.

"Fastest anyone did it was twenty minutes: Narnie. It was because she was small so Jessa and the other little girl have got that on their side."

"Her name's Chloe," Mr. Palmer informs him.

"Slowest?" I ask.

"Forty minutes. One of us fainted down there and by the time we got him out he was having trouble breathing. You've got to understand that you're not actually crawling through a tunnel. You're squeezing through a hole."

"Webb?" I ask.

He nods. "Webb was stocky."

"Why did you let Jonah go, then?" I ask, angrily. "He's massive and he'll get stuck."

"Because he's still smaller or fitter than any of us. Besides he won't freak out and he's got endurance and believe me, Taylor, down there . . ."

". . . you see the devil because it's so dark."

He nods. "I did the whole return trip only once and vowed I would never do it again. It was different when we were building, because we started digging from both ends, so we'd only have to crawl for half the way."

"So how long have they been down there?" Santangelo asks.

"I'm guessing they would have stayed in the room until the smoke became too much for them. I'd say it's already been thirty minutes."

"Wouldn't they have got to this end by now?"

No one says anything. Santangelo's head disappears in the hole again and I look at Jude, wanting to read something, *anything*, on his face.

We sit next to each other in silence while the emergency crew comes in and out and the ambulance officers begin to arrive. Sometimes I see Murrumbidgee faces at the door but Santangelo's dad instructs Richard to take them upstairs to the senior rooms. Because he thinks they're going to be wheeling out bodies through the dorm and he doesn't want the kids to see them. For the billionth time I feel sick.

"She didn't write about being in the tunnel," I say to Jude quietly.

"She didn't write about a lot of things."

"Why? Was being in the tunnel worse than seeing her mother dead . . . or more personal than what happened between you and her?"

I don't think he likes that I know the intimate details of their lives.

"When Webb didn't return from the tunnel and everyone was getting anxious, she went in. Narnie was bloody frightening when she was fearless. I remember their faces when we pulled them out. She was—God, I don't know—stunned."

"Do you think he told her something?" I asked. "Maybe he told her that he was leaving you all. Maybe he'd had enough of Narnie's depression or Tate wanting to consume him. Maybe it wasn't Fitz after all. . . ."

"No, I think he did something in the tunnel that Narnie had done long ago. He lost hope. Webb without hope was like the engine failing on a plane. He was our life force and I think she saw that down in the tunnel and it frightened her."

"Shhh," Santangelo says to everyone. "I think I

hear something." He puts his head and half his body down the hole again and his father holds on to his legs, around the knees.

I can't hear a thing. We wait, my pulse beating out of control and another sick feeling comes over me.

Just say Griggs loses hope down there. And Chloe P. And Jessa.

Just say Jessa never giggles again. Or sings karaoke or pesters me with a trillion inane questions. Just say she never snuggles up in bed with the other girls, whispering about the boys they have crushes on. Just say she never grows up to be my age and just say she never falls in love or gets to know what type of people her parents were. Just say she never gets to be someone's mother and someone's life-long friend.

Just say she never gets to hear me say that I always knew she was something special and that's why I was so horrible to her. Because people with that much spirit frighten the hell out of me. They make me want to be a better person when I know it's not possible.

"Okay," Santangelo's muffled voice says, and they begin pulling him up. He's holding Griggs's legs and there's dirt everywhere. Everyone's hands are grabbing at anything, trying to get them out of there. I see Griggs's torso, absolutely blackened, and then his arms and then his hands and then more hands and I can tell it's Jessa but she's not moving. He's panting and they're pulling Jessa out and the emergency crew are placing breathing stuff over both their mouths and they won't let me near until they have everything in place.

Griggs looks shaken and I know that it's killing him but he can't go down again.

He looks at Santangelo, who looks at his father, who reluctantly nods.

"If you close your eyes, you get to control your own darkness," Jude tells Santangelo. "Do you understand?"

Santangelo nods and they help him in.

I don't want to feel relief, because Jessa isn't moving and Chloe P. is still down there. I go over to Jessa but the emergency crew are working on her and they need their space. I feel useless.

"Will she know your voice?" one of the ambulance people ask me.

I nod. "Of course."

"I think I broke her arm," Griggs says, wincing

from where he is lying.

"Don't you move until we can check you out, too," one of the ambulance officers says.

We hover over them and the ambulance man looks at me. "Talk to her. We need her to respond."

I lie down next to Jessa and take her hand. For a moment I don't know what to say. So I tell her the story she loves best. Of her father who stole a bike and rode down the Jellicoe Road and saved the lives of my parents and Hannah. I tell her that they loved him like a brother and how that night changed their lives forever. I tell her about Tate's sister, who was only eight years old when she died, and how Fitz went into the wreckage for the umpteenth time to carry out her body as well as the bodies of my other grandparents, knowing he could die at any moment. And when I can't tell the story anymore because it breaks my heart, Santangelo's dad takes over, because he was there that night. The ambulance driver has his story to tell about Fitz McKenzie as well and Jude fills in the rest.

I sit there and listen to the history of my family, the Schroeders and the Markhams, who set out on their separate journeys that day not realising the tragic ironies and joys of that collision of worlds on the Jellicoe Road. And of the people they would never have met if it hadn't happened. Like Fitz and Jude.

And me.

Of the people I would never have met if I had just belonged to one half of them. Like Raffy and Jessa and Chaz and Ben.

And Jonah Griggs.

I look at him as they patch him up and he looks back at me and I know that it will be one of the last chances I'll have to see him this close for a very long time.

Again we sit in silence, waiting for Santangelo to emerge and, five minutes later, Chloe P. comes out of the tunnel crying and she clutches onto me while they check her out for any broken bones. Her face is caked with mud and she panics any time they try to put the mask over her face.

And then, for the first time all night everyone breathes in rhythm. Mr. Palmer, like every other adult I've seen tonight, looks a thousand years older but he's relieved and breaks the hands-off rule, hugging me so tight that I almost stop breathing. Again.

"Are they okay?" Richard asks from the door.

The ambulance man gives the thumbs-up and Richard disappears behind the door and a couple of seconds later we hear shouting and cheering and stamping of feet from upstairs and outside and the place becomes a circus.

When they wheel the girls out, the whole school seems to be lining the driveway. Lachlan girls are jumping all over me, flying at me from all directions. I look for Griggs but he gets swallowed up in the mayhem and I feel a weariness that I can't shake.

When we get to the hospital, Raffy and most of the year sevens and eights who had been taken down to the town are there. I don't think anyone has the heart to tell them to stop making a racket.

"This is the best night of my life," Raffy says, crying.

"Raffy, half our House has burnt down," I say wearily. "We don't have a kitchen."

"Why do you always have to be so pessimistic?" she asks. "We can double up in our rooms and have a barbecue every night like the Cadets."

Silently I vow to keep Raffy around for the rest of my life.

I wake up in the waiting room of the hospital, leaning against Jude's shoulder. He's reading a newspaper and glances at me when I move. I look at him for a long time, maybe because for so long, every single time he crossed my path I had looked away. I had misunderstood my anxiety.

"I remember . . . being on your shoulders," I say sleepily.

"I remember you being on my shoulders," he says, putting down the newspaper.

I sit up and stretch, my neck is out in so many places. "You were wrong yesterday in the car, you know," I tell him. "About how every time Hannah looks at you she's wishing you were someone else. I think that every time she looks at you she's scared you won't come back, like the others."

He doesn't say anything but after a moment or two he smiles sadly. "Your mother rang Hannah six weeks ago. Told her that she didn't have much time left but that Hannah owed her. That she wanted to die clean."

He stops for a moment and I know there'll be many of these pauses. For a second or two I close my eyes because I want to go back to the tree but I don't. I go back to the shoulders of the giant.

"Hannah was . . . inconsolable, like she was when we knew Webb was dead and when Fitz died. Worse still, Tate's plan was crazy. If there was ever a time that Tate needed drugs, it was now but you don't know your mother. She had it all worked out. Forget rehab, she wouldn't be able to cope with the affirmations and she couldn't deal with spending so much time in the end with strangers. She was going to go cold turkey, even the chemo was going to stop, and she wanted Hannah and me there with her. So I went and got her and Hannah came down and they've been up in the mountains outside Sydney."

"It's because my mother wanted to die beholden to no one. Like Mrs. Dubose."

"No, it wasn't that. When I signed her out she said, 'I want to die clean for my baby girl, Jude. That's all I want. It's all I have to give her.'"

I wonder about things. Like what she thinks I look like and if she and my father ever spoke about what they wanted for me. But before I can say anything, Jude's looking over my shoulder and I see a change in him. I've never seen this look on his face before but I've imagined it. The way Jude Scanlon would have looked when he saw Narnie standing by the side of the road when he was fourteen.

I turn in the direction of his gaze and there she is, coming through the hospital doors. Hannah.

I stand up and walk towards her because my days of waiting for more are over. If I want more, I need to go and get it, demand it, take hold of it with all my might, and do the best I can with it. I put my arms around her and hold her tight and for once there is nothing between us. I'm holding one of only two people left in the world who share my blood: my father's sister, who one night sat in the same spot for four hours just to protect her brother from a sight that would have killed his spirit.

"Is my mum here?" I ask quietly when she lets go.

"At the hospice. We can drive to Sydney tomorrow."

I shake my head. "Hannah," I say, "I think my father would want her to come home. To the house by the river."

She nods. For once I get to make the decisions. "So where are our little tunnel rats?" she asks over my head, looking at Jude.

He takes her hand and draws her to his side. They don't say anything as they walk with me, but I've been here before, so I know that words aren't needed. I remember love. These two people taught it to me and when I see Hannah lean over and kiss Jessa's sleeping head, I know that for the rest of my life, no matter what, Hannah and Jude are going to be there. Like they always have been. And tomorrow I'll need them more than ever.

When my mother returns home for the last time to the Jellicoe Road.

Chapter 26

Aftermath. Everyone uses it all the time so I get very used to the word. In the aftermath we face the reality that the downstairs area of Lachlan is gutted. No photos, no posters, no fish, no clothing, no books, no diaries. Everything's gone. In the aftermath, when the walls of my world are blackened and the taste in my mouth is of ash, my mother is due to re-enter my life for what will be the last couple of weeks of hers. In the aftermath Jonah Griggs prepares to leave and I have to take it on good faith and a great gut feeling that we will see each other, maybe for the rest of our lives. In the aftermath I finally accept that my father is dead and that the legacy left behind by the person who killed him is a thirteen-year-old kid who clutches my arm as we look at the space around us and whispers, "I knew you'd come and get me, Taylor. I told Chloe P., 'Don't worry, Taylor will find us.'"

I hear Mr. Palmer tell Hannah that it was an electrical fault. Five arsonists in one school and it ends up being something so technically boring. They promise us that the dorm and kitchen will be complete by the time we return from the Christmas holidays in a couple of months' time and I miss the girls already. I miss everything in my world already.

We spend Griggs's last day at Hannah's house with Santangelo and Raffy. It's the first time he meets Hannah, apart from when we were fourteen, and the mood is cool and almost hostile.

"You seem to have a problem with me," he says in typical Griggs fashion.

I can tell he regrets saying it when he is treated to one of Hannah's long cold gazes.

"I think it will be a while before I forgive the trip to Sydney," she says flatly.

"Fair enough. I think it will be a while before I forgive you for what you put her through over the past six weeks."

I watch them both and for the first time it occurs to me that I'm no longer flying solo and that I have no intention of pretending that I am. I have an aunt and I have a Griggs and this is what it's like to have connections with people.

"Do you know what?" I ask both of them. "If you don't build a bridge and get over it, I'll never forgive either of you."

From the verandah I watch Griggs inside, through the window, chatting to Raffy and Santangelo.

I can feel Hannah's gaze on me and I ignore it for as long as I can.

"I know what you're thinking," I say.

She doesn't speak.

"Say something," I say, wanting to take every bad feeling I have out on Hannah because she's so convenient.

"What do you want me to say?" she asks with that ever-patient voice of hers.

"What you're thinking."

"Okay. Why does it have to be so intense between you two?" she asks.

"Because I have an aunt named Narnie and a mother named Tate," I snap, and I want to stop myself from being like this but I can't. I'm too sad. I look at her and I can feel tears in my eyes. "Do you think I don't want him to be gone more than you do? *I do.* Because I need to know that I can still breathe properly when he's not around. If something happens to him, I have to know that I won't fall apart like Tate did without Webb. Even you and Jude. It's not just my father or Fitz or even Tate you've missed all this time. It's Jude not being in your life."

"Jude is in my life, Taylor."

"Then why aren't you together?"

"He's a soldier, Taylor," she says tiredly. "He goes where they send him. East Timor. Solomon Islands. Iraq. Wherever they need to keep the peace. Why is it that we always have to fight?"

"We're not fighting, Hannah. I just don't want to hold back anymore and I don't want you to, either. I'm your only living relative and one day I'm going to have to visit you in a nursing home and spoon-feed you custard and jelly, so I think I'm entitled to know what makes you tick."

She stares at me and I get this feeling of love because I know her history now and understand how it has made her the way she is at times.

"What makes me tick? Tate. Jessa. You. Jude."

"When you look at him, he thinks you're thinking that you'd rather he was Webb or Fitz or Tate. Did you know that?"

"He knows how much he means to me. He wouldn't think that."

"He told me. I asked him why you weren't together and he said you'll always be together but that's bullshit. I've worked it out and I'm presuming that you were a couple until I was seven, but in the past ten years you've been apart and the only time you see each other is when it has to do with me. You wrote the book on all of this, Hannah. Did you never notice that he always felt left out? It's like he wanted to be in that accident or he wanted to be crazy like Fitz. Like being Jude Scanlon wasn't good enough for any of you."

"You don't know what you're talking about."

"Why won't you marry him?"

"Because he hasn't asked me. Maybe it was never meant to be that type of relationship. Maybe it was because we survived. The bond—"

"Hannah, Jude and you don't have a bond because you're the only survivors. Jude and you have a *problem* because you're the survivors. It's like you can't forgive each other. How come you can forgive Tate for what she did and Webb for dying? And Fitz! How come you can forgive him? He killed your brother! He shot him out of a tree! You can forgive all of them but you can't forgive you and Jude for living."

Hannah looks stunned. "What do you want me to say? That if he asked me to marry him, I'd say yes? Okay. Yes. But grief makes a monster out of us sometimes, Taylor, and sometimes you say and do things to the people you love that you can't forgive yourself for."

But I won't let it go. "I'd forgive myself. To be with Jonah I'd do anything."

Jude pulls up at the same time that Griggs comes out of the house.

"I've got to go," Griggs says from the door. Hannah turns and I notice that she's more fragile than I've ever seen her. She's nursed a drug addict for the past six weeks and I can tell by her gauntness that it hasn't been good for her. What went down between her and Tate, I wonder? Was Tate forever envious of the bond between Webb and Narnie? Is that why she wouldn't let Hannah mother me all those years?

"Have a safe trip, Jonah," Hannah says quietly.

"Thank you."

He waits for me. "I'll catch up," I tell him as Raffy and Santangelo walk towards Jude, shaking his hand goodbye.

The plan is that Jude drives down with the Cadets and returns tomorrow with my mother. It's what he always seems to be doing—saving us from ourselves. I remember the saints from Raffy's books in year seven. St. Jude was the patron saint of the impossible—lost and desperate causes. I think he hit the jackpot in that department when he met the Markhams and Schroeders.

"You need anything?" Jude asks from the bottom of the steps.

Hannah shakes her head. "Don't drive if you're tired tomorrow."

"I'd better be going," I say quietly, walking down the steps. When I reach him, I stop.

I want to say a lot of things to Jude and Hannah. I want to thank them and tell them that my life would be like Sam's if it wasn't for them. I want to tell them that the brilliance of that memory of lying between them won't be easily surpassed and that the stories of their love for each other touch me in a way I didn't think possible. I want to convince them that my father comes to speak to me at night and that his love for the two of them is never-ending.

"Jude," I say, taking a deep breath. "Hannah reckons that if you ask her to marry you, she'll say yes."

I pat him on the shoulder and walk away, breaking into a run when I reach the clearing. Griggs is waiting. He takes my hand and we walk.

The Cadets leave from the general store. There is a crowd outside the buses while goodbyes are said and much-needed munchy provisions are purchased. I stay close to Griggs while he talks to people around him and although we don't say a word to each other, we are never more than an inch apart. Every now and again, while he's speaking to Santangelo's mum or some of the Townies, our eyes meet and I dare not open my mouth in case I cry.

One of their teachers calls them from the bus and they begin to file on, calling out last-minute goodbyes. I watch Ben give instructions to Anson Choi, and the Mullet Brothers argue with them at the bus window. They have some gig planned in Canberra and they can't agree on the songs or their order. But I can tell they all like one another so much even if one of the Mullet Brothers has Ben in a headlock, pretending to hit his head against the side of the bus.

Ben pulls away and walks towards us, putting his arm around my shoulder ever so innocently.

"I think you guys need to be on the bus," he says to Griggs.

"And I think you may end up under it," Griggs says, gently pulling me away from Ben.

We stand looking at each other and, as usual with Griggs, it's much too intense.

"So are you going to tell your mother about me?" he asks.

I look around to where Teresa, the hostage from Darling, is crying while her Cadet watches miserably from the bus window.

I shrug. "I'll probably mention that I'm in love with you."

He chuckles. "Only you would say that in such a I-think-I'll-wash-my-hair-tonight tone."

He leans down and kisses me and I hold on to his shirt, wanting to savour every moment.

I hear a few wolf-whistles but he ignores them and we linger.

My insides are in a million pieces and I feel like

someone out of one of those tragic war movies.

The bus driver honks the horn.

"You know on the Jellicoe Road where there's that tree that looks like an old man bent over?" he asks, holding my face between his hands. It's this feeling I'll miss most.

I nod.

"That's the closest mobile phone coverage to the School."

"Griggs, they're waiting," Santangelo says quietly.

"Let them wait."

We kiss again and I don't care who is watching or how late they'll be.

Slowly he untangles himself from me and turns to the others. "See you, Raffy," he says, lifting her off the ground in a hug. He looks at Santangelo. "You drive them down at Christmas," he says. "Promise?"

They grip each other's hands and hug quickly and then he kisses me again and he's on the bus. I can see him walking down the aisle, giving someone the finger, and I can imagine what's being said inside.

Teresa is sobbing beside me and Trini is trying to console her.

"He's in year eight, Teresa," I remind her. "That means he's coming back at least another three times."

"But just say he forgets about me or meets someone else or pretends I don't exist."

I look at her and then at Trini and Raffy.

"Teresa, Teresa. Have we taught you nothing?" Raffy says in an irritated voice. "It's war. You go in and you hunt him down until he realises that he's made a mistake."

Teresa looks hopeful.

"It's not as if men haven't gone to war for dumber reasons," Trini adds.

The Mullet Brothers join us and we watch the bus as it leaves. I can sense everyone's sadness.

We all walk towards town together.

"You want us to be there tomorrow?" Santangelo asks quietly.

I nod.

"Done."

I feel tears running down my face and Raffy takes my hand and squeezes it.

"What are you so sad about?" Santangelo says to me. "We're going to know him for the rest of our lives."

The car pulls up in front of the house and I stand up. In the photos, when she was seventeen, she had lush black hair, white white skin, and dark blue eyes and a plumpness that spoke of good health. When I was young she had bleached the hair, her skin was pasty, her eyes were always bloodshot, and she was skinny. I can hardly ever remember her eating, just nervously smoking one cigarette after another. I don't know which image is stronger in my mind but I know I want the girl with the black hair and the glow in her cheeks.

The person who emerges, though, has neither, courtesy of the chemotherapy. She's even thinner than I remember and I'm amazed that she is actually as young as Hannah and Jude. But I can see from here that her eyes are sharp and bright. She looks beyond the house to the oak tree by the river, a ghost of a smile on her face, and I know she's imagining him there, like Hannah does on those breezy afternoons when it's just her and her thoughts. And like I do when he visits me in my dreams.

She smiles at something Jude says and then she walks towards the house, slowly. I stand at the top of the stairs, looking for any sign of me in her face. I wonder how hard it was for her all that time seeing Webb and Narnie's face stamped on mine and not one single mark of her. When she's almost at the steps, she notices me and stops. There is wonder in her face, like she can't believe what she's seeing. I think she's expecting the sullen eleven-year-old that she left behind and for a moment I'm scared that she doesn't know it's me. But then she starts to cry. Not dramatically but with such sadness, clutching at her throat, looking at me like she can't believe her eyes. She tries to speak but she isn't able to. I walk down the steps of the verandah towards her and with shaking hands she holds my face between them, sobbing, "Look at my beautiful girl."

I take in every inch of her face, the sick pallor of her skin, the dryness of her lips, and I lean forward and I press my lips against hers, like I want to give them colour again. I touch her face and the bristle of her hair that's growing back. I like the feel of it under my fingertips, like a massage.

"It's not good for Tate to be outside," Jude says quietly.

I take her by the hand, up the stairs and inside the house, and she looks around again in awe.

"It's just like he planned it," she says in a hushed tone as Hannah comes over and kisses her gently. I introduce her to Santangelo and Raffy and then Jessa comes running into the house, her arm in a sling, beaming that crazy beam of hers.

"I'm late and I didn't want to be but they had to fix my cast and Mr. Palmer was late picking me up." She looks at my mother. "Did they tell you about the fire and tunnel and how Griggs broke my arm?"

I take Jessa's other hand and bring her forward. "This is Jessa McKenzie. She belongs to Fitz."

My mother looks at Jessa, shaking her head like she can't believe what she's seeing. Hannah comes over and helps her into the chair by the window, putting a pillow behind her, and we hover around her.

"Look at our girls," she says to Hannah and Jude. "How did we get to be so lucky?"

"I think we've earned it, Tate."

Later, she fills the spaces between Hannah's stories and my imaginings. She tells me about the time my father had a dream about me before I was born. How we were sitting in a tree and he asked me my name and I said it was Taylor.

Chapter 27

And life goes on, which seems kind of strange and cruel when you're watching someone die. But there's a joy and an abundance of everything, like information and laughter and summer weather and so many stories. My mother urges me to write them down because, "You're the last of the Markhams, my love." So I record dates and journeys and personalities and traits and heroes and losers and weaknesses and strengths and I try to capture every one of those people because one day I'll need what they had to offer. Worst and best of all, I get to see who Tate Markham could have been and sometimes I feel so angry that I only got to know this incredible person just when I'm going to lose her. She has a belly laugh that Narnie wasn't able to hear in her grief, so Hannah wasn't able to write about it. But if Webb had written the story, I would have known that laugh already. She tells me about her sister, Lily, who was only eight years old when she died, and of how she can still remember the day her father placed her in Tate's arms, when she was four years old, and said, "How blessed can one man be?"

And life goes on.

When some days are worse than others, I find myself walking out of school and sitting at that point on the Jellicoe Road where I can ring Jonah. I'll feel his frustration and his sense of uselessness at being six hundred kilometres away but I need to hear his stories about Danny and his mum and her boyfriend, Jack, and how they have Thai food on Tuesday nights and watch *The Bill*. I'll tell him about Jude moving in and how he sleeps in Hannah's room and of how Tate and I bullied them into going away one weekend by stressing our need to have time alone together. And of how Raffy and I have to share Trini's room while Lachlan House gets refurbished and how we have to join Trini in prayer at night. And I can sense his envy when he hears about our weekends with the Santangelos and how Chaz's mum tells Hannah and Tate about those "two little shits" driving around town in an unregistered car.

And life goes on.

When one day fate visits us again, Jessa comes running into Hannah's house to tell us the news that they've caught the serial killer. Her tone is hushed and I try hard not to look at Jude, who is working on the skirting boards. But I can feel the humour in his gaze as it falls on me and I know that I will never live down the fact that I suspected him. When I ask her, "Who?" slightly curious, she's already out the door looking for Hannah and Tate. "No one important!" she shouts from the other room. "Just some postman in Yass." I look at Jude's face and I see it whiten and we vow never ever to tell the others. My mind that night is full of images of those kids I once saw in the newspaper cuttings on Jessa's bed and of the two who went missing from Yass on the day Jude caught up with me and Jonah. And of the voice Jonah needed to believe was his father, warning us not to go any farther because we would never come back.

And life goes on.

When we know it's close I move into the house

and we lie there, my mother and I. I place the earphones in her ears and I let her listen to the music Webb was listening to when he died. Of flame trees and missing those who aren't around. I tell her that he's been waiting all these years for her and that ever since she's been with me he's visited my dreams every single night. I tell her that the euphoria he feels is like an elixir—one that I believe will be enough to keep her alive.

But one night he's not there anymore, nor is Fitz, and my despair is beyond words and I'm screaming out for him, for both of them, standing on the branch where we'd sit. "Webb! Fitz! Please. Come back. Please." And I wake up and I hold her in my arms, sobbing uncontrollably, "Just one more day, please, Mummy, just one more day, please." And when it hurts too much, I go up to Hannah and Jude's room and tell them that she's dead, and I climb between them and I am raw inside.

My mother took seventeen years to die. I counted.

She died in a house on the Jellicoe Road. The prettiest road I'd ever seen, where trees made breezy canopies like a tunnel to Shangri-la.

God's country, Raffy says. She swears to God it'll change the way I see the world.

Want to believe in something.

But love the world just the way it is.

Some ask me why she didn't give up earlier. The pain without drugs would have been bad. Others say that it was wrong for us not to ease her pain. But my mother said she wouldn't die until she had something to leave her daughter.

So we scatter her ashes with Fitz's from the Prayer Tree and in the summer we finish a journey my father and Hannah began almost two decades ago. Jude arranges a house by the ocean with Griggs and his brother and Chaz and Raffy and Jessa and Narnie and me.

While we watch the others throwing themselves into the surf, I sit with Jessa and Hannah, who cuddles us towards her.

"I wanted to see the ocean," she tells us, "and my father said that it was about time the four of us made that journey. I remember asking, 'What's the difference between a trip and a journey?' and my father said—"

She stops for a moment, to catch her breath. "He

said, 'Narnie, my love, when we get there, you'll understand,' and that was the last thing he ever said."

Jessa leans her head against her. "Hannah, do you think that your mum and dad and Tate's mum and dad and my mum and dad and Webb and Tate are all together someplace?" she asks earnestly.

I look at Hannah, waiting for the answer. And then she smiles. Webb once said that a Narnie smile was a revelation and, at this moment, I need a revelation. And I get one.

"I wonder," Hannah says.

Epilogue

He sat in the tree, his mind overwhelmed by the idea that growing inside Tate was their baby. The cat purred alongside him, a co-conspirator in his contentment. Through the branches he could see Fitz coming his way, his gun balanced on his shoulders, whistling a tune. So Webb closed his eyes, thinking of the dream he'd had the night before where he sat on the branch of a tree and spoke to their child. In the child's voice there was so much promise and joy that it took his breath away. He told her about his plans to build a house. He'd make it out of gopherwood, like Noah's ark, two storeys high, with a view he could look out on every day with wonder. A house for Tate and Narnie and Jude and Fitz and for their families. A home to come back to every day of their lives.

Where they would all belong or long to be.

A place on the Jellicoe Road.

Acknowledgements

Mum, Dad, Marisa, Daniela, Brendan, Luca, and Daniel. Love you guys to oblivion.

Thanks to all who ploughed through the manuscript in its most basic form and still managed to find words of encouragement: Mum, Anna Musarra, Ben Smith, Margaret Devery, Anthony Poniris, Lesley McFadzean, Siobhan Hannan, Sadie Chrestman, Barbara Barclay, Brother Eric Hyde. Special thanks to Maxim Younger, Patrick Devery, and Edward Hawkins for your thorough notes or extensive feedback.

Much gratitude to Laura Harris and Christine Alesich, Lesley McFadzean, and everyone at Penguin Books, and Cameron Creswell, who make my life a bit less stressful!

I am especially appreciative of the hospitality

shown on my Leeton, Colleambally, and Cowra trip in March 2005, which introduced me to the Murrumbidgee and Lachlan rivers. Thank you Margaret and John Devery, Trish and Annabell Malcolm, Neil and Tom Gill, and Vic and Narelle Rossato.

And Patrick and Ben, thanks for coming along and pointing out the rice, citrus, and road kill.